Jutta Goetze was born in a mission hospital in Mwanza, East Africa and soon learned to speak German, Swahili and Indian. She roamed widely – she lived in Germany for two years (where she learned how to ski), in Namibia for nine months, and has travelled around England and Holland on her bike (no motor!). Jutta has nearly always lived in the country, and many of her earlier books have an environmental theme.

For Erika Wettermann,
in loving memory

SNOW WINGS

JUTTA GOETZE

ALLEN&UNWIN

First published in 2005

Allen & Unwin
83 Alexander Street
Crows Nest NSW 2065
Australia
Phone: (61 2) 8425 0100
Fax: (61 2) 9906 2218
Email: info@allenandunwin.com
Web: www.allenandunwin.com
www.juttagoetze.com.au

National Library of Australia
Cataloguing-in-Publication entry:

Goetze, Jutta.
Snow wings.

For children.
ISBN 1 74114 463 9.

1. Snow – Juvenile fiction. 2. Adventure stories – Juvenile fiction. I. Title.

A823.3

Designed by Jo Hunt
Set in Berkeley Book by Midland Typesetters
Printed in Australia by McPherson's Printing Group

1 3 5 7 9 10 8 6 4 2

CONTENTS

PROLOGUE

THE LIGHT BEING

Keep an eye on the weather... it's turning

No one knew how old the Weatherman was. No one remembered there ever being another Weatherman. He had always looked the same – old. If anyone was ever insensitive enough to ask *how* old, he'd smile and say he'd lost count of the years. His face was weathered as it should be. His white hair was longer than other old men wore their hair (if they had any), and thicker than a young girl's. His beard sprouted in an unruly mess, and in a blizzard he could wear it as a scarf. On a clear night his light was seen on the pinnacle of the highest mountain, streaming out, a silver-green star that only dimmed when the clouds sank down.

It was the Weatherman's job to monitor and predict the

weather. He often stood outside the weather hut, which was perched on a rocky outcrop, and studied the horizon. The hut was part of the Mountain Station. Cable cars brought skiers from the valley to this high place. During the ski season the mountain was alive with moving dots in a dance of many colours. The season was due to open tomorrow, and the Weatherman was making last-minute preparations.

A sudden rattle fixed his attention to the weathercock above. It was revolving crazily, as though a wind had sprung up, but there was no wind. The air crackled and vibrated, wires hummed. The Weatherman brought his binoculars to his eyes, and examined the dark cloud cooking over the snowfields, vapours trailing.

'I've never seen such a strange cloud in all my life.' He focussed on its densely woven netting, and grew thoughtful. 'Oh yes I have,' he said then. 'A long, long time ago.' He watched the cloud mass broil across the sun's face until a voice distracted him. A young voice singing a song, with more puffs than notes, and no notes in tune.

One verse later a boy clambered into view and speared his enormous skis into the snow, where they stood, two picket fence posts.

'Hello little one.'

'Don't call me little.' The boy pulled a severe face. *'I'm not little!'*

The Weatherman disregarded the reprimand. 'It isn't a good idea to go out today.'

'I have to learn to ski in all conditions.' The boy gazed at him gravely. 'Practice makes perfect, that's what you always say.'

He was a strange boy; wizened, like an old man whose expressions hung crookedly, as if they'd slipped. His eyes were large and green, luminous and curious. Despite his oddness, he wasn't ugly; his face was too gentle for that. His hair was almost white and fringed across his broad forehead. A silvery curl, a duck's tail, lay softly in the nape of his neck.

'Don't go too far, stay where I can see you.' Always caution from the Weatherman.

The boy nodded, resigned. He blinked into the cold sun, shouldered his skis and tackled the beginners slopes, those nearest the T-bar and poma lifts. The snow was pressed hard and even, prepared by snow-dozers for the ski season.

'See, I'm not going far!' he called.

'Good. And keep an eye on the weather. It's turning.' The Weatherman's attention drew back to the cloud.

In a fresh onslaught of stocks and heavy boots, the boy's skis scissored and tipped as he climbed away from the Mountain Station until he was small as an ant on an enormous sheet of white. His resumed song reached the Weatherman in bursts; his breath was bathroom steam. When he was certain that the Weatherman's eyes were glued to the binoculars, and not fastened on him, he slapped his skis across the slope, kicked his boots into them, pointed them into the valley and, pushing his stocks firmly into the snow, cautiously ploughed down the slope.

Suddenly there was a flash. A shrill whistle pierced the air, and an explosion of steel and glass sent him rolling. Snow on goggles; snow in hair, in boots and all along the zippers of his pockets – and in his pockets where he had forgotten to close them. Scraps of metal lay around him; shrapnel, steaming and hissing. The boy touched a piece. It scalded his glove. He prodded another with his stock and stepped back in surprise.

Under the metal hull was a being, half his size, bedraggled and wet like a drowned cat. Its eyes were closed. Its face was childlike, innocent; it didn't seem to be breathing. It was covered with a mass of angel curls, soft and milky blonde, and was bathed in a luminous golden light that flickered from the pores of its skin. The boy bent to touch it and the being opened its eyes.

A promise given

'It's so cold here.' A bird's sigh kissed the boy's ear and he almost sat down in fright. The being hadn't opened its mouth. He turned around suspiciously to see if someone else had spoken. 'So vvvvery cold.'

The voice sang melodically and light washed over the boy, making him feel happy and at peace. He couldn't look away from the gentle green eyes and found himself smiling.

'We're high up in the mountains,' the boy said, rubbing the being's soft, furry hand. 'Are you hurt?'

'Mmmme? Hurt? Nn-nn-no.' It coughed and shivered

violently. *It was hurt.* Its voice was losing power, its light was fading. It rose, wavering unsteadily in the air, drifting upwards until the boy caught it, so it wouldn't float away. They were eye to eye.

'Are you the Wise Mm-man?'

'No.'

'Oh.' The being's light dipped further as it gave a disappointed chirrup. 'The king said he'd be here.'

'Right here?' The boy scrutinised the emptiness around him.

'Yes. On the highest mountain. I have to find him. The wisest man of all.' The being's song fluted, a canary's trilling, and its light strengthened again.

'Why?'

'The Wise Man has the Key.'

'What kind of key?'

'A key is a key. This one opens all doors.'

'But what –?'

'Questions. Too many questions. Listen.' The being's last flicker of strength went into that one word. Listen. Its light was concentrated in its eyes, a drill boring into the boy's brain. He could see the voice in his mind, as well as hear it. 'Find the Wise Man and ask for his help. He must return the Key to the king. The Key will set us free. But if the Darkness finds the Key first, our worlds will be destroyed.'

'Oh,' the boy said.

'Will you help us?' The being reached out its hand.

'Yes,' the boy promised, clasping it solemnly.

'Then you must take this.'

Letters danced in front of the boy's eyes, a curtain of words shimmered in the air. Momentary maps of mountains shot up like fireworks, popping and hissing as they expanded. The minute he tried to grasp them, they disintegrated.

'How do I –?'

'The Wise Man will know.' The chirruping was so soft the boy could hardly hear it, and the letters disappeared completely. The being sank into the snow, exhausted.

'The Weatherman!' Relieved to have found an answer, the boy surveyed the twists and curls of the wreckage. 'I'll take you to him.' He sifted through the now cooled metal splinters in the hope of finding one large enough to make a sled.

The boy did not notice the dark cloud that had completely covered the sun. It hovered over the snowfield, breathing out and shrinking in, trailing a silver-grey thread that drifted on the freshening wind, before sinking. A dark, bodiless substance oozed from it and landed lightly on the snow. A pool of ink that divided into small globules, black as pitch.

'Run!' the being's small voice cried.

'I can't leave you.'

Spider shapes shivered across the snow towards them. The boy's gaze was drawn to their squirming mass.

'Don't look into their eyes.' High pitched, the bell voice cut into the boy's consciousness and he looked away in time. A yellow eye opened in the largest of the forms, a searchbeam stare swivelled, its wicked gleam flooding him.

Keep the Key safe. The little voice was now only a thought and the happiness the boy had felt drained away. He stamped his boots into the bindings of his skis, and pushed off. The milky being's body pulsed, a fading heartbeat in the formless mist that hovered above it, and with a shuddering cry, it was gone. The Shadows had devoured it.

Stop! The Shadows' eyes refocussed and the spider bodies elongated, stretching sinews after the boy. Stains of darkness discoloured the snow, as they poured down the mountain towards him. He closed his eyes, pushed hard towards the forest and became a streak of speed, flying so fast over the snow's surface that his teeth chattered.

He was skiing too quickly to avoid the snowdrift that lay in his path. Whack! Skis, stocks, hat, goggles – boy – rained down. A tree shuddered and unloaded its snow-laden branches over everything, until it was as though nothing else existed here at the edge of the forest.

The Shadows flew like great, wingless birds of prey across the surface of the snow, but they did not find the boy. Their back to the mountain, their talons pointed to Earth, they disappeared into the grey wool fog that slid in from the other side of the valley. Far away, along the flatness of a riverbed, lay the town of Wintersheim, bustling in the midday hour, unaware of the evil that had arrived on the slopes above.

ONE

ONCE UPON A TIME IN WINTERSHEIM

Failed experiments

Manfred Decker lived at number 13 Nussbaum Strasse, Wintersheim, Germany, with his mother, father and grandma, in a two-storeyed house. There were deer antlers under the eaves. Icicles hung from the drainpipes and the cream coloured walls were decorated with paintings of Saint Florian, patron saint and protector against fires – a useful saint for Manfred's house to have. Flames often belched from the upper window, an unfortunate consequence of Manfred's scientific investigations. In winter, tiny avalanches of snow slid off the roof and landed on the path, which Manfred then had to sweep clean. If he could be found. More often than not, he was in his room experimenting.

Now, a room where a boy can experiment for days on

end can't be an ordinary room, and this one certainly wasn't. It was an upstairs laboratory, full of steel scaffolding that held rockets in place until Manfred finished building them and shot the fiery rainbows out of his window at night.

There wasn't anything ordinary about Manfred, either.

People knew he was coming. He lit up like a Christmas tree on legs. His shirts had moving dots and magnetic press-studs, his pants had clashing stripes, his hats moveable flaps and growing rims. Bow ties twirled, shoes laced and unlaced themselves (and sometimes tripped him). But in his room, Manfred was an inventor with a curious mind. Here he could wear the magnifying glasses that made his eyes too large for his face so that he looked like a serious insect. It didn't matter. He could only have been happier if he were just a brain without a body. Manfred had trouble making his limbs do what his brain wanted.

Today was the culmination of months of hard work. Manfred was close to developing the cheapest, most efficient, non-pollutant rocket fuel ever to be invented in the history of the universe.

'Yes!' His eyes focussed on the computer screen.

'I'm not sure...' Manfred's Calculator was the more cautious of the two.

'Of course, of course – why didn't I see it before?' As always, Manfred took no notice of the Calculator. And as always, the Calculator set out to prove Manfred wrong.

'Be very careful,' it insisted. 'Remember what happened last time, when your mother's hair –'

‘How could I forget?’ Manfred pushed the Calculator aside.

Manfred had built the Calculator years ago and regretted it ever since. It was spiteful, objected when Manfred was right, and wouldn’t keep quiet until it had proved its point. But today Manfred did not let the Calculator interrupt his concentration. He stretched, yawned, cracked his knuckles and hurtled into action. He took Formula A from the fume cupboard, and Formula B from the refrigerator. (They had to be stored separately.) He handled them with the utmost care, and lit the Bunsen burners, which flamed like high-powered Christmas candles. He selected fresh test tubes and sterile spoons, carefully portioning out each ingredient. The Calculator coughed and gave ‘helpful’ hints.

‘I advise caution. B is a key substance. It causes violent chemical reactions if brought into contact with other substances.’

‘I’m being careful.’ Manfred wrinkled his brow.

‘Particular care must be taken if A and B –’

‘All right!’

He only needed six drops. If he could fuse the molecules of A and B – a feat never before achieved – then he’d have his fuel. Each drop had to be measured to a millionth of a gram’s gram, and the fusion temperature had to be exact. Yes, it was correct, so far. The consistency was right, the colour, and the smell. Formula A was turning to fluid at exactly the right moment, and from that fluid he’d be able to distil the six drops he required. And those drops would be added to Formula B.

'I advise caution,' the Calculator repeated.

Manfred placed it on the furthest corner of the table.

'One.'

'Manfred, come here.' Grandma's voice. It didn't register.

'Two.' Everything under control. Manfred's hands were still.

'Manfred.' The voice sounded closer. 'That boy never listens!'

'Three.'

'MANFRED!!!!' Manfred's grandmother fought her way into Manfred's junk jungle, to keep him out of trouble and on time. He was supposed to meet his cousin at the station, but, of course, he'd forgotten.

'Four.' Nearly there.

'I want to see you and I want to see you NOW!' It was a roar.

'Five.' One more and he'd have it. One more and he'd be an Inventor First Class.

'Warning,' the Calculator said in an excitable tone. 'Danger period approaching.'

'Shh. I know. Six.'

'IF YOU DON'T ANSWER ME THIS INSTANT!' Grandma ripped her apron free from the fishhook clasp of the scaffolding and wrenched open the door. Manfred turned.

'Shut the door. Seven. SEVEN?? NO!!!!'

WHOOOOOSH! Purple and green smoke billowed out the windows. Doors slammed, walls shuddered, the foundations of the house shook. Grandma was blown backwards and landed on the collapsing scaffolding in the corridor.

Dust rose, ash settled and Manfred picked up burning papers, threw them in a wastepaper basket and juggled it out the window.

Thppp! The rocket fuel formula landed in the snow beside Manfred's father's car, just as Manfred's father was getting out. His father looked up to the window in the second storey, knowing that burning wastepaper baskets could only come from one place.

After facing three angry adults and a broom, Manfred found himself on the doorstep. His backside tingled – it had paid the price of scientific experimentation many a time. His stomach growled, but Grandma's grim face at the window barred the way back. Even for a snack.

'Can't a person make a mistake?' Manfred gathered his dignity into stiff sounding words.

The door opened briefly and his mother's command issued out, 'Your cousin's waiting! Hurry up.' The door slammed shut.

Cousin! It was all her fault. Manfred waded through the knee-deep snow. He came to the small heap of ashes beside his father's car and extracted what was left of the rocket fuel formula. Flakes of charred paper drifted across the snow. Manfred sighed and stomped off into the cold afternoon, his eyes cast down. He didn't look into the sky.

The sun was red, though it wasn't evening yet. Behind the peak of the highest mountain, like a vulture on its shoulders, was the shadow of something dense and dark. Only a shadow, waiting to form...

Danger alert

Manfred's ears were still ringing from the explosion as he trudged past Christmas trees in shop doorways, and bakeries breathing out the aroma of cinnamon, honey and nuts. Snow had fallen on the fake palms of a nativity scene, giving it a wintry, fairytale air. Around him, people crowded into the narrow cobblestone streets, hurrying to buy presents. Saint Nicholas slid past on a horse-drawn sleigh, a small angel sitting beside him. Sleighbells jingled, the angel's trumpet blared. It was that fir, tinsel and brass time of year.

Manfred paused at the statue in the town square. It was a man, running, pointing to a thing unseen. The horror in the man's face always made Manfred wonder – why? Why was that face familiar? Whose was it? And what had happened in 1405? That was the date at the base of the statue – 1405.

Manfred followed the pointing finger. A chill, more powerful than the cold, slid down his spine. A cloud was blocking the sun. It hurt his eyes to look. He blinked, and when he opened them again there was no cloud, only darkness. His Calculator peeped. Pedestrians gave him curious looks.

'Ssshh!' Manfred was embarrassed. He listened. There were no sounds. No *natural* sounds. Even the tinny music of carols was distant, somehow swallowed up.

'Warning…warning…' The Calculator's voice was muffled as well.

'Oh don't be so melodramatic!' But Manfred swallowed nevertheless. He pressed the pertinent keys. 'Wind strength…humidity…cloud formation…height of cloud…'

Small pin-lights cut tiny holes into the dull afternoon, flashing on then flicking off. The Calculator whirled and clicked uncontrollably. All its stored numerals raced across its screen, a sign that it was overdoing things.

'You've logged in the wrong facts,' it said helplessly.

An uncanny feeling gripped Manfred. He was being watched. A woman scuttled towards him in a sideways gait. Her face was hidden beneath a hood, but he could sense her eyes, staring, hard. Manfred felt weak, as though her eyes were draining him.

What is it? No one was speaking. *What is it you know?*

Manfred was aware of other grey shapes hissing at him, their hands reaching for him. Eye hollows held piercing yellow gleams; greyness seeped through their skin, a sinister aura.

'Danger, danger, danger.' The Calculator glowed hot in his hands.

'Ow!' Manfred thrust it into his pocket. Immediately the hold of the woman's eyes loosened, and the shadow people disappeared. Frightened, Manfred ran, the toes of his boots stubbing the snow.

A sharp wind whistled around the corners of buildings as Manfred continued to run blindly, cannoning into shoppers, skidding on the ice, until he was certain he wasn't being followed. The dread that had threatened to envelop him was weakening, and he finally stopped running and dragged in breath. When he looked at the sky again, the sun was smothered completely.

*

High in the mountains the door of a wooden hut opened and closed again instantly. A tall, thin boy came into a yard fenced by the forest. He wore a leather jacket, boots and a woollen cap pulled well over his eyes, so the world wouldn't see his unhappiness. Smoothing on his gloves, he walked over to the woodpile and picked up an axe to chop wood. Bash. Crack. Woodchips flew. The boy didn't enjoy his chore and pulled a tough, disdainful face. The dislike ran down his arms and was transformed into each powerful swing of the axe. Bash. Crack. A punishment.

Dieter Pfeiffer had lived on the mountain all his life, but the trees and the snow and the cold bored him. His boredom verged on hate. Bash. Crack. He continued to work without lifting his eyes.

When the sound of the telephone cut across the yard, the door of the hut opened and a woman called across to him: 'Dieter, it's for you.' The woman disappeared into the hut again and Dieter continued with his work until he had the kindling he needed. It lay like splinters of ice on the hardened ground. He gathered the pieces and threw them in a cardboard box, put the axe away, and only then answered the phone.

'What? Manfred, calm down. Don't talk so fast.'

Manfred had a tendency to talk extremely speedily when he was nervous or excited or upset. As he was all these things at once, Dieter struggled to understand anything.

'Something weird's going on!' Manfred yelled into the phone. 'Look at the sun! The energy field is sinking, the UV and the gamma rays can't get through.'

'You know we don't get the sun here in the afternoon. I think your brain's sprung a leak.'

'I wish it had. There are some really strange characters lurking about.'

'Tourist season's started.'

'No. People that aren't… Um, they don't…uh…seem to be real.'

'What?'

'I said people that aren't people! It's freaking me out!'

'You don't have to shout. I'll meet you.'

'Town square.' Manfred's teeth chattered. 'Hurry up.'

Dieter shook his head. That Manfred! One explosion too many.

'I'm going to the valley,' he called to his mother as he pulled his sled out from under the hut.

'Isn't it a little late for a trip to town?'

'Have to see Manfred.'

'You'll see him tomorrow at school.' Dieter's mother watched him suspiciously as he pocketed the cloth sack that held his money. 'What about your homework? You haven't finished the chores. There's the chicken coop and –'

'See you.' Dieter jumped onto the sled.

'Don't you play pinball!' his mother warned, but he was already gone.

*

The trip down the mountain was fast. Dieter manoeuvred his sled in easy, practised arcs, sluicing over the frozen ground. He knew every turn of the path, when to lean into a curve, when to use the brakes, and exactly how much pressure to apply without hampering the free-fall motion of the sled. Small heaps of snow were shaken from trees as he passed.

When a small figure stumbled off an embankment ahead of him, Dieter had to plough his boots into the ice to stop the momentum of the sled. He came to a halt within millimetres of the boy.

'Where did you come from?'

'I don't know.' The boy said, confused. His eyes flicked fearfully towards the mountain. 'Danger. Dark…'

'It *is* dangerous in the dark.' Dieter agreed. 'And it'll be dark soon. What are you doing out here on your own?'

'You are.'

'I live here.' Dieter shrugged it off. 'Won't your parents be worried?'

'I don't have parents.' The little boy said it as fact. 'And don't feel sorry for me.'

'All right, I won't. Where are you going?'

The boy didn't answer. Instead, he scrambled up the embankment, tugging at an old pair of skis that were entangled in fir branches.

'Those skis'd be hopeless on this ice. They're far too long for you.' Dieter eyed them critically.

'Have to get away.' There was panic in the boy's voice. 'Before they find me.'

'Who?'

'The Dark.'

He wasn't making any sense. 'Look. You can't stay here. Hop on.' Dieter took hold of the skis. 'Maybe you'll remember when we get into town.'

For a moment the boy held onto his skis, as though he didn't know whether Dieter could be trusted.

'Must help,' he whispered sadly and looked to the mountain.

'Who?' Dieter studied him more closely. 'Is there someone else up there? Is someone in trouble?'

The boy stopped to think. All he could remember was a dark cloud rising above the snow, and a small light flickering. He knew he'd heard a voice, but he couldn't remember anymore what it had said. Then nothing, until he woke cold and alone, his head hurting. 'Too late. Light gone.' A tear slid down his cheek.

Dieter secured the skis to the sled, took his position and told the boy to hold on. He was more careful with a passenger on board. He could feel the boy's grip tighten if he went too fast over the corrugated ice. The air rushed past their ears, fir branches and snow became a blur, and the only sounds were the hiss of the sled and the occasional intake of the boy's breath.

'This is as far as I can take you,' Dieter said when they reached the outskirts of town. 'Will you be okay?'

The boy nodded, uncertain.

'Leave your skis here, no one will take them. You can come for them tomorrow.' Dieter thrust them into the snow, stowing the sled in the doorway of a stable. Cows rustled in straw, cowbells clanked close by. When the village had grown into a sizeable town, the old farmhouses remained nestled among the other houses. Stable-fronts stood beside shop-fronts and manure piles steamed on the footpaths.

'Do you know where you're going?' Dieter asked. Again that vacant nod. 'Is there someone you can call? Someone who can come and get you? A friend?'

'The Wise Man,' the boy said gravely.

'Good. He'll know what to do. Do you have any money?'

The boy didn't answer.

Dieter slid his hand into the cloth sack tied to his belt. 'Here. It's enough for a local call. You're at the south end of Ludwig Strasse. The phone's over there. Get your friend to meet you.' He put the money into the boy's hand, noticing how wet and cold his gloves were. He hesitated. It didn't seem right to leave the boy here, but Dieter wasn't sure what else to do.

'What were you doing on that mountain, all alone?'

'I don't know.' The boy's eyes pricked with tears of frustration.

'You don't know much.' Dieter sighed. 'Go and call your friend.' Without a backward glance, he sauntered off.

The boy took uncertain steps in the opposite direction. He hesitated when he reached the phone and turned, watching Dieter recede into the mist. And then he trotted after him.

The cousin, the cockatoo, the brat and the cat

It began to rain in the valley. Drops of water cascaded over the tiles of the station roof and onto the concrete floor. A train arrived at Wintersheim, its passengers disembarked, new passengers boarded and, full once again, the train departed with the whistle of an unheeded tea kettle.

'Typical!' A cold, wet wind played on the platform and curled around the girl's legs.

'Typical!' her cockatoo repeated. No one there to meet them. 'Typical, typical, typical!' The cockatoo sat on a perch in her cage and whistled tunelessly, casting her wicked eye at fellow travellers. When she felt cheery, she roared out her song in baritone.

'Kookaburra sits in the old gum tree!' Fellow travellers jumped in surprise.

The girl, Anne, remained on the platform with her suitcase and her bird and stared hard at every face to see if it was looking for her. No one was. Anne not welcome. She knew the story, and stamped her foot in annoyance. Anne often stamped her foot wilfully like a horse, tossed her head and shook her mane of hair to create a fearful impression. Anne liked to be feared.

Anne's cockatoo was called Violette. She was a pink bird with white wings and tail and she had a red, watchful eye. Actually, she had two eyes, but as she always regarded the world side on, you only ever saw one eye at a time. When she was content she crowed and murmured soft love words, her crest with its red and yellow bands standing to stiff attention. When she was angry she cussed.

Anne had found Violette in outback Australia, in Oodnadatta. A pink and white package had landed with a thud at her feet.

'Sunstroke,' the package had grumbled, and from that day on Violette stayed with Anne, even though it meant coming halfway across the world to Bavaria.

'Merry merry king of the bush is he!' Violette screeched.

But there was no bush, no wattle seeds or gum nuts in a wintering Germany. No great red plains to fly over or sheep to dive-bomb. Violette was only pretending to be happy to keep Anne's spirits buoyed.

The platform emptied. Anne kicked her suitcase.

'I'm not waiting here another minute!' Maybe this cousin of hers was waiting indoors. More than likely he had forgotten about her. She hitched up the birdcage and entered the vast station hall, but there was no one to greet her there either so, with her chin set at a determined angle, Anne marched out of the building and the little warmth it offered.

Outside the rain diffused the streetlights which turned the snow orange, and from on high a church bell chimed the hour.

'13 Nussbaum Strasse.' Anne referred to the crumpled and damp piece of paper she was holding. 'Nut tree road, what an odd name for a street.'

'Nut tree road is odd!' Violette repeated.

Anne looked in either direction and couldn't decide which way to go.

'Nussbaum Strasse is that way.' A tall, thin boy in a leather jacket and a cap pulled well over his eyes pointed up the street. 'About two kilometres.' He looked at Anne's unsuitable shoes. 'It's on a hill, so it's a bit of a climb.'

'I'll manage,' Anne said primly. 'Thanks.'

'Not a problem.' The boy continued on his way.

Two kilometres! Anne opened the cage and Violette had the honour of riding on her shoulder.

'Watch it – ice!' The cockatoo called out strategies.

'I can see.'

'Not there – there!' Violette's voice could point.

'Let me decide where – they're my feet!'

Anne had barely stepped off the pavement when she jumped back again. A long, black car, shiny as a Christmas beetle, sailed past, oblivious of the wave of slush it splashed onto Anne's shoes and coat. She was vaguely aware of a face, framed by flaming red hair, pressed against the tinted window.

'Idiots!' Anne yelled after the car, but her voice was lost in the mist that was turning the air into soup.

The occupants of the limousine hadn't noticed the girl with the thin coat and tattered suitcase. And they didn't see the thickening Shadows, licking along the streets, treading softly, hugging the walls. Their vehicle pulled into a side street, like a ship steaming into harbour, and slipped into a parking space marked VIP Reserved. Porters descended, a platoon executing precise manoeuvres. As people from the street stared, the fur-clad party was reverently escorted from the car to the entrance of the Grand Hotel.

*

Ziggi was accustomed to being stared at. Her behaviour demanded it. Look at me, said the arch of her eyebrows and the swing of her bobbed hair. She glanced, uninterested, at the onlookers, then held out her long, slender hand.

'Daddy.' The party stopped at the foot of the hotel stairs. 'I need money.' The usual request, couched in the usual way. Ziggi's father gave Ziggi his credit card, which she snatched without comment. Then she turned towards the shops and clicked her fingers.

'Epsilon!' It was an imperial command.

After a long minute, a cat, large and white, and with more fur than Ziggi's mother's mink coat, appeared from the leather interior of the car.

'Come with me.'

The cat stretched, her diamanté collar winking. She arched her back and licked her paws, revealing claws that were as sharp as knives.

'Come!'

Epsilon was the only creature in the world that didn't do what Ziggi demanded, when she demanded it.

'Now!'

A vacant green-eyed glance flicked over its owner. Ziggi grabbed at her cat but Epsilon eluded her – a white flash with a tail in the air, an exclamation mark to her intent.

'*Epsilon!*' Her voice plaintive now, Ziggi had no choice but to follow.

Bee-stings and Gugelhupf

Georg didn't notice the silence or the shadowy forms, the pouches of darkness crouched in corners, seeping into drains. He was oblivious to the yellow eyes that flickered feverishly from face to face, searching. All Georg saw was the cream-cake, a sweet, squishy Bee-sting sponge, close, closer, gone. Georg was eating outside his father's bakery on the north end of Ludwig Strasse, and the grinding of teeth was loud in his ears. He opened his mouth again, took another bite, and his fourth cake disappeared. Then he greedily turned to eye the chocolate and vanilla Gugelhupf in the window. Wiping his mouth he retraced his steps to the shop door.

The padding of feet in the snow and a cold, wet nose distracted him. Georg turned and encountered the liquid brown eyes and lolling tongue of a small dog. The dog investigated Georg's leg and gave a bark of approval when he found a drip of cream. He was foxy red and not yet filled out, although he was fully grown. His fur was long and thick, his ears and paws were daubed with black, and his bushy tail wagged effusively.

'Where did you come from?' Georg eyed the people in the street. 'Don't you have a home?' The dog whimpered.

'Are you hungry?'

'Orff,' the dog barked.

'I suppose you want me to feed you?' Georg spoke slowly, thoughtfully, considering the situation.

'Orff!' The dog gave Georg a push towards the door, for good measure.

'You're always eating, Oh Mei.' Dieter had arrived and stood watching, shaking his head.

'Yep,' Georg replied, unconcerned, or so he liked to appear. 'I don't know where he is,' he said next, unexpectedly. Dieter frowned, then smiled.

'Who says I'm looking for him?' he asked.

'You're always looking for Manfred,' Georg replied. 'He flip out again?'

'Something like that. He said he's in the town square.' Dieter moved off. 'So I thought I'd –'

'Play pinball,' Georg concluded, knowing the Fun Parlour was on the way.

'Want to come?' Dieter asked.

'I ought to go home.' Georg collected his bike from where he'd left it leaning against a lamppost. 'Dinner. You know.'

'All right. Go.' Dieter strode out and Georg had to trot to keep pace. The dog was forgotten.

'I suppose half an hour won't hurt.' Georg increased his speed. It wasn't often that Dieter invited him anywhere.

'Well, come on. Don't stand there,' Dieter said, although Georg was practically running.

'Oh Mei!' he gasped, as they crowded other pedestrians off the footpath. It was an Austrian expression; a piece of slang that came out in a sigh. When Georg said it, he rolled his eyes and looked to heaven. 'Oh Mei.' Two deeply felt words.

The dog remained at the door. Its tail stopped wagging and it sighed audibly. Still hopeful, it looked to the many feet passing, but not one person stopped to give it a smile or a pat, or even a second glance. Then it shrank into the shop doorway as the night's chill took the rain in its cold grip and transformed the drips into sharp teeth.

When the little boy entered the street, the dog pricked its ears. The boy stopped, unsure of which way to go, and gravitated towards the shop window. He gazed hungrily at the vast assortment of pastries. The dog whimpered; the boy saw it and smiled.

Suddenly a dark form glided in from above, hovered, and slowly sank in front of them. The dog's hackles rose. It growled and backed up against the boy, baring its fangs. Around them the street lights fizzed, the town's lights went out and the shadowy form lunged.

'Help! Hel –' A hand clamped over the boy's mouth, and the cry was cut off.

TWO

THE SHADOWS' QUARRY

Run!

'Did you hear that?' Dieter stopped to listen.

'Orff. Orff.' There was a note of urgency in the bark. The dog barrelled around the corner of a building. It wheeled around behind them and, nipping them on the heels, herded them back in the direction it had come.

'Orff orff.' Its barking grew more urgent.

'It wants us to follow!'

As they turned into Ludwig Strasse, Dieter saw strange, indistinguishable figures looming over a cowering boy. Then something cold brushed past him, as more grey figures converged on the boy and blocked him from Dieter's sight.

'Help me!'

Dieter recognised the voice.

Silence. The command was dark and rasping as the boy was pulled along the footpath. The dog tugged at the boy's hand, growling and snapping, but the figures overpowered it.

'Distract them while I grab him,' Dieter hissed to Georg. 'I'll meet you at the station.'

Georg nodded and, without thinking how many attackers there were, waded towards the group, using his weight and swinging his fists. The dog was by his side, biting ankles. Together they allowed Dieter to take advantage of the confusion, grab the boy's hand and run.

The rain fell harder and the footpath was slippery and difficult to see in the gloom. Dieter wasn't sure who was chasing him, but he could sense them getting closer. Vague shapes of people veered out of his way as he ran, the sharp corners of house walls jumped at him, blocking him. His breath was running out and he could feel the heavy tiredness of the child he was pulling. He was about to turn into an alley when an old man loomed out of the rain, a greenish glow throwing a halo on the slush at his feet.

'Not that way, it's a dead end.' The voice was familiar, but Dieter was breathing so hard he couldn't place it and he couldn't see the man's face, which was obscured by a white beard. 'Turn left, then straight ahead.' The voice pushed him on, and without thinking, Dieter followed its directions and disappeared into a narrow space hemmed in by house walls. When he turned to thank him, the old man had gone and there was only the monotonous dripping of the rain.

When he could no longer hear the echo of footsteps following, Dieter let go of the little boy's hand. They hurried towards the station, the older boy checking behind them every now and then. They finally stopped beside an old waterwheel that was turning slowly so the stream wouldn't freeze.

'All right. Tell me what's going on. What did you do?' Dieter asked sternly. 'Why are they after you?'

The little boy stared at his boots and wrinkled his brow. 'I don't know.' His ears were red from the cold.

'You must have done something,' Dieter prodded.

'I don't know,' the little boy repeated. He turned his head, first one way, then the other, listening for the soft chirrup of a bird's voice that would remind him.

'I thought your friend was going to meet you?'

'Hey!' Wobbling wheels skidded in snow and an almost overbalanced Georg arrived, the dog close behind him. 'What was that all about?' He swallowed and rolled his eyes, too breathless for the usual, 'Oh Mei.'

'I don't know,' said the little boy. 'I didn't do anything.'

'Do you know who they were?' Dieter asked.

'No.'

'Have you seen them before? Were they chasing you on the mountain?'

'I…'

'…don't know,' Georg concluded. 'They weren't friendly. They were really strange.'

'Manfred warned me about strangers.' Dieter gripped the handlebar of Georg's bike. 'Have you noticed anything weird in town in the last few days?'

'No.' Georg hated questions he didn't know the answers to. 'Just the usual Christmas chaos.'

'Do you remember anything?' Dieter asked the child.

'No.' The boy's voice was small. 'I need to find...'

'What?'

But the boy didn't know. Above them a church-bell chimed. Georg sighed, hungrily. Quarter to five. The boy shivered.

'Here.' Georg pulled off his hat. The oversized wool drowned the boy's small head. 'Keep it. I have plenty.'

'Thanks.' Then the boy turned to Dieter. 'And thank you for helping me again,' he said shyly.

'No problem.' Dieter shrugged his shoulders. 'Is that friend of yours going to show?'

'I don't think so.' The boy held Dieter's change out to him. Dieter waved it away.

'What are we going to do with you?'

Neither the boy nor Georg had an answer.

'We can't abandon him,' Georg suggested helpfully.

'I know that, Oh Mei.' Dieter's lips thinned into a grim line. 'You'd better come with us till we can think of something,' he said to the little boy.

The dog flicked Dieter with its paw.

'Yes, you too.' Dieter sauntered off.

'Orff!' The dog barked happily at the passing world,

running ahead of the boys, behind them and through their legs, as they headed towards the town square.

Moments later, the Weatherman emerged out of a dark doorway, listening for movement behind the fog. When he was certain nothing was following the boys, his watchfulness eased. He even allowed himself the luxury of lighting his pipe, before strolling after them.

'Yes,' he murmured into the stem of his pipe. 'I think they'll do.' He was quite pleased with himself.

Cat fight

'Can't trust anyone nowadays!' No one took any notice of the bad-tempered boy grumbling to himself. Manfred was more ice-block than boy now. He tried to keep warm by slinging his arms around himself and hitting his shoulder blades with mittened fists. 'What's the time?' His breath came out like dragon's smoke.

'Five minutes later than last time,' the Calculator peeped.

'Zttch!' Manfred's eyes darted both ways along the street. 'It's the last straw! *The Last Straw!*' He stomped off, his lips tight and blue.

A bell sounded. A church steeple loomed in the mist. Manfred skidded to a stop as the last chimes rang out. Oh no. Oh no, no, no, no, no!!!! There was a reason he was out here in the grey-soup day freezing his fingers, the cold threatening to shear off his nose. His cousin. Three o'clock. On the dot. And five chimes had rung.

Two hours too late (unless the train was delayed by falling snow, or perhaps an accident – a derailment could add hours – no, that would be too much to hope for). Manfred did a rapid succession of calculations and kept coming back to one fact. He was in trouble. Again.

To make matters worse a cat momentarily tangled itself in his legs, tripped him up, extracted itself, and raced away. Manfred shook his head. He'd been shaking it a lot today.

'Mad,' he muttered. 'The whole world's mad.'

*

'Look out!' Violette called as a white flash shot past Anne, and cold fur tickled her legs.

'Enemy at close range!' Violette shot off as the cat sped past.

'Violette!' Hitching up her belongings, her feet sinking into mush, Anne gave chase.

She was running so fast she tripped over the grey figure that had caught hold of the cat. Epsilon growled, her tail lashed, her ears flattened, but it was no use – the grey boy had her by the scruff of her neck and was stuffing her into a sack.

'You can't treat animals that way!' Anne marched straight towards him but he ignored her, winding string around the opening so the cat couldn't escape.

'Open it up!' Anne yanked the sack out of his spidery hands as the cat wailed and struggled.

What do you think you're doing? The whispered hiss hit her with force. She was aware of the boy's yellow stare, burning into her. *Get away!*

'You'll suffocate it.' She was mesmerised by the boy. His face was hidden by a collar and a hat, and there was a strange grey shimmer about him, but it was his feverish yellow eyes that left her barely aware of anything else.

'Get away! Quick! Run!' Violette screeched, beating her wings.

Cover the bird. The order came to Anne, and she obeyed – this girl who disobeyed orders on principle. She caught Violette and covered her with her coat, holding her as though she were in danger.

Leave! The thought pressed into her brain and, without resisting it, she stumbled away, until the weakening miaows of the cat broke the glittering hold the boy's eyes had on her.

'No.' Anne stuck her chin out stubbornly. 'Let the cat go. You're hurting her.' She knelt to pull at the opening of the sack.

Leave her alone.

Anne didn't see the boy kick the cat, but he must have, for she yowled and flew along the footpath with the force of the blow. Furious, Anne clenched her fists and pummelled the boy hard, realising with a shock he was more a shadow than a boy. The cat stopped wailing and wriggled a paw into the opening of the sack, tearing at it with her teeth and finally struggling free. Fur on end, she sprang at the boy and stretched out her pitiless claws. The cat spat, the boy yelped, and Anne gave him a kick for good measure.

You can have it! He backed away from the group of people who had gathered around them. As he melted into the dark, Anne saw he had no mouth.

She crouched to run her hand over the cat's body, making sure it was unhurt. The cat mewed pitifully.

'Nothing's broken,' Anne tried to read the name on its glittery tag.

'What do you think you're doing?' a sharp voice demanded.

Anne straightened. A red-headed girl stood over her.

'I saved your cat's life.' Anne waited to be thanked.

'Get out of my way!' Ziggi had no talent for creating good first impressions. She pushed past Anne. Epsilon purred loudly and wound herself around her legs. Anne seethed. Ziggi cast a disdainful glance in Violette's direction.

'What's that supposed to be? Is that fleabag yours?' (The second impressions were rarely any better.)

'Yes. Violette's a Pink Cockatoo,' Anne retorted, her blood pressure rising.

'*Cacatua leadbeateri!*' Violette landed on Anne's arm.

'She's also called a Major Mitchell cockatoo in Australia,' Anne added proudly. 'Named after Sir Thomas Livingstone Mitchell, a Scottish explorer who led expeditions through New South Wales and Victoria in the 1880s.'

'Attention!' Violette paraded along Anne's arm, sticking her chest out, saluting with her crest. 'Move out!' That was aimed at Ziggi.

'What a feather duster.' Ziggi smiled sweetly, which always meant the worst. 'I've never seen such a stupid bird in all my life.' Her face took on a pained look as she measured Anne from top to toe. 'In fact, you're not exactly a fashion statement yourself.' Every word gleeful. 'Plaits. They are so not cool.' And with that, she turned on her heels and flounced away.

Anne heaved the cage and her suitcase in a determined manner and followed. Her mouth was set in a disapproving line, her eyes were firmly fixed on Ziggi.

*

'Two hours is too much!' Manfred was terse. He glowered at Dieter, ignoring Georg and the little boy who had stopped beside him.

'I was held up.' Dieter's grin made Manfred madder.

'It's not what you think,' Georg was quick to point out. 'We didn't get to the Pinball Parlour.'

Manfred gave the fat boy a disbelieving look and turned away in disgust. As far as he was concerned it was a poor excuse for having stood up a friend. But he didn't say it. An angry squeal stopped him.

'If you call her stupid once more…' a voice threatened, and a bird hovered above a hedge close to the footpath.

'Murder, murder,' it yelled excitedly, made a dive and darted up with a beak full of red hair.

'Yeeoowww!!'

Manfred forgot his anger, Georg let his bike drop and, with the little boy trailing, the boys ran in the direction of the yelling. A girl with torn tights, and plaits flying, had another girl in a headlock. Squirming, high heel boots slipping in the snow, Ziggi flailed with her arms like a broken windmill.

'Let me go.' It didn't occur to Ziggi to say please. And it didn't occur to Anne to let go.

Dieter laughed. Georg smirked. Manfred folded his arms and studied the scene. The little boy stood quietly by the hedge, guarded by the dog he'd found.

'Do something, she's killing me!' Ziggi glared at them.

Anne struggled and swung her fists, but Dieter was stronger and pulled her away from Ziggi by her plaits. He ducked a rain of blows in time and had to juggle the wild girl to stay out of her firing range.

'Leave me alone! Let me go! Don't you dare touch my hair!!' Anne was so angry she could spit.

'She is so rude. Listen to her.' Ziggi scrambled to her feet and dusted the snow from her cashmere sweater. 'She attacked me. For no reason!'

'Take it easy.' Dieter was unfazed. He let Anne go and rubbed his arm. 'Not a bad left hook…for a girl.'

Georg looked surprised. That was the first time he had ever heard Dieter praise a girl. But Anne didn't accept it as praise. It was a matter-of-fact comment to her.

'I can look after myself,' she said, dryly.

'I was talking to you.' Ziggi hated being overlooked and stamped patent leather.

Dieter regarded the two girls. 'What's the problem?'

'She's mad. They ought to lock her away.' Ziggi flicked out the accusation. Anne kicked at her.

'Enough!' Dieter's expression was hard and his voice final. Anne's mouth pulled a grim line; she had plenty more to say but thought better of it – for the moment.

'You wait,' slipped out in one last, angry whisper. Anne's hands were still fists.

Dieter gave her a warning glance. 'What's your name?'

'What's your name?' Georg asked Ziggi at the same time, and because Ziggi's voice was louder, she drowned out any answer Anne may have given.

'Zigrid, but with a Zee,' she pronounced the name precisely. 'Zigrid Anita Elizabeth Renate Loretta Jennifer Olivia Twigg.' Said with pride. 'I'm here on holiday, from LA.'

'Couldn't your parents decide on one name?' Anne asked. Ziggi glared.

'A name for each day of the week.' Georg was peacemaker.

'Very individual.' The mechanical voice of the Calculator was quick to add an opinion. There was a moment's surprised silence. Ziggi glowered in Manfred's direction and Anne viewed him suspiciously. Manfred shrugged, innocent.

'It's a status symbol.' Ziggi said archly. 'None of you would know anything about that.'

'Ziggi Twigg.' Manfred savoured the name. 'A chip off the old block.' He grinned widely. 'Block of wood, get it?'

'You're barking up the wrong tree.' Georg joined in, smiling too.

'That's not even remotely funny.' Ziggi wrinkled her nose in disgust.

'Mmm,' Manfred drawled. 'We'd better *leaf* her alone.'

'Ztt!' Ziggi glared. 'How juvenile.' She turned her back on

them to favour Dieter. 'This is Epsilon.' She indicated her cat. 'Which means Y in the Greek alphabet – right next to Zee.'

'Zed,' Anne corrected her.

'If you're a luddite,' Ziggi said smoothly. 'Moron, for those who don't know.'

'No it's not,' Manfred cut in. 'Luddites are anti-machine, anti-technology, but you'd have to know your history.'

'Which she obviously doesn't,' Anne chimed in triumphantly.

'Oh!' Ziggi was close to crying because nothing was going the way she wanted it to.

'Why are you making such a drama of it, Ziggi?' Dieter enjoyed the game. He was measuring Ziggi, and Ziggi didn't measure up.

'I insist on Zigrid.'

'We don't call Georg by his real name. He's Oh Mei.'

'I don't care what you call that tub of lard,' Ziggi exploded, but Dieter was no longer listening.

'We didn't get your name,' he asked Anne again.

'Anne.' Flat reply.

'Anne who?'

'Anne will do.'

'And?' Dieter pointed to the tree, where Violette had settled a healthy distance from the cat.

'Violette.' Anne disregarded Ziggi's snigger.

'Uh-oh.' Manfred searched the ground as though he'd lost something at his feet. 'You're cousin Anne, with the cockatoo.'

'And you're two hours late!' Anne flared.

'Anne, Ziggi.' Dieter had to raise his voice. 'This is Manfred. That's Oh Mei, I'm Dieter.' His attention returned to the little boy who stood to the side. 'I haven't asked your name?'

'I...I don't know.' It was a whisper.

'What do you mean you don't know? Everybody knows their name.' Ziggi laughed nastily.

The little boy inched behind the dog, as if it could protect him from their questions, and the dog growled at them.

'Well, do you know his name?' Dieter asked, pointing to the dog. The little boy's face remained blank.

'He's a stray...like me.'

'Orff orff orff!' the dog barked impetuously.

'Orff. Well, that's a start.' Dieter scratched his head.

'Where do you come from?' Georg asked kindly.

'I don't know.' Very small voice.

'We'll have to call you something,' Manfred announced. 'Names can be convenient.'

'What do you want to be called?' Dieter leaned towards the boy.

'I don't know.'

'I don't kno–' Ziggi mimicked in an ugly voice.

'I know!' Dieter said. 'We'll call you I Don't Know. Until you remember your name.'

'What kind of name is that?' Ziggi was critical because she couldn't think of a suitable name for him.

'Why don't you give him one of yours?' Anne asked. That silenced her.

'I Don't Know.' The little boy weighed the name.

'Yes. IDK for short.' A Manfred abbreviation.

'IDK?' The boy smiled. As he did, his face lit up, the glow of light radiating from his eyes and his skin, and it made them all want to smile – everyone except Ziggi.

'How stupid is that?' she said.

'If you say that one more time –' Anne didn't finish the threat. The tree beside them suddenly rattled. Snow fell, pink and white feathers fluttered. Epsilon held Violette pinned by her wing and the cockatoo beat her other wing, squawking fearfully, pecking at the cat. Epsilon hadn't reckoned on the strength of the bird's beak, just as Ziggi hadn't reckoned on Anne.

'If anything happens to Violette I'll make a fur coat out of that cat!' Anne climbed the tree and pulled Epsilon's tail, while Violette gave her a pincer-like nip. With a spitting hiss, Epsilon let Violette go, her fur standing on end.

Violette hurtled skyward. Treading air, like treading water, she smoothed her ruffled feathers. Ruffled? She looked a cross between a pincushion and a porcupine, and so did the cat. But everything was in order, hurt pride the only damage.

'No, no, no, no!' she lectured, landed on Anne's shoulder, and lightly rubbed Anne's cheek with her beak.

IDK laughed. Georg laughed. Dieter. Manfred. Last of all Anne. They were all laughing. Except Ziggi. She'd had enough. Her sense of humour didn't extend to laughing at herself. She glared at them all and stomped off. Her cat followed her and the two disappeared around the corner.

'Stupid!' Violette yelled after them.

The laughter stopped as suddenly as it had begun. The day had ended, people were in their houses, warm; children belonged there too. Breaking from the group, Anne retrieved her suitcase and handed it to Manfred.

'It had better not be far,' she glowered. Georg picked up his bike. With the dog running ahead, the group filed out of the park.

'Does he have a place to stay?' Georg nodded in the little boy's direction.

Dieter shook his head.

'We can't leave him,' Anne said, firm. 'Manfred.' It was a tone of voice that didn't accept 'no' as an answer.

'I'm in enough trouble as it is,' Manfred countered, knowing what Anne wanted.

'Manfred!' she said again.

'I suppose he can sleep in my room.' Manfred sighed and turned to Dieter. 'And you'd better stay as well.'

Anne nodded, satisfied.

'Good. Now come on. I'm starving. I've had nothing to eat since Perth.'

Dark rumblings

'So you're Manfred's cousin from Australia?' Dieter remarked to Anne.

'Yes,' Anne replied nimbly.

'Australia's just around the corner,' Dieter joked.

'Aus-tra-lia,' Anne enunciated it slowly. 'Not Austria. People always get that mixed up. It's in the southern hemisphere,' she added primly.

'That was a joke,' Georg interrupted, kindly. 'Around the corner…like…it's not.'

'That's right. Not a good joke.' Anne was glad it was dark, so they couldn't see her blush.

'Are you on holiday?' Dieter continued.

'No. My parents are…scientists.'

Dieter looked sceptical.

'This year they had to visit…the Antarctic, so they sent me here,' Anne continued unperturbed. Manfred tuned in. He crowded Georg off the footpath so he could listen. 'Well, what would I do at the South Pole?'

Oh no, Manfred thought, a cousin and a cockatoo, both with big mouths. A cousin and a cockatoo who argued and thought they were always right. A cousin and a cockatoo who were liars to boot! The situation threatened to become overwhelming. Manfred shot a warning glance at Anne. Before she could reply they arrived outside his house. A glow spread into all parts of the garden and the circus of instruments set up there.

Anne was fascinated. She pointed to the glittering objects. 'What are they?'

'Highly technological data-gathering equipment. If your parents were scientists, you'd know that.'

'It looks like junk to me.'

Manfred was easily insulted by comments concerning his

experiments. He was about to give his red-faced and excitable opinion when Dieter quickly diffused the argument.

'What are you going to tell your parents? About us staying?'

'Leave it to me. I'll talk them round.' Anne was always confident.

'We'll do it my way or not at all,' Manfred said. He turned to IDK. 'Don't worry about a thing.' He was clearly worried. 'They like me to have company.'

'Looks like you already have visitors,' Georg pointed to a light stabbing out of the skylight in Manfred's bedroom.

'The light turns on automatically at seventeen hundred hours,' the Calculator chipped in.

'What *is* that thing?' Anne demanded. Georg coughed. But before Manfred could retort, a growl sounded. Loud and long, muffled thunder came from the roots of the earth and reached into the sky.

'Avalanches,' Georg said. 'The ski patrol's setting them off.' His face was pale.

'No, Oh Mei. Not at this time of night.' Dieter knew the lore of the mountains.

'I tell you they're exploding avalanches.' But Georg knew it wasn't true. He'd lived through every winter when avalanches were exploded in the mornings, to make slopes safe for skiers. He knew their sound. This was different. It had a deeper tone, it was more threatening.

Dieter looked into the sky. 'It'll snow soon.' The conversation stopped uncertainly, their thoughts full of private fears. The dark rumbling sounded again.

'You had something important to tell me,' Dieter remembered.

'It'll have to wait,' Manfred said, disappointed. He could always rely on Dieter for common sense, but now he had new fears. His garden instruments were whirring strangely.

'What's the matter?' Dieter recognised Manfred's perplexed expression. Manfred selected an erratically ticking black box, and moved out of earshot of Anne, Georg and IDK.

'This measures electro-magnetic waves,' he explained to his friend in a whisper, and held it out towards the wall of fog. 'I invented it to warn me about meteorites. It tells me when foreign objects are approaching... So far I've only identified aeroplanes.' He was about to explain the difference between aeroplanes and meteorites and how, in theory, meteorites could be detected by an increase in the volume and frequency of the ticking. But he didn't, because the volume and frequency increased to such an extent that the box jumped out of his hands.

'It's going haywire!' Manfred turned it upright with his foot, the ticking so quick it formed a single stream of noise.

'Maybe it's broken?' Dieter sounded hopeful.

'No. A large and dense object is approaching.'

'I can't see anything.' Dieter peered into the fog.

'Can't you *feel* there's something wrong?'

'What are you talking about?' Dieter looked at his friend doubtfully. He knew Manfred was far less certain of feelings than he was of scientific facts.

'I can't put my finger on it...' Manfred scanned the dark

as if he could see through it. 'I have this strange feeling we're not alone. I'm sure we've been followed.' He tried to keep his tone even. 'And there's evil out there. Pure evil.'

'Slow down.' Dieter recognised the fear in Manfred's voice, though he didn't understand what he meant. 'You haven't been making sense all afternoon.'

'It's hard to –' Manfred was seldom lost for words. '*Nothing* makes sense.'

'Then why don't you sleep on it? It might be better in the morning.'

'Yes, and it might be worse,' Manfred said, gloomily.

'Well, there's nothing we can do tonight, is there?'

'Georg. G…E…O…R…G!' A mother's voice. 'Georg Woerndle!'

'Have to go.' Georg reacted as though jumping up out of sleep. 'Dinner.' He grinned at the thought. 'See you tomorr –' He pedalled off before he'd even finished speaking.

'I'll tell the folks there's two more for dinner,' Manfred swallowed, not relishing the task. 'Stay here.'

It started to snow, a curtain of it extending from the mountains across the valley, saturating space with movement and a smothering silence. Manfred rubbed flakes off his anorak. Standing in the light of the porch, he watched the snow swirling around him, and examined the flakes on his glove. They were smeared, shot through with a sticky grey substance. They weren't at all how snow should be.

THREE

THE BLACK CLOUD

Black snow

The sun didn't appear the next day and it was still snowing. Snow covered hedges and trees; it silently fell onto cars in the street, and onto rooftops. But where the town had once been clean and tidy in its white winter wrapping, it was distorted now. Wintersheim was choked in the underbelly of a black cloud that hid the tallest mountain, hid everything from everything else, and the snow that oozed out of it was black.

Anne woke early to find Dieter and Manfred already gone, and IDK sitting on the side of his bed watching her with frightened eyes.

'It's worse than Melbourne weather!' She dressed hastily. 'I thought this was a resort town. I wouldn't have come if I'd known about this pollution.'

'It isn't pollution.' Manfred's voice drifted in through the open window.

'What are you doing?' Anne had to lean right out to spot him. Manfred was standing on the third-highest rung of a ladder, balanced against the chimney. He was reaching into the sky, grasping at handfuls of air with one hand, holding a pair of scissors in the other.

'Hold the ladder steady – I can't reach!'

'I'm not climbing up there.'

'Whoa!' The ladder tipped sideways, threatening to send Manfred into orbit. Quickly feeling her way along the snow-laden gutters, Anne inched towards the chimney and held the ladder in place.

Steady now, Manfred plucked a snowflake from the air and inspected it. He squeezed it between his thumb and forefinger. It wouldn't squash. An intense cold emanated from it, and an unpleasant odour, like burnt rubber. Manfred wrinkled his nose. He stretched further until his fingertips finally reached into the cloud. Grasping a handful of mist, he pulled it towards him, cutting at the strands of gossamer netting.

'It has the consistency of black fairy floss.' He sniffed it. 'But it smells like tar.' He turned to his cousin. 'Whatever this is, it isn't a cloud.'

Keeping a careful hold of his sample, he climbed down the ladder, jumping awkwardly onto the tiles, nearly causing a roof avalanche. From this vantage point he could see out over the street. His heart gave a thump. They were there again, right outside his house!

'Look out!' He ducked behind the chimney, dragging Anne down with him, then cautiously peered around the corner. He recognised the shadow people from the night before. They gathered in the gloom, barely visible, their faces turned towards his window, the light of their eyes probing, as if they could see through the drawn curtains. But they had changed. Their greyness had grown darker, more intense; their eye-light was more vicious. And there were more of them.

'What's the matter?' Anne poked her head out from behind the chimney.

'Don't show yourself.' Manfred pulled her back. 'On the footpath. Have you seen those…those people before?'

Anne sighed. There was something seriously wrong with her cousin. She couldn't see anyone on the footpath.

'Where?' She gave him an annoyed look.

'There.' Manfred ventured another peek. The grey people had gone.

'You need new glasses,' Anne grumbled and lowered herself onto Manfred's balcony. When Manfred thought it was safe, he followed. Returning to his room he immediately placed the piece of cloud under a microscope.

'It's artificial webbing.' He snapped on the radio. It was barely receiving the local station.

'Wintersheim is inaccessible to outside traffic,' a newsreader's voice blared into the room. 'Overnight avalanches have blocked both ends of the valley. Council workers estimate clean-up operations will last weeks.'

'We can't get out.' Manfred's voice was tense. He picked up the phone and listened. 'The line's dead.' He bit his lip. 'Means we can't use email either.' He tried his mobile phone. There was no signal.

Manfred paced the room, flicking switches and setting dials. A whirring started.

'An electronic force field?' Manfred chewed his pencil. 'Something's causing severe interference. It started yesterday; it's as though this cloud is blocking out everything.'

'Manfred, Anne, little IDK?' The intercom crackled. 'Breakfast is ready. Hurry! You'll be late for school.' Grandma's voice was polite this morning because Manfred had guests.

'In a minute.' Manfred flicked out a reply.

'Where's Dieter?' Anne asked.

'He's gone to reconnoitre, to see what's going on.' Manfred gathered his school case, books, pencils and sports clothes.

'Manfred!' Grandma's politeness was wearing thin.

'All right!' The temptation to check one more instrument was too much for him. 'You two go,' he said to Anne. 'I'll be there as soon as I can.' But Anne had no intention of going without him. She was as concerned as Manfred, and as frightened as IDK. She stared at the machine Manfred was adjusting.

'It's the sonic scanner.'

Sounds filtered into the room. Creaking noises like a door opening in a breeze. The crackling of static, a grinding of steel against rock. Suddenly there was a crackle and a roar from a closer source.

'Manfred, you get down here right now!'

Manfred sighed. 'Anne, ask my mother to lend you some skis.' He herded Anne out of the room.

'Take me, take me!' peeped the Calculator, who would never forgive Manfred for not giving it legs.

As Manfred reached for the Calculator his foot kicked a shard of light, which glinted brightly and skittered under the bed. He retrieved it, then nearly dropped it in surprise. Letters of light hung in his hand like limp spaghetti. They pulsed feebly, forming a word. *Help*.

'Do you know what this is?' Manfred asked, puzzled, and held it out to IDK who had remained behind.

The boy's forehead puckered as he tried to recall where he'd seen those words before.

'I don't know.'

'Of course you don't.' Manfred was immediately suspicious. 'If you're playing games with us...'

'No,' the little boy said. 'I don't know any games.' He furrowed his brow and thought really hard. 'I...I don't remember anything, not since...since...'

Manfred waited, but nothing else came, so he gave up. He lowered himself onto the floor and lifted the hem of the bedspread. There were more pieces of light, balled in a corner, under the bed. He carefully inched them out, untangled them and spread them on the carpet. They formed perfectly drawn words, graceful letters, scraps of a map that grew brighter when he shut the curtains and switched off the overhead lamp.

'I don't get it.' Manfred blinked in amazement. 'They're solid. But what are they saying?'

'Ahem.' The Calculator switched itself on, tiny lights and cogs moving.

'What?'

'If I may suggest?' The polite voice was an indication it was about to show off.

'Yes, all right.'

'Take a photograph. Then study the permutations.'

Too proud to admit he was stumped, Manfred switched on the Calculator's digital camera. Images whirred. The letters and words flashed across the screen in many different sequences, until they finally slowed, and settled into a beautifully written paragraph. There was also a map of a mountain range, but Manfred focussed on the Gothic calligraphy that shone like the northern lights.

'It's a letter.' He squinted at the screen. 'To the Wisest Man. I wonder who that is?'

'Maybe it's for you?'

'I'm not wise. Clever, smart maybe.'

'Of course you're wise.' The Calculator insisted. 'You're a scientist, aren't you? And you have me.' The Calculator was never in any doubt about its talents. 'Is it addressed to anyone in particular? A name?'

'No.' Manfred knew what the Calculator was leading to.

'Then there's no reason to believe it's not for you. It's in your room, isn't it?' The Calculator could be extremely pushy. Manfred hesitated. 'Go on. Read it.'

Manfred's glasses flashed, reflecting the light-drenched words on the screen. He did want to read them; he'd found them, after all, and now they were on his Calculator. They might even provide an explanation for all the weird events of the last twelve hours. Manfred was good at convincing himself he was doing the right thing, and those sentences shimmered enticingly. So he jammed his glasses up onto the bridge of his nose and, as he read them, the words flowed out soft as spoken thoughts.

This is an intergalactic SOS. We are looking for the Wise Man who has the Key. Only the Key can save us. If it is not turned at the midnight hour, when the Years pass one another, then the Light Star will be destroyed. Our light will expire. Please help. Return and turn the Key. Time is scarce.

Manfred read the words again. '*Only the Key can save us.* Obviously the Key is the solution to this problem, and we have to find it,' he said to himself, to the Calculator and to IDK. But he was baffled. How?

Wagging school

Dieter and Georg were waiting at the gate as Manfred and IDK trudged through the confusion in Manfred's garden. It was like a shipwreck: smashed, lopsided plates wedged into the snow; tatters of windsocks, frozen and hanging stiff;

wires lying coiled; nothing whole was left, and black snow covered everything.

'This is terrible!' Manfred groaned. Years of work lay scattered and broken.

'Oh Mei,' Georg sympathised, and rolled his eyes until only the whites showed.

'What happened?' Dieter surveyed the mess.

'Some kind of electrical disturbance.' Manfred stabbed his skis into the snow. 'An accumulation of energy which...exploded. But these...' He pointed helplessly at his broken instruments. 'Vandals destroyed these.'

He searched for clues on the footpath, and quickly found them. There were eight indentations in the snow where the grey people had been standing earlier: not footprints, but narrow, deep holes. His entire garden was covered in them. Manfred bent to examine the evidence. He pulled back quickly. The cold that seeped from the holes was unbearable.

Dieter joined him, grim-mouthed.

'It's not just a mess here.' His expression was serious. 'When I went for a walk this morning I noticed all the animals have gone.'

'They can't disappear!' Manfred was shocked.

'There are no pets anywhere. No wild animals, no birds, foxes, rabbits; the deer in the forest have gone. All their hay's untouched.'

'They probably have enough to eat,' said Georg.

'No.' Dieter could read the signs of nature clearly. 'There's no food about this year. The whole valley's in chaos. Come and look at this.' He led them to the spring that flowed behind Manfred's house. When he broke a hole in the crust of ice, oily, brackish water percolated out. 'It's never been this polluted.'

Manfred nodded. 'We have to find out what's going on.'

'Do you have a plan, Dieter?' Georg asked.

'No, Oh Mei, but one thing's for sure.' Dieter's pause added weight to his words. 'School's out of the question.'

Georg stole a glance in Manfred's direction. Seeing he wasn't worried, Georg tried not to worry either.

'Sure,' he said casually. 'It's only sport today anyway.'

Manfred realised he had to show Dieter the words of light as soon as possible.

'The disturbances came from behind the cloud.' He turned his back on Georg, who eased in closer, as if that would include him. 'So I suggest –'

'I'll meet you at the Valley Station.' Georg jumped on his sled.

'That we go to the Valley Station,' Manfred concluded at the same time. 'From there we can take a cable car onto the mountain.'

Dieter turned to IDK in dismay. 'We forgot to get your skis.'

'He can come with me,' Georg said at the same time as Dieter told IDK he could go with Georg. IDK eyed Georg's sled. There didn't seem to be room for the two of them, but Georg had already pushed off and he had to run to jump on board.

'Dieter, I need to talk to you.' Relieved they were finally alone, Manfred reached for his Calculator.

'What are we waiting for?' Anne stomped across the garden in a big pair of boots, carrying Manfred's mother's skis. Violette balanced expertly on her shoulder. 'Your mum *gave* me the skis,' Anne called triumphantly.

The gate creaked and Orff shot past, kicking up snow as he went, chasing Georg's sled.

'Where are your stocks?' Manfred asked Anne, trying to buy himself time.

'My what?'

'Poles. You need them to balance and push off when you ski. Haven't you skied before?' Whenever Anne was around, Manfred became exasperated.

'I can ski as well as you can!' Anne retorted. 'Where are these poles?'

'At the front door.' Manfred waited until she was gone. 'Girls! She's driving me crazy!' He motioned to Dieter. 'Come on.' Without waiting, Manfred pushed off.

*

The old man peered in the window at the front of the house.

'Can I help you?' Anne asked in a disapproving voice.

'Where is the boy?' The Weatherman wasn't perturbed by Anne's tone.

'What boy?' Anne was instantly suspicious.

'The little one.'

'You're at the wrong house.' Anne kept her expression neutral.

'Protect him from the Darkness.' The old man stepped onto the footpath towards her. 'He is in great danger.'

'I don't know what you're talking about.' She didn't drop her guard.

'I'd like to show you something, if I may.' The Weatherman's smile disarmed her. He beckoned her to a sheet of black water lying on the path. 'Don't look at it for long,' he cautioned. He hadn't spoken a moment too soon, because from the instant she looked into the pungent water, she felt herself being drawn down, as though she was falling into a bottomless pit.

'You're a sensible girl,' the Weatherman said. 'This is what you must protect him from. The boy, the others, yourself.'

'I'm not scared of anything.' Anne nudged the hardened puddle with her toe. Her foot was instantly chilled to the bone.

'I know you're not,' the Weatherman's voice remained grave. 'Which is why you have been chosen. But when you encounter it – and you will – think about what I am about to say: fear is like a shadow, it clouds our minds and makes our hearts grow cold. But the fear in our hearts is always worse than the reality. Remember that. Do not listen to their words. Do not look into their eyes.'

'And if I do?' She thought of the grey boy's yellow eyes and the force of his will, pushing itself at her.

'You will be eaten by your own fears,' the Weatherman said.

Anne stared at him blankly. 'They can't control me.'

'How do you know? You have negative thoughts.' He looked at her keenly, then continued. 'We all do. And they are the gateway. Once the Darkness gets in, it requires great strength of will to dislodge it. Often we can't do it all on our own.'

'Well, I'm used to handling things on my own.' She gave the puddle a disdainful look. 'Could I have my stocks, please?'

'Of course.' The old man held them out to her. As she reached for them, a silvery green sheen seeped from underneath his coat, dazzling her, and for one moment she was happier than she had felt in a long time. Then the glow was extinguished, and she felt less certain.

'Now, are the boys inside?' The Weatherman peered into the house again.

'You've missed them.'

'Could you get them please,' his voice remained kindly, even when he gave a command. 'We don't have very long.'

*

As she approached the back gate, Anne saw that Dieter and Manfred had left without her. She knew she would have to ski fast to catch them, so she pointed her skis downhill, crouched low over them for least wind resistance, and hoped for the best.

Anne wasn't frightened of the snow or of speed. She wasn't frightened because she didn't know any better. But when the broad slope she was on became a narrow, winding track, with moguls – a series of small humps – Anne's determination wasn't enough to keep her upright. Her knees jarred, her skis slipped sideways, scraping over patches of ice. One moment she was standing, the next she was sliding on her stomach.

Bedraggled and snow-stained, she collected her stocks and her hat, pulled her pride about her like a winter coat and pushed off a second time. As suddenly as the slope had narrowed, it opened out again. Anne breathed a sigh of relief – no ice here – and squatted on her haunches, shooting across the slope so that her skis rattled. Slope, skis, girl and plaits were one straight line, as Anne's confidence (and her smile) returned. For safety's sake Violette opted to fly.

*

'It's staring us in the face.' Manfred was jumping on the spot waving the Calculator in front of Dieter's nose, talking quickly. 'I can't believe we didn't figure it out, it so obviously adds up to –'

'What?' Dieter had to calm him.

'An invasion!'

'You're nuts!'

'No I'm not.'

'You're nuts.'

'Listen…' Manfred waited, expecting Dieter to interrupt. People often interrupted when Manfred made unbelievable statements – and he could hardly believe this himself. But Dieter didn't cut him off; Dieter listened, and there was a moment's heavy silence.

'It's to do with the sun, or rather, the sun's energy field. When I checked it yesterday it was falling. As though something had come between it and us. Then this cloud appeared, but it's not a normal cloud. Look at it. Look how densely matted it is. And now the snow's black. It's a smokescreen.' His voice grew more urgent: 'We're trapped! There's no communication between us and the rest of the world. There's no way in, and no way out. Whatever's happening on that mountain, no one else knows about it!'

'Hold on. Stop!' Dieter halted the waterfall of words. 'What's all that have to do with this letter? I mean pieces of light…'

'But I told you.'

'Who is it addressed to?'

'Us.' Manfred saw the count-me-out expression on Dieter's face. 'Me.' And then he looked away, because that wasn't quite true either. 'They need help,' he said in a small voice.

'Who does?' Dieter asked tersely.

Manfred felt foolish. This was why he had been so secretive in the first place. And what he wanted to say next sounded even sillier, so he sheepishly pointed at the sky.

'Clouds don't need help.'

'But whatever that cloud's hiding might.'

'That's right,' said the Calculator, agreeing with Manfred for a change.

'There's a mountain behind the cloud, nothing else,' Dieter said quietly. 'I don't know where you get your ideas from. That cloud's pollution.'

'No.' Manfred answered, emphatic. 'It's an invasion.'

*

Nearby, a tree shuddered, releasing its load of dark snow. The pool of shade at the tree's feet lengthened, its darkness deepened. Only the brittle gleam of yellow eyes was visible.

There. Shadowy tongues flicked from hollow trees, claws pointed at Manfred, malevolent shapes flitted across the snow-littered earth. *They know.*

*

'There they are!' Violette squawked as Anne came to a shaky stop on a plateau. She saw Manfred jabbing his finger at Dieter, and at his Calculator. Then malign forms emerged from the tree trunks, to surround the boys. For a moment Anne's voice stuck in her throat, then she shouted, 'Dieter – look out!' But he was too far away and the blanket of snow absorbed her warning; the valley wind caught it and flicked it in her face.

'Oh…' With a hefty push she turned her skis into the valley towards them.

*

Where is the boy? A dark wraith towered in front of Manfred.

'What boy?' Manfred jumped at the unspoken words and was caught in the glare of yellow eyes. 'It's them!' He tried to alert his friend.

'Who are you?' Dieter asked, but the grey being ignored him.

Where is the child? It grew taller as it spoke.

'I don't know what you're talking about.'

You're lying. A snake's tongue licked uneven teeth. *Where is he?*

Manfred retreated two steps, his knees weakening.

WWTTUMmmmmmmmmm!!! A girl on out-of-control skis cut between Manfred and the dark form and crashed into the snow.

'Run!' Anne screamed.

Enough! Dead eyes stared at her.

'But…' Small defence, small voice.

You're not wanted here. The eye-light pierced Anne's skull. Too late she remembered the Weatherman's warning, and felt the Shadow's command take hold. Suddenly uncertain, frightened, she stood up, unsteadily, as if in a trance.

'Wake up, wake up!' A throaty bird whisper. Violette fluttered onto her shoulder and pinched her nose. 'Anne, wake up.' But Anne stamped her feet back into her skis and continued down the slope.

Manfred had been taken prisoner. Not with rope or wire, but with thoughts. His head was empty. He couldn't look away from the yellow eyes and stood trembling and afraid. Dieter wasn't caught so easily. Dieter was defiant. There was a strength in him that fought them. The Darkness continued to probe Manfred's brain until it hurt. When it realised Manfred was the weaker of the two it concentrated more forcefully on him.

Tears rolled down Manfred's cheeks. Tears from trying to

escape, from battling a force too strong for him. He shivered, grew hot. His determination wilted.

Where is the boy? Tell me! –

'Don't. Don't tell it anything,' Dieter whispered, but the thought-voice was louder than any words Dieter could say.

Manfred's hands were balled into fists. His face was white, his lips ashen. His eyes were vacant. He had to tell; he couldn't stand it anymore.

'I... I...'

'Don't. Manfred, please!' Echoes of words swirled in his brain.

'The letter...the letter said...we... It said we have to...' Manfred's teeth chattered uncontrollably as he tried to force his mouth shut.

*

'There you are.' The Weatherman's voice reached Anne, the green glow he carried with him thawed the cold that had settled around her heart. 'I thought I'd lost you.' He skied down the slope, nimble on old Nordic skis.

Anne blinked, and slowly refocussed.

'Manfred and Dieter are in terrible, terrible trouble,' she blurted, remembering. 'I looked into their eyes. I listened to them. I know you warned me not to, but...' She hadn't protected them, and now Manfred and Dieter were snared, and she didn't know what to do.

'Send the bird.' The Weatherman's voice stilled her panic. 'Animals can withstand them. Make as much noise as you can.'

'Manfred Decker, Dieter Pfeiffer!' Violette catapulted into the air, shooting across the slope until she hung above the boys, squawking at them, breaking the heavy pressure that was concentrated on Manfred. She dive-bombed him, fluttering around his face, darting out of the way of the reaching shadowy hands. Manfred's mouth snapped shut. Colour returned to his cheeks.

'Manfred Decker! Dieter Pfeiffer!' Waving frantically, Anne called their names too.

'Decker! Pfeiffer!' The Weatherman added his voice to the clamour, and the dark forms faded into the trees. Violette landed on Manfred's shoulder and gave his ear a tweak, just to be certain.

'Ow!' He swiped at her and managed to grin shakily at his rescuers.

'You were lucky this time.' The Weatherman ran his eyes over Manfred, then motioned to Violette, who landed on his arm, rubbing her beak in the old man's beard. 'Well done,' he praised her softly, then turned to Manfred and Dieter. 'You two. Go home and pack. Anne, you find Georg and the little one. Tell Georg to do the same and meet us at the Valley Station. Tell him to hurry. Bring the little one back.' He lowered his voice and, looking towards the trees, added: 'Make sure he's safe. I'll meet you at Manfred's house in half an hour.'

No one reacted. They all glanced nervously towards where the dark beings had disappeared, remembering the hypnotic, glittering eyes.

'I'll deal with them,' said the Weatherman firmly.

He watched over the children, as they filed out of the forest. Then, brandishing his stocks as swords, the old man skied after the Shadows.

FOUR

THE KING'S CRYSTAL

1405

'It talked to us without moving its mouth.' Manfred's whispers fled to the corners of his room. 'Weird.' He pushed the last of his belongings into his rucksack and secured it.

'I heard it,' Dieter gave him a reproving look.

'You heard thoughts, not a voice. That's how they speak.'

'Don't start that again.'

'You saw them! Who – or what – are they? Why are they after us?' Manfred strode to the window and surveyed the street. Although it was still early, the dark cloud had turned day into night. 'How are we going to stop them?'

'Who said anything about "we"?' Dieter laughed nervously.

'Well, I can't do it alone.'

'You don't have to do anything.'

'We *do* have to!' Manfred was exasperated. 'The Weatherman agrees.' Dieter stared fixedly at the floorboards. 'Dieter! Two heads are better than one. We can't do nothing!' With a pounding heart Manfred thought about the Key they were supposed to find.

'Why not?'

'As soon as the going gets rough you always back away!' Disgusted, Manfred paced the room. 'Well, I'm not like that!' He realised he had hit his mark because Dieter's face burned.

The stove rattled in a gust of wind. Manfred stacked more wood into it, his eyes flicking over an enormous leather-bound book he'd found beside the woodpile when they had returned. It was very old. He carefully opened it. The Gothic writing inside resembled the letters of light.

'I found this on the verandah.'

'Tttch!' A small sigh of annoyance from Dieter. As they weren't talking, Manfred took no notice of the friend who wasn't a friend right now, and started to read.

Strange rumblings and other noise began in the mountains in the year the cloud came, the year of 1405.

1405. Six hundred years ago. Why was that year familiar?

Scrapings in the night, of such power houses shook and the people were afraid. Rock hit rock and a thunder called deep and loud into the day.

'Hey Dieter – listen to this.' Manfred's eyes were glued to the page. Dieter stood by the window, indifferent, so Manfred read out loud.

The world is a changed place since the arrival of the cloud. The sun no longer shines. The trees in the forest grow ill. Death steals across the land. The winters are colder than any in our memory; snow turns black and hides things fearful from the eyes of woman and man.

Manfred stopped. Dieter had stepped from the window and was listening now.

'This has happened before!' Manfred's eyes, wide with the discovery, snapped back to the page.

A measure of good came with the passing of the cloud. In spring, flowers in the field grow more beautiful than ever humankind has seen them. Lantern lights on summer hills glow at the midnight hour, to disappear should any mortal venture near. There are voices too, songs of birds, carried on air. Voices so faint they seem a part of the air itself, intangible as scent, without body or shape. But the winters are bitter and deadly and a great harm has come into the world.

'Manfred...' Dieter interrupted, but Manfred was oblivious to him, and to the low drumbeat of knockings that had begun to underscore his words.

Both an ill intent and the warmth of hope were left behind once the black snows melted and the cloud dispersed. There is an equal measure of dark and light that had not been on Earth before, and yet neither woman nor man can speak of what it is.

'Manfred –'

Or why it is.

'It's happened before!' Manfred closed the book.

'It's a fairy story.'

'It's a history book.'

'Fairytale.'

'All stories take root in fact.' The Calculator insinuated itself into their conversation.

'I suppose there is a similarity.' Dieter sighed. 'And it would help if we knew what was causing it…'

Manfred nodded, relieved. They were talking to one another again, a good sign. And Dieter had said 'we', which was more promising than 'you'. Putting the book on the desk he became aware of the knocking. His eyes swivelled to the door.

'Has our visitor arrived?' Now Manfred's voice sounded accusing.

'Yes. I tried to tell you.'

Manfred was halfway to the door when it flew open, and the old man stood in the doorway.

'Good,' the Weatherman said. 'I see you've packed.'

The demise of the Light Star

'First things first.' Manfred tried to take control with stiff-sounding words. 'You are the meteorologist, are you not?'

'I'm an old man.' The Weatherman deflected Manfred's formality gently.

'Yes, but you know what's going on.' Manfred's voice rose by a decibel. 'Your instruments –'

'...were destroyed.' The Weatherman's face was grim. 'Like yours.'

'You were near the alley yesterday; you warned me that it was a dead end.' Dieter studied the Weatherman's face thoughtfully.

'Brrr, it's cold.' The old man chose not to answer. 'Colder than usual. It's a sign.' He warmed his hands over the stove and saw the book that still lay on the desk. 'An excellent edition, don't you think? I take it you found it instructive?'

'So it's yours?'

The old man nodded mildly.

'It would help if we had a context,' Manfred added.

'Yes,' the Weatherman agreed. He looked sheepish. 'I owe you an explanation.' He didn't speak again until he'd turned on all the lights in the room. When he was sure nothing remained in shadow, he called the boys over. 'There are certain things you need to know.'

'Just tell us what's going on.'

The Weatherman overlooked Dieter's frown.

'A long time ago there was a little planet...'

'How long ago precisely?' Manfred asked, emphatic. 'Are we talking six hundred years?'

'No, long before that. So long ago you couldn't even imagine.' The Weatherman waited until Manfred was seated. 'This little planet was from another galaxy altogether. It was made completely of light. The Light Star had no solar system of its own, no suns or moons to steal sunlight or moonlight from. It was a planet that had no place on astrologers' charts, it simply trundled across the night sky and was gone by morning. Well, that's the way things used to be,' he added, his voice growing sad.

'The folk of the Light Star were called Light Beings. They were a little people who loved to laugh and sing. They never felt the cold, for if it grew cool, they drove their home to the shoulder of another sun and nestled in its warmth until their world had absorbed enough light and energy to move on. They were happy, this little race, skipping across the universe from one sun to the next, gathering light the way bees gather honey.'

'Recharging their battery cells?' Manfred asked.

'You could say that,' the old man replied. 'And in the great stretches of darkness between the suns, the king used an ancient light that had been caught in a crystal prism, fashioned before time began, which he wore around his neck. This light is why we find ourselves here.' For a moment the Weatherman fell into silent contemplation.

'Go on.' Manfred had to prod him.

'The Light Beings were a peaceful people, without

substance or shape, very like the light they gathered; shimmering creatures that could rise and fall softly, coasting on air. They were smiling, glowing creatures who were unafraid. Then, six hundred years ago –'

'Aha!' Manfred exclaimed. 'Six hundred years. 1405.'

The Weatherman paused, hesitant.

'Yes or no?'

'Yes.'

'I knew it. The date on the statue.' Manfred had remembered where he'd seen it. He contemplated the Weatherman's face. 'It's where I've seen *you* before!'

'A distant relative,' the Weatherman admitted.

'What was he running from?'

'Let him explain!' Dieter said.

The Weatherman gave him a grateful look.

'Six hundred years ago the planet of the Light Beings crashed into Earth. They left the orbit of the sun and flew too close to our planet. Our gravity caught them and a storm pulled them to the pinnacle of the highest mountain, where they were stuck.'

'Sound familiar?' Manfred gave Dieter a significant look.

'Once they had overcome their fear of being on another world, the king decided to explore it. They glided down on the drops of summer rain, while their little planet remained anchored, hidden by cloud on the mountaintop. And here they found a truly beautiful world.'

'"One day," said their king. "You may have one day, and then we must leave."'

'They had never seen trees before, nor flowers; they had never felt the touch of grasses or heard wind sigh through leaves. They had never seen sunlight glimmering on water, or the way the light grew thick and green in a forest glen. They were enchanted and gathered armfuls of everything they could find, leaves and grasses and flowers, to take with them so that these might grow on the Light Star. Soon the Light Beings were dispersed like the seeds of a dandelion flying on the wind.

'The king and the queen and their son remained in a field of red poppies brighter than any colour they had ever seen. They breathed the colour in with all their senses. They knew this was a way of taking it with them, in their hearts. Winking and blinking on the breeze, all who encountered them felt happy and at peace. The power of the crystal the king wore drew people from far and wide. It reached deep into their hearts and souls, and it stirred old longings. But dark things woke too, which the Light Beings couldn't know about, for in their world there had never been malignant intentions. While the sun was high, the dark stayed in the shade, watching them with yellow eyes.

'As the sun set, the king and his family were on their way back to the highest mountain, when they were met by a Shadow who barred their way. It coveted the king's crystal; it had been called by its ancient magic, its power.'

'Is that what they are? The grey people? Are they Shadows?' Dieter asked softly.

'Shadows. Shades. Demons. Sometimes you can't give

evil a name.' The Weatherman contemplated both boys. 'Creatures that fear the light.' He knew they understood.

'The king and the Shadow fought, and the battle drew villagers from their homes. But a wall of shade surrounded them, a sense of desolation halted them and the Earth people could only feel the tremors of the great battle. There was nothing to see in the dark that had risen, and a black fear was born on that night, a black death stole across the land.

'The king would have been killed had it not been for the power of the crystal he wore. It grew fiery and bright, it blinded the Shadow and made him powerless. But not before he had breathed a mist of darkness into the king's heart. The mist spread through the king's being, and he lost all sense of hope. He no longer cared for himself, his wife, his son, or for the crystal that had fallen in battle. The Shadow snatched it out of the grass. Its light grew wicked, a great sword flashing, opening the night and cutting at the hearts of all those whose eyes it touched. The people ran in terror from the things they had seen, but were frozen by the light to become statues of stone.'

'Is that what happened to the man in the town square?' Manfred asked softly.

'Yes. To many of my forebears.' The Weatherman sighed before continuing. 'And having felt the crystal's great power, the Shadow vowed never to let it go. But the light grew hot and burned its hands, and the crystal fell. The queen took it and held it high.

'"We must go," she cried to the king, "for only time will dissolve the darkness in your heart."'

'More Shadows stole out of the woods and surrounded the king, so that the queen could not reach him.

'"I will find a wise man," she promised her husband. "He will know what to do."'

'She took her son, not knowing that his eyes had also been tainted by darkness. Keeping the crystal, she kissed the king goodbye. They would never meet again.

'By nightfall the king's people gathered at the foot of the mountain. The summer had ended. Ice lay on the ground. Shivering, the Light Beings waited for their king and queen. When they did not return, they sent messengers to every corner of the fields and forests. They found their king wandering alone in the woods. All he had in his pockets were the seeds he had gathered, and a handful of flowers. The queen and her son and the crystal had disappeared.

'When they could no longer tolerate the cold, the Light Beings ascended with their king to the peak of the mountain, leaving only the queen's servants behind. Using what light energy they had left, they pulled their planet free. Sadly they watched the beautiful, treacherous Earth recede into the clouds. It vanished like a dream, and with it their happiness ceased.

'The king's councillors drove the Light Star into the spheres of the brightest suns, far away from the Earth and the influence of its Shadows, in the hope that they would melt the dark on the king's soul, but they did not. And the dark things that had crept on board, like thieves through a window, took hold. The king surrounded himself with his people and fought the Shadows with what little strength he had left. To ease his wounded heart he grew trees from the seeds he had collected, planting them in a secluded valley and protecting them with what magic remained.

'On Earth, the queen searched far and wide until she found a shepherd, an old man who tended goats and sheep high on the mountain. She knew that a man who worked in harmony with the lore of nature, who understood the stars and could read the wind and clouds, would best know the signs that would tell when the planet returned.'

'Like me!' Manfred gave Dieter a pointed look. 'Well, I didn't know it was a planet, but I knew it was some kind of celestial commotion.'

'Perhaps you too are a wise man.' The Weatherman paused to allow for Manfred's pride.

'Before the queen gave the crystal into the shepherd's care, she looked into its light and knew her world would be saved, and who would save it. Once she was certain, she entrusted the prince to the shepherd.'

'As a caretaker?' Manfred asked.

'Yes. It was his duty to keep the prince and the crystal safe.

'The queen had chosen wisely. The shepherd remained faithful to her and the child. From that time on, the crystal's light could be seen far away, a small star glimmering on the pinnacle of the highest mountain.

'Once a year the queen and those few who were with her, lit fires on every mountain and every hill, and strung lights on every tree in an attempt to draw the Light Star back to Earth. The queen whispered her hopes to the stars, but the king did not hear.

'While the planet had light, the Shadows stayed small, but slowly their will pushed the Light Star away from the suns, the light ebbed and the distance between the stars widened. The further the Light Star travelled into the universe, the bolder the Shadows became. Like spiders, they spun their dark web, and as it grew, the planet's ability to absorb warmth weakened and lethargy lay heavily on the Light Beings. Light turned to ice, which formed on the planet's surface and could not be swept away. Centuries passed. The Shadows grew fierce and warlike, the king weaker.

'The Light Beings faded; their shapes changed. The cold gave them substance, and they sprouted fur that grew long and wavy, angel's hair. Gradually their shimmer was extinguished; only their eyes spoke of the light inside, glowing a luminous green, and their faces, which had always known how to smile, showed only fright.'

'Why didn't they stay?' asked Deiter. 'Wouldn't they have had a better chance if they'd stuck together?'

'And ruin our world?' The Light Beings knew what they had unleashed and they tried to draw the evil away. At the time they still had light energy and thought it was enough. It was not.' The Weatherman nodded towards Manfred. 'Like batteries, their energy is running out. They've returned in a state of extreme emergency. For when the years pass each other, the light that remains will be extinguished. The Light Beings will never again feel the beam of the crystal that has called to them all this time, because they will no longer exist.' The Weatherman's story concluded heavily.

'What happened to the queen?' Dieter asked softly.

'She died of a broken heart.' The Weatherman's eyes were moist.

There was a long silence while Manfred and Dieter digested what they had heard.

'Most of what you say sounds plausible,' Manfred admitted at last. 'But for the sake of any doubters in the room, do you have proof?'

'Proof?' The old man indicated the dark snow outside. 'What more proof do you need?'

'There could be other explanations,' Dieter cut in.

'No, he's made his point,' Manfred conceded, and addressed the Weatherman again. 'How is it you know all this?'

'From time to time an emissary returned to Earth, to search for the queen.'

An expert at avoiding tricky questions himself, Manfred knew when someone else was being evasive.

'How do *you* know all this?' he asked the old man expectantly. 'Exactly how old are you?'

The Weatherman laughed. 'I'm old. But not as old as you think. Stories get passed down through generations. My father told me. His father told him, and all the fathers and grandfathers and great, great grandfathers before them told their sons and their grandsons. Unfortunately,' and now the Weatherman sighed, 'I don't have a son to tell my story to. So I'm telling you.'

'Were you looking after the prince too?' Manfred came straight to the point.

'I…inherited him for a short time.'

'But?' Manfred could sense he was hedging.

'He's with the next caretaker.' The Weatherman's reply was vague.

'What about the king's crystal?' Dieter asked quietly. 'Do you have that?'

'Yes, I do.'

Manfred turned the Calculator on and re-read the words of light.

'Is the king's crystal the Key referred to in this intergalactic SOS?'

'Yes.'

'And you want us to find the king and return the Key?'

'If you will.'

'And the prince?' Dieter asked thoughtfully. 'Does he have a role in all this?'

'He'll find you when the time is right.' The Weatherman's face folded into a smile.

'Why us? Why can't you do it?' Dieter still wasn't convinced.

'There are other forces at play,' the old man admitted.

'The Darkness has grown too powerful for one man alone to staunch. It can only be overcome through the work of many.'

'Two heads are better than one.' Manfred looked across at Dieter. 'That's what I'm always saying.'

'Six heads in this case,' the Weatherman corrected him.

'There are only two of us.' Manfred was perplexed.

'The Queen's Prophecy says six have been chosen to save the worlds.' The Weatherman observed both boys keenly. 'I place great trust in fate.'

'Well, there's Oh Mei.' Manfred cleared his throat.

'Here we are!' The door crashed open and Anne arrived with IDK in tow.

'Orff!' A furry red nose eagerly sniffed the Weatherman's shoes and a tail wagged excitedly.

'Have we missed anything?'

'No.' Manfred's lips pursed and he gave the Weatherman a worried glance.

'That brings it to five.' The Weatherman smiled.

'I won't be long.' Anne had seen Manfred's rucksack by the window, and started packing her suitcase. Manfred sighed. He lowered his voice, aware that the little boy was staring at him.

'And with you, we're six?' he addressed the Weatherman, who smiled enigmatically. 'Where do you propose we start looking?'

'Where do *you* think you should start?' The Weatherman turned the question back on Manfred.

'Well, if the planet of the Light Beings is on the highest mountain, then that's where we should go.' Manfred considered the map of the mountains on the Calculator's screen. 'So I say we start at the Valley Station and take a cable car from there.'

'Good idea!' The Weatherman looked hugely relieved.

'Right.' Manfred rose, eager to get going. 'I think I'm the best equipped to look after the Key.'

The Weatherman smiled at his enthusiasm. 'You will get the Key when you are ready to receive it. First I must throw a little light on what you're doing. I'll need the Key to tear a hole in their web to let the sun's light in, for they fear light, and it will be your greatest ally.'

'That means we can only travel during daylight.' Manfred looked outside. 'Not that I'd call this daylight!'

'You don't have a choice.' The Weatherman had risen. He touched each boy on the shoulder and stroked Anne's cheek. For a moment they were enveloped by a green aura that made their hearts feel easy. 'Learn to act in concert. Trust is all you can count on. But remember, trust must be worked for, and won.'

He reached the door, which opened of its own accord, and before they knew he was gone, he was.

Flight to the stars

'Trust! How do we know we can trust *him*?' Dieter's words were carefully measured. 'Are you really sure about this?'

'Yes.' Manfred heaved his rucksack out the open window and stole a glance in Dieter's direction. 'Are you coming?'

'Have to see you get there safely,' Dieter replied, and at last Manfred breathed easily. He reached for the second rucksack.

'I'll take that.' Anne grabbed it. She had a strong suspicion that whatever they were planning, they weren't going to include her.

'No, Anne. Give it back,' Dieter said quietly. 'Manfred, you take the rucksack.'

'I can carry it!' Anne flared.

'I know you can. But you have another job to do.'

Reluctantly, Anne passed the rucksack to Manfred and he dropped it over the balcony.

Dieter turned back to Anne. 'You're staying here.'

'What?'

'What?' Manfred echoed.

Dieter cut them both off. 'You and IDK are staying at home. We need you to keep an eye on things here. To make sure they don't get out of hand.'

'But the Weatherman said –' Manfred tried to intervene.

'I want to come with you.' Anne's voice was shaking.

'It's too dangerous, Anne. We don't know what's out there. We might be gone for days.' Dieter hoisted himself out the window onto the balcony and then shimmied down the drainpipe.

'I'm not sure that was such a good idea,' Manfred mumbled, following him. 'He did say six.'

'They can't ski.' Dieter had made up his mind. 'They'd only slow us down.' His answer was final.

Anne watched Manfred and Dieter disappear into the gloom of the garden. The clash of disappointment and anger were loud in her head. *Anne, stay home. We don't need you. You're not wanted.* The same old story.

'I'll show them!' she said to IDK, to them, to herself, and grabbed her things.

❋

A suitcase, a rucksack, a girl, a cockatoo, a dog and the little boy landed in the snow below Manfred's balcony. Two pairs of skis were collected from the back door. Quickly packing their belongings onto Manfred's old sled, Anne set a course straight ahead, her eyes fixed on Dieter and Manfred's tracks.

'Hey!' Suddenly an obstacle blocked her path. Ziggi. Laden with skis, parcels, her father's credit card, the white cat wrapped around her shoulders – a living scarf. Epsilon bristled.

Anne crossed the street. But Ziggi's brand of impertinence wasn't easily shaken. Ziggi wouldn't leave Anne alone. Oh no, Anne would pay for making a fool of her.

'You and your stupid bird.' Ziggi's words were needles.

Anne kept walking. Ziggi hurried after her and her possessions rattled. Anne moved to the edge of the footpath, forcing Ziggi into the gutter. But even weighted with purchases, she overtook Anne, yanked the rope out of her hand and grabbed hold of the sled. With one swipe, Ziggi pushed IDK off, and loaded her own packages on it.

'Take us to the hotel,' she said emphatically.

'Nasty piece of work!' Violette scolded her from a safe distance. 'Bad, bad, bad.'

Orff growled, defending Anne's belongings, and Ziggi soon learned that little dogs have a talent for biting ankles.

Reluctantly Anne called Orff to heel. Ziggi brushed off her dishevelment. Her ankle hurt but she wouldn't show *Anne* that. And she could still annoy her. She could see Anne was in a hurry, so she attached herself like a leech.

'Go away,' demanded Anne.

'Don't want to.'

'Leave me alone.'

'No.' And so it went all the way along the street. The more Anne cursed and scolded, the more determined Ziggi was to stay.

*

In the murky glow of fog lamps on snow, Dieter and Manfred struggled through town, aware of a scrabbling behind walled fences, of stones rattling on the pavement, as though a thousand rats were gnawing at them; running feet, hushed voices and wicked whisperings. A seething ocean swell of sound surrounded them. They could see nothing – the Shadows were invisible in the dark – but they were aware of an intense and terrifying cold.

They ran through the empty town square, hampered by their skis and rucksacks, which they carried awkwardly. They passed the statue. Their faces were as pale and harrowed and as afraid as the tortured man who pointed in the direction they were going. There was no mistaking the Weatherman's face, etched on the stone features. The statue was running, half turning towards the blackness behind, which was threatening to overwhelm them. Both boys realised the statue was a memorial for future generations to remember what had been. Now they clearly saw that the future had arrived.

'This way!' Dieter cut through a lane between two houses and headed for the forest beyond the town. They passed the last house. Trees bent against the dark weight on their boughs. The paths were choked with snow; even the larger paths that were cleared regularly were heavy with snowdrifts. The dark was unrelenting, the sun could not pierce the cloud, and there was nothing to point the way. But the forest and fields were Dieter's playground and workplace; he'd been this way often enough, and he knew every turning. He quickly passed between the trees, recognising the vague shape of an oak, the blurred contour of a hill; he knew that fence, that sty, this hayshed; he could read the signs of the land as he read a book, and he forged ahead, certain, with Manfred following close behind.

At a fork in the path, they found Georg, pulling a laden sled that knocked against his heels.

'Oh Mei, what a racket!' was all Georg could manage. He bent double, his breath wheezing, chin near his stomach, eyes wide in surprise. He was scared, but he didn't know of what.

Georg looked around once he'd caught his breath. 'Where's Anne?'

'Can you keep going?' Dieter cast his eye over the supplies in Georg's sled.

'Sure,' Georg said, sounding uncertain. 'But shouldn't we wait for –'

Dieter didn't wait. He strode off again and Georg fell into line behind Manfred and was soon huffing through snow-drifts that reached his chin.

*

Anne managed to skirt around the town square. No Dieter, no Manfred, no clues about the direction they had taken. All she could see was the snow boiling with pockmarks along the footpath.

'Which way do you think they've gone?' Anne caught IDK's eye. Above them the streetlights weakened.

'Who? Who's gone where?' Ziggi demanded.

'Are you a cockatoo?'

'No!' yelled Ziggi.

'NO!!' shrieked Violette.

'I've had enough of this!' Ziggi's lips pursed. 'Don't think I'm going to let you steal my things! I want them taken to my hotel!'

'Shh!' Anne could feel the cold formlessness around them and, clutching IDK more tightly, followed Orff, who ran through a lane between two houses and into the forest.

'My father is a very important man!'

'Shut up!!'

Now Ziggi heard the seething too. Saw the Shadows

move from their hiding holes in the trees, a wasp-swarm forming. They had multiplied.

'What are they?' A note of uncertainty crept into Ziggi's voice.

Anne peered ahead, not daring to make a sound. She felt as though she was caught in a room with no windows or doors, in a dream with no hope of waking.

'Watch out!' Violette screeched and in the next moment the wind had her and sent her like an arrow into the sky. She was gone, but she didn't stop her warning call. 'Look out, look out, look out!'

'Quick!' Anne's scream was lost in the sighing of wind rushing through a thousand sharpened teeth. She pushed IDK into motion. 'Don't let them separate us.'

Ziggi didn't move.

'Come on!'

Ziggi stared, transfixed.

'You're afraid!' Anne tugged Ziggi's sleeve.

'Am not!' Still Ziggi hesitated. Shadows were welling, lapping, nipping, as though a dam wall had broken and dark, rancid water was pouring in from all sides, threatening to drown them.

'Ziggi!'

But Ziggi had frozen.

Anne bent, tied a piece of string through Orff's collar, and whispered 'find them'. There was a tone in her voice, Ziggi was suddenly aware of – an earnest, frightened tone she couldn't ignore.

'Don't leave me!' Her hand found Anne's at last and, holding onto IDK and the sled, they stumbled downhill, through the trees.

Suddenly, hoary fingers reached for Anne. Tendrils, solid and wide as tree branches, passed sticky threads across her face, and she was pulled off her feet. She dropped the string, had enough presence of mind to push IDK and Ziggi away from her, and then she disappeared.

'Don't stop!' her voice came from inside the thicket. 'Keep going downhill.'

Anne struggled, aiming blows behind her, fighting with her elbows and nails. But she was enveloped by a black film that glued her mouth and her eyes closed. She tore at it, gasping for air, wiping her face clean. More threads wrapped themselves in her hair, lassoed her so that her elbows pressed into her sides and she couldn't fight. The threads curled around her throat and tightened, bark arms pulled at her, this way, that way, backwards and down.

'Help me!' Anne was alone. She had always been alone. It was nothing new and she would not give in.

Twig hands reached for her plaits. Anne wriggled and pinched. But the renewed energy didn't help. The blackness swallowed her voice and she couldn't shout. Her determination drained. Weak arms, weak legs. Feet without the energy to kick, her head without the strength to toss. She let it drop forward. Her hands were tied to her sides. Her will ebbed.

'Please help me.' Her voice was rough and small. Only her fingers were free, could move at all. She wriggled them into her pocket and grasped her pocket knife. She held still, very, very still; gathering the last of her strength. Then she cut at the threads of the cocoon that held her, heard them snap, brittle, one after the other. She kept going until her arms were free, and her legs, until she could breathe again. Now she was being held only by her hair.

She stabbed at the thing dragging her down, down. Sticky acid burned her skin. She had found her mark. But it held tight to her hair, and she was pulled along, deeper, further away from Dieter and the others, and no matter how hard she fought, she couldn't reach the bindings with her knife.

Anne continued to stab. Then she tried sawing and cutting. She felt her hair ripping at its roots as she desperately cut at it and she was suddenly free. No horse's mane now. The cruel tendrils, the suffocating membrane released her. With the last of her energy she ran as fast as she could towards the voices, towards the sounds of life. She broke from the trees and cannoned into a clearing and the group that was huddled there. She scattered them.

'Anne!' Dieter cried out and the others looked at her with fear-filled eyes.

Anne stood among them, not breathing, not crying. She couldn't cry. She had disobeyed Dieter, she was here, where she shouldn't be… She looked around. At Georg, Dieter, Manfred, Ziggi. And realised IDK was missing. IDK, Violette, Orff and Epsilon. She had lost them.

'There's something out there.' She could still feel the net

of tendrils flowing out, capturing her, a fly in its webbing. 'It's hideous!' She didn't trust herself to continue.

They stood in a circle, back to back. The black snow hid the Shadows and the children realised it was their cover. To blind the world to what was happening.

'There's something out there,' Anne repeated softly. She didn't take her eyes off the forest. 'It's alive and it pulled me. It wouldn't let go.' A branch snapped, whip-crack shots fired nearby. They jumped.

'Where are we?' Ziggi asked.

'Valley Station.'

Anne could barely see the outline of a building, low-lying. Two strands of thick cable grew out of it, and disappeared into the dark mass across the valley.

'We won't make it. We're surrounded.' Manfred's heart hammered loudly in his chest.

Anne felt a wet nose nuzzle against her hand. Orff wagged his tail for her, then growled, barking sharply at the trees, daring anything to come close.

The forest suddenly opened. The Shadow army broke into the clearing, holding the children in a gaze of yellow.

'Don't look into their eyes!' Anne warned, but it was too late. They stood frozen, looking on horrified as the grey half-people massed around them. Their shapes were changing, their stolen bodies bending, stretching, and finally peeling off. Skin dropped like pieces of discarded clothing, and the darkness inside joined together, to hover, incorporeal in front of them.

Breathe me. The voices came from no one place, the Darkness drifted closer and the cold became more intense.

'Hold your breath,' Dieter yelled. The others turned to him in horror as the black vapours swirled around them. Anne covered her mouth and nose, squeezed her eyes shut, but she had seen too much and the fear in her mind took hold. She wouldn't breathe, she wouldn't think, she wouldn't feel again – ever! She knew she was going to die.

Then, in the dark spaces of her own mind, she saw the green star glow.

'Anne!' Dieter's elbow was digging into her ribs. 'It's all right. Look! He's here!' Anne opened her eyes, and the green star became real.

'This way!' An old voice ripped into the darkness. The glowing light he held speared across the snow. It pulsed, a trickle of silver, a flood of green, a star-prism coming from inside the Valley Station. The Weatherman stood behind the light, his hands cupping a crystal.

'I've been waiting for you,' he called in a voice that beat down the mutinous whisperings of the Shadows. Warmth flooded out from his hands; green light bathed him. 'Come.' The light grew stronger; the darkness that had been threatening them cowered back.

In a mad dash they sped across the space between them and the Valley Station, and the doors, which had been locked, opened to admit them. They stumbled inside, dragging their belongings in after them.

'In here.'

They threw themselves into the cable car, which swung like a pendulum on wire. In the green glow, its cables appeared sharp as the edges of a knife cutting into the dark, until they disappeared up the mountain.

'Quick.' Manfred shouldered his way to the controls, as Georg and Ziggi pulled the sleds in, while Anne pushed from outside.

'We can't leave him behind.' Anne stopped short of the door and hurried to the circle of light. 'IDK?'

'Here!' A cockatoo's cry lifted from the forest.

'There isn't time to go back!' Ziggi tried to jiggle the controls out of Manfred's hands.

'Go get him, Anne!' In the flickering light the old man looked taller than the mountain, his beard swinging long and low and glistening with green. A swarm of dark things were wound in his white hair, writhed in it. The old man was unperturbed. Anne looked towards him but she couldn't see his face.

'I'm frightened.' Her voice quivered. The Shadows spat laughter at her. Anne summoned the last of her courage. 'Shine the light over there!' she ordered the old man, as though the crystal star were a torch, and she pointed to the trees. The receding tide of light barely reached the trunks and touched IDK, who was cowering there. A faint glow emanated from the child and enveloped him. The cat and the bird stood fast, defending him.

Epsilon spat, arching her body. Her hisses were fiercer than those of the Shadows, her needle teeth gleamed, her claws were daggers. She was a green-eyed fiend with an indomitable will. Violette made flying attacks on any Shadows that eluded the cat.

'Anne – get in the cable car!' Ziggi shrieked.

'No!' She ran forward.

Suddenly, Georg was at her side, wielding a torch like a rapier, and Dieter, holding a flare. The small pin-lights stabbed through the darkness and united with IDK's pale, shimmering light. Warding off the Shadows once more, they fenced off a safe passage through. They reached him and lifted him to his feet, then turned to the cable car, running low, fast, eluding shadowy hands, their feet barely touching the hard-packed snow. They dived into the cable car and Anne pulled the door closed.

Shadows surrounded the capsule and hammered on the windows with the force of crashing waves. Only a pane of glass separated them from their prey.

Manfred pushed Ziggi out the way and pulled at levers and shifted gears. He pressed the ignition button, pressed it again and again, as dark hands pummelled the glass and more and more faceless shapes crowded in on them.

'It's no use. It's broken,' Manfred screamed against the rising tide of noise. 'We're trapped.'

'No!' The old man's voice boomed. He was bent over the motor that powered the cable car and it sprang to life before that one word was out. A whirring of bolts and screws, iron teeth and claws, stiff with cold, was called into a fast tempo and the cable car glowed a vivid green. The dark creatures fell away, burned by the light, leaving a grey residue sticking to the glass. The ghostly howling increased as if the sound alone could break the glass, but the car pulled away from them.

The children turned to the front, ignoring the things outside, knowing that the only escape was up there, on the mountainside. The tightly stretched cables slackened. They snaked, shivering, harp-strings playing. There was a sawing, then a splintering, a vibration so highly pitched that they had to cover their ears. Iron screamed. Ahead of them was the cloud, the cables stretching into it. One final shudder and the cables snapped, recoiling in a whiplash action that flung the cable car in a high arc, further than the Shadows could reach. The capsule was out of control, rolling through the air, hulled in an aura of green light, without a sign of ever coming down. The black cloud came closer, closer; its smoking fingers reached out to it, held it and pulled it in. The cloud swallowed the cable car whole.

FIVE

PLANET OF ICE

Defiance

The sun's light was thin gold; the cold was so brittle it threatened to snap. The cable car had landed halfway up the slope, a black crust of dirt outlining the shape of it. It looked like a dead beetle lying on its back. Snow was piled high around it and crowded in the door. Nothing moved for a long time. Then, from inside, a small hand wiped away the sticky crusting. The cable car moaned and tilted a few degrees closer to toppling over completely. The door was flung open. A load of snow was dislodged and shimmered in the air, like the flakings of tiny mirrors.

Anne brushed it off and hoisted herself into the doorway. She had to disentangle herself from the mass of bodies inside, and from the knot of rope, boots, skis, loose pieces of clothing and scientific apparatus that had spilled out of the rucksacks. She jumped clear. Ancient mountains stood around her, bearded in frost. They dominated the horizon, blanketed in pristine snow, and etched out of deep blue sky.

Anne shook her head to clear it. She pulled her coat about her ears. Her nose stung, her breath came short, her chin was frozen so that she couldn't open her mouth to speak. It was a still day, but there were clear signs that a strong wind had swept across the rippled snow, tilting the trees on the downward slope. Fir needles, bark and small twigs chequered the landscape brown and green.

The cable car behind Anne stirred and groaned again. The crusting of black snow broke and fell like collapsing chain mail. A shout of laughter rang out.

'You look like a plucked chicken!' Ziggi, hands on hips and mouth wide open, stood in the doorway and flicked her hair. Anne's hands hurried to her own. The plaits were gone, there was only stubble.

'I don't know what's worse – before or after!' Ziggi taunted her, and was immediately toppled off her perch and landed face first in the snow.

The cable car shook. Angry squabbling penetrated the icy cabin and the others stirred. Dieter jumped out and catching hold of two separate ear lobes, pulled Anne and Ziggi apart.

'Can't you two get on for five minutes?'

'She started it!' Ziggi hissed.

'I did not.'

'Shut up!' Dieter let go, but not without a warning glower.

'What happened to you?' Georg's head appeared from inside the cable car, and with a struggle of heaves and kicks he managed to tip out. He was followed by Manfred, then IDK. They all looked at Anne curiously.

'Is anyone hurt?' Dieter asked. No one was.

'Anne?' Manfred jumped down beside her and touched her cheek. 'What's this?' A black substance stuck stubbornly to her skin.

'It's soot. She's a grub.' Ziggi proclaimed.

'It is not! I am not!'

'It isn't soot. It looks more like dried blood.' Manfred tried to wipe it off with his glove, and when it wouldn't come off, he tried with a handful of snow.

Anne's cheeks smarted. The cold lay on the nape of her neck where her hair should have been. She shivered. Her eyes filled with tears.

Manfred finally succeeded in carefully scraping some of the substance off her cheek with his scalpel, and smeared it onto a glass slide that he took from his rucksack. He placed it under a small microscope, which was in the rucksack too, and examined it.

'Where are we, Dieter?' Georg stared out into the white wilderness. Dieter jumped onto the cable car and studied the mountains. He could easily identify those he knew. But in the spaces between the familiar peaks there were other peaks he'd never seen before, as if the valley hollows had been filled with new mountains.

'Do you know where we are or don't you?' Ziggi demanded.

'Yes…no. I don't know.' Uncertainty played on Dieter's features.

'You're as bad as he is!' The toss of Ziggi's head indicated IDK. Suddenly there was a loud gurgle.

'I'm starving!' Georg turned on his heel, embarrassed, and disappeared into the cable car. His voice drifted out, plaintive. 'If I don't eat I'll go nuts!'

After a great deal of commotion, he reappeared pulling the rucksack laden with supplies out behind him. Georg promptly overbalanced and fell into the snow. Before he could sort himself out, Epsilon had secured a salami and, lifting each paw tentatively, stalked across the deep snow out of reach.

'Will you control that cat!' Georg yelled, glaring at Ziggi. He gathered the remaining provisions, making it absolutely clear that food rationing was his responsibility.

'You shouldn't have brought her,' Dieter said softly to Ziggi.

'She goes where I go.' Ziggi bristled as Epsilon sometimes did. 'And what about Anne's mouthpiece? And the dog?'

'You'll have to carry her.'

'Tell me something I don't know!' Ziggi said archly, and swept off after her cat.

A string of equations and hurried conferring came from a sheltered corner behind the cable car. Manfred, hunched over his microscope, was in consultation with his Calculator.

'It's just as I thought,' he mumbled when Dieter joined

him. 'This is blood. But it isn't Anne's.' Low, worried words. 'The question is, whose is it?'

'If it's blood, it's an animal's.'

'Not from our world. Didn't Anne say something had caught hold of her in the forest?' Manfred inched closer to Dieter. 'I think we're up against more than these Shadows, you know.' He lowered his voice even further. 'And another thing. How come we weren't broken into pieces when we crashed – have you asked yourself that?'

'We landed in a deep snowdrift,' Dieter surveyed the mountains unhappily.

'We were enveloped by that green light.' Manfred corrected him. 'It cushioned us. While we were catapulted onto the Light Star!'

'Don't be ridiculous.'

'Now look here!' Manfred raised his voice in frustration. 'What gives you the right to call me ridiculous?' Flecks of spittle formed at the corners of his mouth. 'Didn't you listen to a word the Weatherman said?' He could see doubt beginning to build in his friend's eyes.

'There has to be another explanation.'

'Okay, I'll prove it once and for all.' Manfred keyed the map into the Calculator's screen. He had to turn it several times to find the right way up and the mountains of light floated in the air in front of him like a hologram. He pointed at them, then to the mountains around them. 'Do you see the similarity?' Dieter had to agree. Manfred reread the light-letter again, his lips moving as in prayer.

This is an intergalactic SOS. We are looking for the Wise Man who has the Key. Only the Key can save us. If it is not turned at the midnight hour, when the Years pass one another, then the Light Star will be destroyed. Our light will expire. Please help. Return and turn the Key. Time is scarce.

'It's pretty vague.' Dieter still sounded critical. 'What midnight hour? And what's "turning it" supposed to mean? It doesn't even say where the king is.' He thrust his hands deep into his pockets. 'How much time do we have?'

'They're not going to spell it out, are they? What if this falls into enemy hands? We have to use our ingenuity.' Manfred grinned. 'This is incredible! We're about to explore another planet!'

Dieter didn't think it was incredible at all. Not if the recent attack was an indication of the behaviour of the life forms on this planet.

'It does explain the extra mountains,' Dieter conceded. Then he looked puzzled again. He had a fair idea where they were, even with the planet's extra mountains surrounding them. 'But where's the Mountain Station? Where's the Weatherman's hut?'

The Mountain Station wasn't anywhere. Only the broken threads of ski-lift cables lying in the snow, and posts that had snapped like matchsticks. Dieter followed their trail along the ridge-line. He found the Mountain Station at last. Or what was left of it. A stew of molten steel had coagulated in the snow. Shards of glass glittered fiercely. A once-moving road of metal lava had cooled and stopped, sluggish, halfway down. The Shadows had blown up the only contact with the valley.

'We can't take that route,' Manfred sighed. 'Once we're ready to leave.' He searched the sky. 'At least the Weather-man kept his promise. He's used the Key to cut a hole in the cloud.' Dieter looked at him, curiously. 'It's still daylight here.' Manfred faltered. 'But I don't know how he plans to get the Key to us, and without it –'

'Here, I've made a sandwich,' Georg interrupted. Dieter shot Manfred a warning glance, and Georg wondered at the almost imperceptible nod Manfred gave in return.

'Thanks, Oh Mei.' Dieter said, before Georg could ask.

'And drink lots of fluids to stay hydrated,' Georg reminded them. 'We're very high.'

Dieter nodded. 'We have four hours, at the most, to find shelter,' he murmured to Manfred.

'Hey!' A shout from Ziggi distracted them.

Georg turned to confront the loudmouth before she could make any demands.

'This is all we have,' he said firmly.

'I want duck liver pate, caviar and camembert cheese,' Ziggi insisted. 'Not this muck! And goat's milk for Epsilon, she's allergic to cow.' Ziggi bit into the slice of pumpernickel bread Georg had given her and screwed up her face. 'It's disgusting.' She tossed it to Orff. Then a movement caught her attention and her eyes glittered dangerously. Georg forgotten, she stalked over to Anne, who was sorting the cable car's contents into two piles. The 'useless' pile had grown to gigantic proportions, made up entirely of Ziggi's and Manfred's belongings.

'What do you think you're doing?' An accusing hand snatched a pair of goggles out of Anne's hand. 'Get out of my things!'

'You don't need two pairs.' Anne held a second pair out of Ziggi's reach.

'Who says?'

Anne took no notice. She turned to IDK.

'Do you have any goggles?'

The little boy shook his head. He was scared and cold, and he was poorly dressed, so he huddled in the doorway of the cable car and didn't dare move out of the little warmth it afforded. Anne threw the goggles to him. Ziggi's expression hardened into anger. They were *her* things Anne was giving away.

'You can't do that!' Ziggi spluttered. But Anne did, and handed him a bright orange ski suit and two jumpers. IDK mumbled a thankyou. Ziggi grabbed Anne's arm. 'I said stop it!'

'He has to be warm too.' Anne shrugged her off.

'Sweetie.' It was offensive, the way Ziggi said it. 'I wouldn't, if I were you.' Her eyes narrowed when Anne ignored her. 'Fine. Don't say I didn't warn you.' She minced daintily across the snow towards Manfred. 'Oh Manfred,' she cooed softly. 'I think you should take a look at this.'

Manfred's eyes opened to his immediate surroundings. He saw the two piles of objects in the snow, recognised his equipment, and paled. For a moment his mouth opened, but no noise came out. Then he pushed his glasses onto the bridge of his nose and, with his elbows and chin out, marched over to Anne.

'I really have to lodge a protest.' Manfred's voice rose several octaves.

'She won't listen.' Ziggi gave Anne a superior smile.

'I'm sorting the essential supplies from the junk.' Anne remained unperturbed.

'Junk?!' was all Manfred could get out.

'We can't take it.'

'We have to take it! It *is* essential. It's of the highest scientific importance!'

'I told you.' Ziggi smiled coyly as Manfred, handling his instruments lovingly, repacked his rucksack. 'What would a layperson know about science?' Ziggi stooped to help him.

'Especially a girl.' Manfred sighed heavily. 'Of course I don't mean you, Ziggi.'

'Of course not.' Another poisonous smile was aimed at Anne.

'You'll have to carry it all.' Anne knew she had been outmanoeuvred. Ziggi stole a victorious glance in Manfred's direction.

'The birdcage comes too,' said Manfred. 'But *you* can carry it, Anne.'

Dieter had been watching them.

'Why don't you rely on what's in there?' He pointed at Manfred's skull. 'It wouldn't weigh as much.'

'It's not that simple, Dieter. This "junk" might save our lives!' Manfred filled the pockets of his anorak with gadgets, pulled the string of his rucksack to secure it, and hoisted it onto his back. Ziggi packed her extra racing skis, bags of clothing and a tube of lip-gloss. The others did the same with food and warm clothes, and sorted their skis from the jumble in the cable car.

'We should talk about the ground rules,' Dieter said quietly when they had straggled into line. 'Animal owners are responsible for their own animals.' His eyes met Ziggi's. 'Orff can ride on the sled and I'll pull it. Manfred and Oh Mei can alternate pulling the other sled. We have a fair distance to cover, so unless you're exhausted we'll keep going. But let me know if you're having difficulties.'

He waited for Violette to settle on Anne's shoulder. Ziggi clicked her fingers and Epsilon sprang onto her head, to become a furry turban. They all faced the two crags that formed a gateway to the valley below. For a moment they could see Wintersheim, a tiny grey dot shimmering faintly, water at the bottom of a well – then just as suddenly, it was enveloped by the black cloud.

'We're not going that way.' Dieter called their attention away from the valley and focussed it onto the mountains.

'Yes we are,' Ziggi said sharply. Georg was inclined to agree with her. Skiing downhill was better than climbing up. He kept his fingers crossed.

'We're heading inland.' Dieter's voice remained firm.

'Why?' An explosion of disbelief.

'We can't stay in the open, and we can't get down, so we're going into the mountains.'

'Now listen to me.' Ziggi lost her temper. 'I start training tomorrow, and I can't miss a single day, so I'm going down.'

'How?' Dieter asked, staying calm.

'That way.' Ziggi jabbed her fists in the direction of the crags, and the valley beyond.

'It's too steep.' Dieter persevered. 'Too unstable.'

'You mightn't be able to ski it, but I can.' Ziggi tightened her boots.

'Hold your horses for one second.' The authority in Manfred's voice slowed her preparations. 'Ziggi, we do have our reasons.'

'I don't care.'

Manfred's mouth snapped closed. Ziggi glared.

'I think we'd better tell them, Dieter.' Manfred slowed the pace of his words. 'I haven't said anything because I didn't want anyone to be unduly alarmed. But it might be dangerous if you don't know.' He handed his Calculator to his cousin. 'Read the letter and make up your own minds.'

Anne read the letters of light that flimmered on the Calculator's screen, then passed it on to Georg, who considered it silently, taking a long time to digest it.

'Wow! I knew something was up,' he said finally, before handing it to Ziggi. 'Who do we give this Key to? Where do we have to take it?'

'We know who. And we know where – roughly…' Manfred admitted. 'Which is why we have to climb up, not ski down. Ladies and gentlemen. Dog, cat and bird,' he took a deep breath, 'we are about to explore a new planet.'

'NEW PLANET!!! You tell bigger stories than your cousin,' Ziggi accused him.

'What sort of planet?' Georg quickly interceded.

'You don't seriously believe this rubbish!' Ziggi took up her skis.

'What do you think those things were that chased us?'

'It was a Fasching Parade. All those silly hats and wooden masks they put on.' Ziggi had worked it all out.

'Fasching isn't until the new year. And you can't tell me –' Manfred suddenly stopped in mid-sentence. 'What did the message say about the passing of the years?'

'When the years pass one another…' the Calculator scrolled through the letter again. 'The Light Star will be destroyed.'

'That has to be New Year's Eve!' Manfred gasped, excited. 'Midnight, New Year's Eve – I bet that's what it is.'

'You're loopy. You're ALL loopy!' Ziggi made a few more inarticulate sounds and marched away from the group. Her skis hit the snow. She peered into the grey-black mass of cloud that lay in the valley beyond the cliffs, lifted her cat off her shoulders and placed her on the snow.

'I'll send a valet for Epsilon.' She flung the words at Dieter, defiantly kicked her boots into the bindings of her skis and flipped the clips forward.

'Not that way, there could be avalanches.'

That infuriatingly know-all voice again. Ziggi ignored it. She stamped each ski once, and pushed off. Snow smoked behind her, the trail of an arrow that shot across the mountain.

'No!! No, no, no, no.' The echo threw the frightened voice from stone to stone until it returned to Dieter, unanswered.

Avalanche

They were all secretly relieved Ziggi had gone. Except Dieter. He coiled a length of rope about his waist and collected his skis. There was an urgency in his actions that couldn't be questioned. He rummaged in his rucksack and dragged out a second anorak, which he put on. Then he tightened his boots and stepped onto his skis and fastened them, ignoring the safety-bindings. Anne looked on critically. He wasn't holding his stocks properly. The loops of leather weren't around his wrists, the way they should be.

'That's not right,' she ventured, and was cut off.

'Yes it is. In this case, Anne, it's exactly right.' Manfred spoke gravely. He was as concerned as Dieter.

'What's going on?' Anne looked from one to the other.

'Skis and stocks are anchors in an avalanche.' The Calculator turned itself on.

'I will not be lectured by a machine!'

'In an avalanche,' said Manfred, 'skis and stocks pull you under, if you can't let them go.'

'But there isn't an avalanche.'

A dull, deep-throated roar thundered below them. Clouds of powder lifted off the slope to envelop the cliffs. For a moment the single tone of a girl's scream rose above it and was held thinly pitched in the unstable air, thrown above the growl, then as suddenly it was cut off.

Dieter pushed off towards the gateway in the cliffs, following Ziggi's trail as straight and fast as he could. He stopped suddenly as a broken piece of mountain surged down the slope. Manfred and Georg skied to where Dieter was standing and the three looked on, silent, pale. Great sheets of ice and loosened rock slipped below them, pulling trees from the ground, like rotten teeth, turning, churning, bringing the forest crashing into the valley.

'She skied as far as that fir tree.' Dieter pointed to a spruce, its roots exposed, slowly moving in the weight of the snow. 'Keep watching it.'

Anne and IDK eased the sleds down in a careful snow-plough to join them. After what seemed an eternity, the roaring lessened; the thunder becoming a grumble, then a low moan. Slowly the mass of snow and the matchstick trees came to a halt where the slope flattened.

Dieter turned to the others. 'We have to rescue her.'

'It's too late,' Manfred said.

'No! Not if we find her quickly.' Dieter wouldn't take on his pessimism. 'One at a time. IDK – you and Anne stay put. The snow is still unstable. It's too risky for the sleds. And we all have to be quiet. No sounds. Anything could set it off again.'

Nobody spoke. Dieter saw their hesitation.

'She might still be alive.' He whistled to Orff. 'Anne – watch me. If anything happens to me, watch the spot I go under. Keep your eyes on that exact point as it moves down.' Dieter faced Manfred. 'Come down when I get to that tree.' He indicated the tree he'd singled out before.

Anne pointed out one of Ziggi's skis, further down the slope.

'That's where she'll be,' she interrupted.

'No,' Dieter disagreed. 'Her ski is light. Ziggi's heavier. She'll be above it.' He turned back to Manfred. 'Come down the quickest way you can, but be safe. If another avalanche starts, go to the edge, where it's slower.'

Manfred nodded.

'What if it catches me?' His voice quavered.

'Get rid of the stocks. Start swimming.' Dieter made breast stroke motions. 'The swimming should get you to the surface. Oh Mei?'

'Understood.' Georg nodded.

They put on extra clothing. Dieter collected the tent. Anne handed over Orff's lead and Dieter clipped it onto the dog's collar. It was hard for her to send the dog into danger, harder to watch Dieter go.

'Be careful.'

Dieter skied without faltering or changing the course he'd planned. The slope was riddled with obstacles; in places earth had broken through the dislodged snow, and rocks gravelled the path, scratching into his skis. Orff stayed calmly in his arms, nose in the air, tail fluttering, a fan. They finally came to a halt beside the fallen tree, where Dieter let the dog down. Orff immediately sniffed the rubble.

Manfred pushed his glasses back and swallowed hard. It was his turn. He had never skied as well as Dieter, even on good snow. It wasn't good snow now, it was broken pieces of ice. He was tense and aware of the danger, not only to himself, but to them all, should he fall. Not sure of himself, he didn't ski fast. But he kept on course. He made it to each of the safety points Dieter had pointed out, the natural anchors: a large rock, a surviving tree, a plateau where there was less likelihood of snow dislodging. Manfred arrived finally, safe.

'Your turn, Oh Mei.' Anne's voice made Georg jump. He stared into the valley, but didn't move. 'You can do it.'

Georg doubted it. He couldn't ski well – not like Dieter, not even like Manfred. He was unsure and unbalanced, and he was afraid. But hesitating meant time lost for Ziggi, so Georg breathed in deeply, wiped the perspiration from his forehead and cautiously pushed off.

'Keep an eye on him,' Anne nudged Violette into the air, and silently the bird trailed him from above.

Georg tried to follow Dieter's advice; he tried to lessen the braking motion of his slow snow-plough stance, so he'd go a little faster. He tried to recall all the skiing lessons he'd had, but couldn't remember anything. He wobbled, his knees weak, his mouth dry. No confidence, no experience, except on baby slopes, and they didn't count here. He jolted over a bump, slowed to steady himself, and missed the first anchor point altogether. He brought his skis together carefully, so they no longer formed a V. The brake of the plough was released and he immediately gathered speed, his fear growing as his pulse raced and he lost his control and his balance.

Georg fell, rolled, slid, and came to a halt with his nose in the snow and feet in the air. His eyes were shut tight. Any minute the world was going to cave in. Any minute he would be buried in darkness. He didn't dare breathe, didn't dare move. Up above, Anne held her breath too. Down below, Manfred and Dieter exchanged a look, waiting, all waiting for the earth to crack and swallow Georg. Nothing happened.

Georg opened one eye. He opened the other. A full flood of light hit his snow-blurred vision. He squinted and rubbed his eyes. He stood, searching for his stocks and cap and the bits and pieces he lost in his fall.

'Oh Mei!' Violette hopped anxiously from one leg to the other. She tugged at the leather strap of a stock half buried in the snow. 'Oh Mei!'

'Thanks, Violette.' He reassembled himself and set off again.

He was even slower now, with less confidence and less control over his direction. His turns were wide; he skied right over branches, into boulders. Dieter couldn't call out to him and he didn't want to wave in case he distracted Georg's frightened concentration.

When Georg finally arrived he was red in the face, his lips pale. Beads of sweat pearled the rim of his hat. His knees were shaking so badly he could hardly stand. But he'd made it. Georg surveyed his path down the slope and grinned, just for a moment, until he remembered why he was there.

Everything broken, no signs of life, and no indication of where to start searching. Side by side the three boys slowly pushed up the slope, at regular intervals, using their stocks as probes, gently pressing them into the snow, feeling for life, for Ziggi. With each step Dieter stopped, bent, listened, but there was no sound except their boots crunching. Cautiously they stepped, stopped, listened, stepped and stopped again. They had to depend on one another and most of all on Dieter's experience and Dieter's lead. But time was passing, and with it Ziggi's chances of survival diminished.

'There! *There!*' Violette's squawks drew their attention away from the slope.

'The dog,' Georg pointed. 'He's found her!'

Orff was scratching, biting at the snow. He whined and ran in a circle. He knew he mustn't bark.

'Dig!' Georg used the ends of his skis, Dieter a piece of wood, Manfred his hands. They worked as fast as they could. The snow was heavy and they had to be careful – they didn't want to hurt Ziggi.

Anne couldn't bear the waiting anymore, but she knew she couldn't leave IDK. Her hands went to her hair in frustration, but she could only tug at the short tufts, and let out an annoyed hiss instead.

'Tsst! Do you think you can follow me, IDK?'

IDK nodded, tentative. He knew he had no choice. Anne tied the sleds to a tree, adjusted IDK's stocks and his skis, swung the cat and a rucksack onto her back, hunched her shoulders against the extra weight, and took a deep breath.

'Do exactly as I do.' Again the boy nodded, and one behind the other they slowly slid down. There was no time to be frightened, to worry about ice. If Ziggi had been found, Anne wanted to help, so she kept her thoughts focussed on that. IDK focussed his thoughts on her.

The boys were still digging around Ziggi when they arrived. Now they grabbed her arms and pulled her from her bed of snow. Carefully they put her onto the tent, which they had spread out on a level section of the slope. Ziggi appeared to be asleep, curled with her knees to her chin, pale and small. Georg began mouth-to-mouth resuscitation.

'Get her out of her wet clothes!' Dieter ordered Manfred, and pulled at Ziggi's boots.

'Is…is…she –?' Anne couldn't finish the question.

'There's a faint heartbeat.' Georg glanced up briefly. 'Blankets.'

'In my rucksack,' said Dieter.

Anne found them quickly and soon Ziggi was cocooned in them. Anne rubbed Ziggi's fingers. They were colder than the snow.

'Wait. If you only warm her fingers you'll burn her skin.' Dieter stayed Anne's hand. 'She's suffering from hypothermia. We have to get all of her warm at the same time.'

Dieter directed Anne and IDK to lie beside Ziggi. Violette, Orff, Epsilon and Manfred snuggled in around her. Dieter patted Orff. Without the dog they would never have found Ziggi. And then Dieter lay down too. They all lay still, listening to Georg breathe air into Ziggi, stop, gauge its effect, count, and breathe again. It took more than an hour before Georg was satisfied that Ziggi's system could do the work on its own.

SIX

FOLLOWING THE LIGHT

The bivouac

Silence. No bickering now – only shallow breathing and a slow beating of hearts. They had lain in a small huddle beside Ziggi for a long time, as if they were also asleep. A light spread from the pores of IDK's skin, like a blanket wrapped around Ziggi, suffusing her with heat. Gradually her heartbeat became regular and her breathing less shallow so Georg could rest from the strain of helping her breathe. A little colour crept into her face. But her eyes remained closed.

'Well done, Oh Mei,' Dieter squeezed his shoulder and Georg beamed with pride.

They gathered up their skis and drew their clothes tightly around them. The extended period with no movement had made them cold and stiff.

'We have to get off this slope,' Dieter said. The shadow of the mountain had descended; the sun had long since disappeared.

'Can we move her?' asked Manfred.

'We can't stay here.' No one argued with Dieter this time.

They used the pieces of Ziggi's broken skis, tying them as struts across two unbroken skis to make a stretcher. They lay the tent across the crude framework and Ziggi on top. Every blanket they had was piled onto her. Then each of them took hold of one end of the stretcher. Stocks in hand to lean on, their boots kicked into the snow, heavy and unyielding and rubbing their shins; they were dwarfs walking across a giant's brow.

They stopped at the foot of the cliff and retrieved the sleds. Once they had caught their breath they secured the makeshift stretcher across the two sleds.

'Where are we going?' Anne looked around critically. 'Where will we sleep?'

'In the snow.' Dieter pointed to a plateau, above them.

'We'll freeze to death.'

'Haven't you slept in a bivouac?'

'Of course I have.' Anne hated it when people thought she was ignorant. 'When I was in the Rocky Mountains –'

'Liar. You've never been to the Rockies!' It was a feeble voice, but unmistakable.

'Ziggi!' All at once, and all pleased, even Anne.

'I must look a mess!' Ziggi tried to sit up.

'How do you feel?' Manfred steadied her.

'Fine. Fantastic. I just didn't want to walk,' Ziggi tried to joke.

'Oh Mei, I can think of better ways of getting out of it.' Georg rolled his eyes. 'Oh Mei, Mei.'

They continued toiling upwards until they reached the plateau, which was high enough to still be in sunshine.

'Try to stay awake, you'll lose less body heat,' Dieter cautioned Ziggi. He turned to the others and issued instructions. First the rucksacks had to be placed side by side; then the sleds were pushed against them and the tent on top, so that Ziggi had enough protection from the cold. Dog and cat had to keep peace and nestle in as Ziggi's hot-water bottles.

'Fleas!' Ziggi complained about Orff, but no one listened. Violette took it upon herself to keep Ziggi awake.

'Kookaburra sits in the old gum tree…'

'Oh Mei.' Ziggi sighed like Georg.

'You could help us dig,' Dieter joked, knowing how weak Ziggi was.

'No thanks. I'll leave that to the serfs.'

It was hard work. They scooped snow, clearing an area one and a half metres deep and as wide as their skis were long, and shovelled the snow to one side to make a wall. When Dieter was satisfied, he instructed them to dig a ditch down the middle.

'For cold air,' Manfred announced.

'Cold air sinks,' added the Calculator, not to be outdone. 'The ditch channels it out.'

'We need stones.' Dieter was quick to spot a brewing argument. 'Flat and round, all about the same size.' They searched in pairs. It took a long time, and the snow was so deep they could only find four stones. They placed them at the base of the dugout, with the skis on top, to make a platform to sleep on, off the snow. One pair of skis was put aside for the roof beams. Once more the tent was useful – it became the ceiling. Snow was shovelled on top of it to keep the freezing air out of the snow-house. Only a small opening was left as doorway.

'It isn't the Hilton,' said Ziggi. Carefully they helped her inside. One by one they entered as the last of the sun's rays turned the snow around them pink.

It was a tight fit and they could do no more than sit with elbows on their knees and their feet together.

'Be careful.'

'Watch it.'

'You're standing on my foot.'

'OH MEI!!'

'I'm hungry,' Georg complained, looking for his rucksack. He pulled at something. Orff growled. Georg let go of Orff's tail.

After they had eaten, Ziggi declared she was going to sleep and she didn't care what anyone said.

'I promise I won't die.' She glared at Georg.

'You'd better not, I'm too tired to revive you,' Georg was quick to reply.

'I don't need your permission to sleep!' Ziggi wriggled and squirmed to make a more comfortable position for herself, taking more space than anyone.

'You know, you could say thank you.' Dieter's voice was so soft only Ziggi could hear. 'You wouldn't be alive except for Oh Mei.'

Ziggi didn't say anything; she pretended she was already asleep. But before Georg dozed off, his chin to his chest, her hand found his and gave it a small squeeze.

'Thank you, Georg,' Ziggi's whisper was softer than even Dieter's, but Georg knew who it was and his face turned bright red.

Soon they were all breathing evenly and deeply. Only Dieter and Anne were awake, eyes open in the faint glimmer that lingered above the faces of the sleepers. The light came from no place in particular, and yet was everywhere at once.

'What's that glow?' Anne asked.

'It's Ziggi's watch,' Dieter said.

Anne didn't agree. The light was more intense around IDK.

'IDK's glowing,' she mumbled and shook her head to clear it. But try as she might, she couldn't find the source of the light. 'I must be snow blind.' Then she focussed on Dieter again. 'Where did you learn that? Building the bivouac, I mean.'

'My father was a *Förster* – a forester. Animals and trees were entrusted to him. He taught me. He used to take me into the mountains. We had to travel light, so we couldn't take a tent.'

'Oh.' Anne's voice had a tone of envy in it. Her parents didn't take her anywhere – they sent her places. 'How come you know so much about avalanches?' Dieter didn't answer. 'Dieter?'

'What? Why? How come? Why do you have to know so much?' His reply was unexpectedly harsh.

'Can't learn anything if I don't ask,' Anne answered, haughty. Her feelings were hurt.

'I'm interested in avalanches,' Dieter said at last, stonily. 'The white death. My father died in an avalanche.'

'Oh. I'm sorry.' There was nothing else she could add, and Dieter moved his hand away when she tried to touch it in sympathy.

Outside the moon had drawn a circle in the sky. It lay at the shoulder of the mountain, its light shining onto the bivouac, which stood lonely and small on a wide expanse of snow. It was a full moon and the shadows were chased away. The night was clear. Big and clear and empty.

Journey into the ice planet

Ziggi was the first to wake.

'Hey! Fatso! What's the big idea? Roll over.'

'Hmm?' Georg woke from a comfortable dream. His father's bakery receded.

'You're squashing me.' Ziggi gave him a mighty shove. 'Bug eyes! Get off!' Her elbow made contact with Manfred's ribs as she wriggled on top of the pile of bodies. Her efforts woke the others, who weren't on the ski-platform anymore, but on the snow floor where Ziggi had pushed them. Their noses were blue and their cheeks red. Ziggi ripped the roof off their bedroom. A sheet of light fell in, along with a cascade of snow.

'I'm ravenous,' Ziggi announced. She jumped out of the bivouac with the food supply and threw herself at it as though she hadn't eaten in a week.

'Food is my responsibility.' Georg reacted faster than anyone imagined possible. 'I wish I hadn't revived your appetite!' he added as he wrestled a loaf of bread from her. The others emerged, blinking in the sun, realising the same old Ziggi was back.

'My beautiful skis,' Ziggi complained bitterly. She lifted the broken skis and inspected them. Luckily they weren't her racing skis or there really would have been trouble. She slapped those onto the snow. She wanted to ski straight-away, to go home, but she said nothing of heading into the valley now.

Instead she limbered up, stretching to get the blood flowing through her body. The others joined in, even Georg, until the lure of breakfast made him hungry, and he trotted off to sort out the food. There wasn't a great deal left, and he stared sadly at the remainder. Manfred and Dieter quietly discussed their plans.

'Can't we stay here?' Georg asked when he overheard that they were intending to move off.

'We'd be spotted too easily.' Dieter glanced around. 'And the weather's going to change. There's not enough shelter here.'

'How can you tell?' Georg doubted that prediction. The day was beautiful and still. Dieter indicated the mountains. The trees on them were black, distinct. The mountains themselves appeared closer than they really were, as though they had taken several steps forward.

'The air is unusually clear – it magnifies things,' he explained. 'That means it's going to snow. Have you worked out where we're going yet, Manfred?'

'I think we should go to the highest point on the planet. If the king is hiding anywhere we might be able to see him – or at least signs of him.' Manfred referred to the map of light.

'He's not going to be in plain sight.' Dieter dismissed the idea.

'Ahem,' the Calculator interjected.

'There is another reason,' Manfred admitted, cutting his machine off. He pulled out his black box, which was loudly ticking. 'Listen to that signal. It's measuring the density of the planet.' He faced the box in the direction of the planet's tallest mountain, and the signal changed. 'But if I point it at the mountain and key in the co-ordinates, it's fainter.' Manfred tapped the map, his hand passing through bands of light. 'There's definitely something up there. I can't tell whether it's alive or not, but I'm keen to see what it is.'

Dieter wasn't convinced. 'It's too difficult for the others. We need a safe base camp. What about that valley the Weatherman was talking about? Where the king planted his trees?'

'There's no way of telling where it is, and we can't waste time looking.' Manfred stared at the map for a long time. 'I think we have to risk it. We have to go up,' he insisted, and the Calculator did too.

Soon they left the last of Earth's mountains behind and were surrounded by the planet's unknown ranges. The children were tiny specks of life on a sea of ice, steadily climbing. When they did stop it was to consult the map and re-establish their bearings. Georg handed out drinks and pieces of chocolate, which they savoured, knowing there wasn't much left – of chocolate or anything else. Then they set off again, their eyes upwards, where their hopes should have been. But hopes had a way of plummeting under a heavy load in an unfamiliar land, and most especially when the clouds rolled in.

'My boots hurt.'

'Epsilon's too heavy.'

'When can we stop?'

'Will someone take this sled?'

'Why not send the bird?' Manfred checked his compass and scanned the horizon. 'Maybe Violette can spot what's ahead.'

'Not a bad idea,' Dieter agreed.

'Violette?' Anne summoned the cockatoo.

'Yes, yes, yes, yes.' Violette squawked and took off.

The low clouds swallowed her immediately. For a

moment they could hear the swish of her wings cutting the air. Her pterodactyl cry receded, and then that was gone too.

It started to snow. Big wet flakes tickled their skin and landed softly on their eyelashes and hats. Manfred put on his glasses with wipers; the earflaps on his hat drew down and his collar up, so that only his nose poked out. Anne shivered and wrapped her scarf more tightly around her neck. They all pulled on their wet-weather gear, bunched close together and kept moving. IDK hummed softly, to cheer himself up. The melody drifted over them, the tune, light and birdlike, left no room for unhappy thoughts. Stepping in the rhythm of his music, they didn't stop, didn't once look behind them, and didn't see the gloaming on the horizon.

Chasm of ice

The Shadow came out when the snow began to fall. It hovered at the feet of the sentinel cliffs. It was dark here; a wind slunk up from the valley, hissing in the firs. Another avalanche broke from the face of the slope, and roared. Then everything was still.

'Laugh, Kookaburra, laugh, Kookaburra…' Violette was a small freckle breaking through the clouds, her red eyes scanning the ground. Nothing below her moved, except the cloud and the snow it was disgorging.

'Snow blindness!' Violette complained. 'Gay your life must be.' She wanted to help Anne, so she pretended to be brave.

Violette didn't see the thin hands steaming towards her, fingers hanging in the air, transparent, until she felt their pull on her. The hands grasped the cockatoo around the neck, and plucked her out of the sky, so that no complaints, no anger, no cussing could help her. One moment she was there, the next she was gone, and nothing was left behind but vapours.

*

They were on the ridge of one of the lower mountains, small silhouettes that clung tenaciously to the rock-face, Dieter urging them on. Only Anne made no attempt to increase her pace, stopping often to scan the empty sky for Violette.

'She's lost her way.' Ziggi dropped back to walk alongside her. 'She'll never find us now. Cockatoos aren't used to the cold.' For once Anne didn't retaliate. So the others jumped to her defence.

'Shut up, Ziggi!'

Orff growled at Ziggi and pressed himself close to Anne's ankles. She patted him, distracted.

'We have to keep going,' Dieter was apologetic.

'She'll find us.' Manfred said. 'She can see a long way from up there.'

'Maybe she's already found someplace safe and is eating sunflower seeds.' Georg would love to be eating sunflower seeds too.

'Violette hates sunflower seeds,' Anne replied, annoyed.

'She's probably found a hut.' Dieter joined Anne and brought her thoughts back to earth.

'No.' Her voice was listless. 'If she had, she would have told me. We've never been separated since the day I found her.' Her eyes were bright. 'What are we waiting for?' She turned away and kept climbing. The others followed her silently. Anne continued to peer up every now and then, in case there was a small pink and white dot to be recognised in all that falling snow. But there wasn't.

They travelled on through the afternoon, stopping only once for Manfred to check the map, take out his binoculars and examine each mountain face. There was no indication of where the king could be, no sign of any other form of life. And the highest peak was shrouded in cloud.

'We'll have to stop soon – I can't keep pushing the others.' Dieter looked into the failing light. 'And we're not safe here once the light goes.'

'Did you hear that?' Manfred lifted the flaps of his hat and held his head this way and that, listening.

'No.'

Manfred hurried on, but at the earliest opportunity he whispered tersely to Dieter. 'I think we're being followed.' He pointed to a patch of dark, stained snow that slithered towards them.

'More than one?'

'I can't tell.' Manfred adjusted the binoculars. 'That's the problem, it's using the mountain's shadow as cover.'

'We can't let it catch us.' Dieter turned off the path they were on and pointed to a slope running to the right of them.

'Our only chance is to outrun it.' He faced the others, keeping his tone even. 'Okay everyone. Change of pace coming up. We're heading downhill.'

'Do we have to?' Georg whined. 'Can't we stay here for the night?'

'Go!' Jumping off the rise Dieter snapped on his skis. 'Move!'

They could all feel the paralysing cold now, could hear breath hissing and knew the Shadow was stalking them. The whites of Georg's eyes showed. Every muscle in IDK's body hurt as he tried to get away. Anne forgot about Violette. The instruments in Manfred's rucksack rattled. Ziggi's breath came in rasps. And all the while Dieter skied behind them, shepherding them. They were moving faster than they had all day, now, at the end of it, when they were tired.

With the steeper gradient their pace increased and the gap between them and the Shadow grew larger. For a while they were safe, but then the slope evened out and they found themselves on a great plateau, with no sign of the land falling away again.

'Dieter?' IDK was the last in line. His legs were too short to keep up with their ice-skater tempo. Dieter steered towards him and held out his stock. The boy grabbed hold of it and, with Dieter pulling him, was able to keep pace. But they were losing ground, the sleds hampered them and they could only glide forward slowly, and so the gap narrowed, the Darkness steadily moving in behind them.

'Look out!' Manfred, in the lead, suddenly teetered on the edge of a huge chasm, the others slipping to a stop. There was nothing but air and cloud in front of them, the land starting again fifty or so metres away, as though it had been split open by an axe. It was impossible to see what lay at the bottom.

'Danger!' the Calculator peeped.

'It's dividing.' Manfred indicated the multiplying forms of the Shadows.

'Stay together.' Dieter inched closer to the edge of the gorge. 'They won't do anything until nightfall.'

'I'm not jumping across that.' Georg felt his way to the edge and peered over.

'We're not going to. Our rope's not long enough.' Dieter took off his skis and threw them over the lip of the chasm. His rucksack followed. Twenty metres away they landed on a ledge in deep, soft snow.

'And I'm not jumping down there!' Georg looked as though he would rather take on the Shadows. His mouth was a grim line and his face blotchy.

'No, we're not jumping,' agreed Dieter. 'We're abseiling.' With Manfred's help, he lowered the sleds until they rested beside the rucksacks. He then hammered his stocks into the ground. 'We don't know what's under the snow or if the ledge will hold us. We'll have to abseil.' He worked quickly, tying rope around his stocks and fastening it.

IDK and Anne tied ropes around their bodies too. Orff and Epsilon were bundled into empty rucksacks, which

Anne carried. Ziggi, Manfred, Dieter and Georg held on while she and IDK began their descent. Anne disappeared over the side, IDK following her lead, his feet edging down, pushing off. Suddenly, there was just air and the deep canyon below as he dangled, a spider on its thread, while the four above braced themselves.

'Hurry!' Anne's pulse hammered in her ears and drowned out the sound of her own voice. A professional monkey, she bounced off the ice-face and landed lightly in the snow. The ledge held.

IDK wasn't as nimble or fast. One moment he was right side up, the next upside down. Everything in his pockets fell out.

'Use your feet for balance,' Anne instructed. 'Tsst!!'

He righted himself, tried again, the rope around his waist squeezing the breath out of him. Cautiously, he bounced off the walls, as Anne had done. At last he lowered himself onto the snow. Now it was Georg and Manfred's turn.

Anne stood on tiptoe to peer at the cliff wall. Manfred's head appeared, worried eyes behind fogged glasses.

'Turn around, Manfred. Step over the edge backwards so your feet swing into the cliff,' Anne called out.

Manfred turned and lowered himself cautiously, as if he were getting into a hot bath. He kept an eye on the sun, which was fast slipping behind the horizon. Georg followed. Anne almost couldn't bear to watch him hanging on his rope, his hands and feet squirming in the air.

'Kick off. Get up a rhythm, Oh Mei. Hurry!' Anne

instructed. Georg pulled himself together, his chest heaving like blacksmith's bellows. He tried to bounce.

'Watch Manfred.' He wasn't the best example to follow, but he was at least a touch more co-ordinated and reached the ledge ahead of Georg. Finally Georg jumped the last few metres. It was more like a fall but he landed safely in the snow. The ledge was broader than it looked from above. Manfred immediately scraped away the snow and examined it.

'It's a type of brickwork?' He looked surprised.

It was Ziggi's turn. She already had the rope around her waist. Dieter was waiting until last. They had to be fast – the Shadows were creeping closer.

'Don't look at their eyes,' Dieter whispered, but Ziggi was already snared by a Shadow that had drifted in front of her.

Zigrid. The Shadow's voice was velvet. *Zigrid Twigg, you're a great skier*, the voice licked warm honey into Ziggi's ears.

'Don't listen to it, Ziggi.'

You will win many races, but you cannot climb into the gorge.

'Ziggi, please.'

Zigrid. A dark smile hung above Ziggi. *There are rocks there, sharp as shark's teeth. You'll fall. Death waits for you there. You don't want to die, do you? Think of all the prizes you'll miss out on.*

Ziggi blanched. She stood, frozen on the edge. Took a step forwards, towards the Shadow.

'I don't want to die,' she whispered.

Then come to us, the voice continued, silken smooth.

'Ziggi – go!'

'No.' Ziggi sat cross-legged in the snow. Her eyes could look nowhere else but into the depth of the Shadow.

'Ziggi?' The four on the ledge craned their necks. The space above them remained empty.

'I can't move her.' Dieter's sorrowful face suddenly appeared. 'A Shadow's caught her.'

'Tell her she's a coward.' Anne's face was pinched. 'She hates that. Go on. Tell her. COWARD!' She yelled with all her might. 'Ziggi you're a coward!'

'Coward!' the others joined in. 'Ziggi is a coward.'

The small word rose from the ledge to lift into the air. It reached Ziggi, hung for a moment, helpless, hopeless, before dissipating. But they didn't let up. Again and again they shouted the word, their voices getting louder with every breath, so that at last, for one split second, it broke through the force of the Shadow's power.

'I am not a coward!' Angrily, Ziggi faced Dieter, whose voice resonated loudest. Dieter took his chance. He pushed Ziggi and for a moment they were locked in an awkward embrace, their feet slipping on the ice, both pushing and pulling at one another. Ziggi was strong, but Dieter was stronger, and inched her towards the precipice, until she finally disappeared with a yell. Now Ziggi hung in the air and cursed even more than Violette could curse. She kicked and gesticulated, throwing a tantrum; then, with her mouth a grim line, eyes sparking, she took control and let herself down.

Once the fuming Ziggi landed, Dieter quickly released her rope. He knew to turn away from the Shadows, to concentrate on what he was doing. They were dangerously close now, had almost reached him, the cold of their hands searing into his shoulder, numbing him.

Dieter. One whispered his name.

'I'm not listening.' Dieter balanced on the edge, sending lumps of ice and snow into the gorge.

You're frightened, aren't you?

'No, I'm not.' He kept his eyes closed.

'Dieter? What's happening?' George called.

'Hurry, Dieter!' they all called out. The light suddenly blotted out as night fell. They held their breath.

Dieter jumped, roped to his stocks, which were deeply embedded in the snow. The Shadows lunged for him. He could feel the vibrations in the rope, and the gnawing at his stocks, then the snap as the stocks and the rope broke and he had no hold. He fell with nothing between him and the valley floor far below. The group on the ledge watched, horrified.

'Catch him!' IDK threw himself at the dangling end of Dieter's rope, his voice calling the others into the present. 'Don't let go.' He held tight to the rope.

The others threw themselves at IDK. Their combined weight was an anchor and Dieter jerked to a sudden halt. He hung in the air like a broken doll until they hauled him up. Georg, the strongest, gripped him under the arms when he appeared, and pulled him all the way onto the ledge.

'Is he alive?' Manfred asked. Georg listened for a heartbeat and nodded.

'Barely.'

'It's your fault.' Anne's temper snapped and she turned on Ziggi. 'It's always your fault.'

'Shut up, Anne,' said Manfred, but Anne wouldn't listen. 'Dieter risked his life to save her and she doesn't even care.'

'Hey, steady on,' Georg said. 'You don't know that.'

'She's a trouble-maker!' Anne looked sadly at Dieter's pale face before renewing her attack on Ziggi. 'We don't want you here. Why did you have to come? All you ever think about is yourself!' And then there weren't any more words; there was only the anger of unspoken hostile thoughts. Anne sat next to Dieter and stroked his hand.

There was nowhere to go, so Ziggi stayed where she was, sat on the ledge dangling her feet, hanging on tightly to her cat. After a short time, Dieter opened his eyes, squinting at their glum faces.

'What was all the shouting about?' He sat up cautiously and rubbed his head.

'Nothing important.' Anne glared at Ziggi, who looked away. 'I thought you weren't going to make it.' Her voice quivered. 'I thought you were dead!' She immediately grew embarrassed.

'It'd take more than a Shadow to stop me.' Dieter gave her a small nudge but Anne just blew into her cupped hands and shook the cold from her fingers.

'That was a close call.' Georg flexed his own stiff fingers. 'But we've made it in one piece.' Then he suddenly laughed and pointed. The moon had risen; the Shadows had fled.

SEVEN

THE GREEN VALLEY

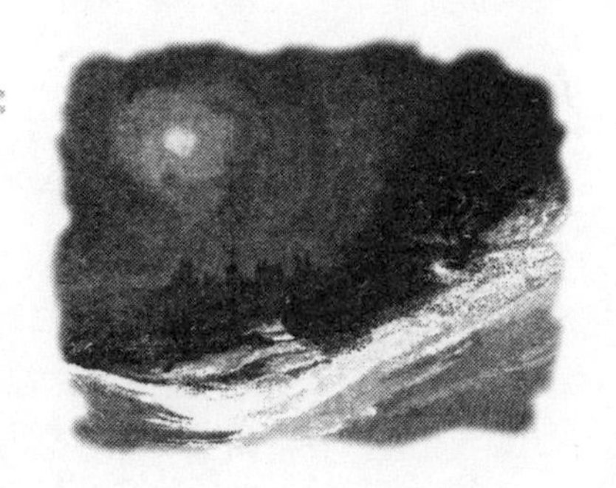

The cottage in the woods

The chasm was perpendicular. They had to inch their way, one careful step at a time, along the staircase ledge that had been hewn into the icy wall, until it ended and they were on level ground once more, at the foot of the cliffs. They could see that water had once coursed down the wall, the way they had come, but it was now frozen in its fall, like crystallised foam. Ice broke from the hardened waterfall to shatter around them.

A second wall of ice rose up on the other side of the narrow valley they were standing in, the two cliffs forming a high corridor. Only a strip of night sky was visible above, a broken seam, a rip, which let in a trickle of moonlight.

'It's like being in a sheep race.' Anne tried to make out where they were. She couldn't see very far into the gloom.

'A broader valley opens out further along.' Manfred referred to the luminous map on the Calculator, then indicated beyond the walls of the gorge. 'Follow the stream. It's the only way we can go.'

'Tomorrow.' Anne said. 'I'm freezing. Can we camp here?'

'Here's as good a place as any to build an igloo.' Dieter rammed his skis into the snow.

'Igloo?' Anne knew she shouldn't have asked.

'I'm hungry,' IDK ventured. They were all hungry.

'There's no food left.' Georg was the hungriest of all.

'Yes.' Manfred hadn't been listening. 'It's more sheltered here.' He followed the course of the stream and saw that it was beginning to thaw.

'Doesn't matter where we starve,' Ziggi grumbled.

'Will you stop it?'

'I'll say what I want!'

'Dig!!' Georg interrupted the bickering. It was the kind that could go on all night, and they had more important things to do. He thrust a shovel at Ziggi. But Ziggi handed the shovel back.

'You dig,' she said.

They took it in turns. It was slow and tedious, trying to break the hardened ground. The shovel struck the ice and echoed as though it were striking rock. They didn't even dent it.

'Keep going.' Dieter handed the shovel on. 'It'll crack eventually.'

When it was Ziggi's turn they discovered she had disappeared.

'She's got a nerve!' Even the usually placid Georg was annoyed.

'Wait till I get my hands on her,' Anne fumed.

'That's if I don't first,' Manfred joined in, but before he could say what he thought of her, a puffing Ziggi returned.

'Hey! Stop digging!' She wasn't sulking anymore. 'I've found a hut.' There was a note of pride in her voice. 'It's warm and dry and fully stocked with blankets and food and everything we need! It's unbelievable!' She jumped around on the spot and threw her arms about. They had never seen Ziggi so excited. She noticed their hesitation. 'All right.' Her voice grew sullen again. 'If you want to freeze, fine, but I'm sleeping in comfort!' She stomped into the darkness.

'Orff, orff.' Orff wagged his tail. Epsilon hurried after Ziggi, rabbit-hopping across the snow. The others exchanged glances.

'I don't believe her,' said Manfred, ever cautious. 'Do you?'

'I don't know.' IDK would have liked to.

'It's an excuse to get out of work.' Anne continued to dig.

'But what if she's telling the truth?' asked an ever-hopeful Georg.

'We *are* exhausted.' Dieter weighed their responses.

'Ziggi!' Five voices called out.

They ran carefully across the ice, following the burbling stream beside the cliffs until the valley opened out. A forest grew near the mouth of the gorge. Anne eyed the trees mistrustfully, and tugged at the ragged ends of her hair, remembering what lived in dark forests. But Ziggi kept on, jiggling ahead of them, weaving through the trees, returning every so often, to make sure they were still there.

The hut was at the edge of a clearing. It was built of living wood, its roof sloped by branches that hung thick and thatched, its walls the trunks of trees that had grown tightly together. The stream they had been following flowed underneath the roots of the tree that formed the wall beside the door, which stood open to them. Inside, it resurfaced in a steaming pool in the centre of the hut, bridged by a row of stepping stones.

'Thermal baths!' A wide smile spread across Manfred's face. He dropped the sled rope and hurried forward.

They stood in awe, not believing what they saw. Warm light glowed through windows of the one-roomed hut, six carved, wooden chairs stood around a table that was already laid, six beds were lined against a wall. A fire crackled and jumped, firelight spilled onto the dark snow outside and from a pot suspended on a hook above the flames, the sweetest smell ever drifted across cold air and touched their noses. Then Georg said, 'Rice pudding!' and headed straight for the pot.

Anne eased out of her boots and rubbed tired ankles. IDK flopped onto a soft feather quilt and sighed, contented.

Orff and Epsilon quickly fell asleep in a corner near the stove. Ziggi bagged the best bed and unpacked her belongings.

'Where's the –'

'No electricity,' Georg replied before Ziggi could ask about the light-switch. 'It's firelight and beeswax candles.' He opened every cupboard door, surveying their contents. 'Wow, a fully stocked larder!' He craned his neck and saw dried fruit and herbs hanging in branches that doubled as rafters, and two chickens, roosting. 'Fresh eggs, pots, pans, tinned asparagus!' His voice rose with every new discovery. 'It has everything!'

'But how am I going to plug in my hair-drier?' Ziggi wailed, appalled.

'Batteries,' Manfred supplied. 'You can borrow mine.' He was walking around the pool that was sunk into the stone floor. By now Anne was soaking her feet in it.

'This is heavenly!' She reached for a towel that hung from a hook on the wall. 'There are even six towels!' She looked around. 'And a dog bowl, a cat dish and a bird…' Her voice trailed off.

'She'll find her way,' IDK's voice warbled softly and he squeezed Anne's hand.

'A series of pipes takes the water to the stove and back.' Manfred had finished his perusal and was clearly impressed. 'We have our own personal spa.' He splashed water onto the hearth and it hissed. 'Simple but ingenious.'

'The Weatherman must have known about this hut.'

Dieter joined him. 'He's prepared it for us. But why didn't he tell us it was here?'

'He couldn't chance it,' Manfred replied. 'Not if the Shadows can read our minds, and we can't defend ourselves.' He chewed his lip. 'I can't help feeling he's testing us. Making sure we're up to scratch.'

'I don't blame him. It's a big responsibility, saving a planet.'

'Yes. First thing we'll have to do is learn to outsmart the Shadows. Fortify ourselves.' Manfred eased himself onto the last unoccupied bed. 'Tomorrow.' He groaned with pleasure as he sank into the quilts.

After that there wasn't much movement until Georg ladled spoonfuls of – he was right, rice pudding – into bowls. They threw themselves at their food, warmth returning to their bodies and smiles to their faces. When they had eaten they fell asleep in firm beds, under warm feathers.

Ashes shifted, sparks glowed briefly then winked out. A log settled. The lid of the pot beat softly with a pp ppp ppp of escaping steam and a rattle of cast iron. Then that stopped too, and the brightness of the fire faded, leaving a small glimmer of light, a mist of it, drifting above the sleeping IDK.

Outside, the moon peeked out from behind the clouds and, satisfied, stole back. For a time, the night was black and heavy in its own darkness. Then the clouds blew in, great silent shapes that swelled and burst, the air growing alive with the thronging of snowflakes. Thick, tickling flakes filled the valley, driving down in a constant veil of white.

Valley of the trees

It stopped snowing the following morning. The clouds shook the last of their feathers in a fine drizzle, then ripped apart and revealed a royal blue. One metre of snow had fallen.

Anne was the first to wake. She threw open the shutters and went to the door. Cold air stroked her legs, winding like a cat about her ankles. She scanned the sky.

'What's happened to you, Violette?' The hurt that had been building in her rose to the surface. Tears streamed down her face. She had lost her friend, the one creature she had depended on, and she sobbed inconsolably. But only for a minute. When she heard the others stir inside, she pulled herself together, and by the time they came out to gauge their surroundings she had wiped away all evidence of tears.

The valley was bordered by hills, a dense forest growing along their ridges and feathering down. The trees near the hut were clothed in frosted garments with ermine collars and sleeves. On the upper slopes, snow clung to fir needles, long, limp shapes dragging the boughs down.

'They're like sleeping lizards.' Anne took hold of a fir branch and shook it. Snow slid off.

'You're such a child!' Ziggi said from the door.

'Snow looks different in Australia.' Anne immediately grew defensive. 'On gum trees.'

'This must be the Valley of the Trees!' Manfred scrutinised the vegetation. 'The Weatherman said the king planted trees and protected them with magic.' He indicated the sky-scraper cliffs of the chasm, which stood high and pale blue behind them. 'That's where we were last night.' Then he pointed to the mountain at the opposite end of the valley, 'And that's where we have to get to.'

The mountain stood brittle white, and a long way off. It was in sharp contrast to the vivid blue of the sky, the lesser mountains around it slinking away. It began to rise at the point where they stopped, too far, too high to contemplate.

'What are we waiting for?' Ziggi's jaw was set at a dangerous angle. 'The sooner we go, the sooner we get there.'

'And the sooner *you* can go home,' Anne finished off for her. Ziggi glowered.

'I would normally be inclined to agree with Ziggi.' Manfred kept his voice neutral. 'Time is of the essence. Except for one thing.' He switched his Calculator on, focussed it on the mountain and zoomed in. 'That mountain is made completely of ice. It's as treacherous as glass. You'd have to be more than good to ski that.'

'Can you see what's on the summit?' Dieter asked him.

Manfred shook his head. 'The peak is shrouded in permanent cloud.'

Dieter weighed what Manfred had said. 'Then we'll stay here and improve our skiing,' he said at last. 'Or there's no point going anywhere.' He contemplated the skis stacked against the wall, touching the edges, examining the wax covering on their underside. Notches had been bitten into most of them and the surfaces were criss-crossed with gouges. 'First thing we have to do is fill the cracks in our skis.' Dieter's manner was businesslike. 'Did we bring wax?'

'In my rucksack,' Georg volunteered. 'There's a battery-powered iron too, to melt the wax.' He saw Anne's perplexed expression. 'To give the underside of the skis a protective coating. Wax makes them slide smoothly.'

They set to work immediately. What Manfred and Dieter had said resonated with all of them. If the quest was to succeed, they had to be able to ski, and to do that, not only the equipment, but they themselves, had to be capable.

'Sunscreen, everyone.' Anne handed around the tube. 'Tip of the ears, back of the neck,' she hounded them.

The first practice session began. Dieter took on the role of teacher, instructing Georg and Manfred, concentrating on IDK and Anne. It was exhausting without lifts, side-stepping up the hill and then skiing down all too quickly, but Dieter made them do it again and again.

Ziggi refused to join in. She had portioned off a part of the run and was practising slalom, wending between a line of poles she had found beside the hut and placed at irregular intervals down the slope. Ziggi wanted to race. It was the only thing she had ever wanted to do, so she knew everything about it. She had even waxed her skis with racing wax that helped them move faster across the snow. Tucking herself into a small ball, stocks angled back, chin up, she was the image of a fast, professional racer. She flew past Anne.

'Hey kangaroo.' Skis and stocks in all directions, backside out, body tipping forward, Ziggi imitated Anne's skiing. 'What a marsupial!' She swung so close that Anne lost her balance, fell onto the snow and slid all the way to the end of the slope.

'Ziggi!' Anne's face was a thundercloud. Ziggi laughed and held out her stock to help her to her feet. When Anne reached for it, Ziggi pushed her, so that she landed in the snow a second time.

'Big show-off!' But Anne's voice didn't have its usual sting, although she would never admit she was impressed with Ziggi's athletic style.

Laughing, Ziggi raced off, executing perfect turns and running up the hill almost as fast as she skied it. She was fit, she was enjoying herself, and she knew she was good. Anne, red in the face and puffing, was left to attack the hill with steely determination.

Manfred skied until the niggling in his brain undermined his concentration. He had heard unusual sounds each time he had fallen, sliding down with his ear to the snow. A rumbling in the bowels of the planet, followed by a high-pitched whine, light and clear and definitely mechanical. Finally he couldn't take it anymore; he had to identify what it was.

The door of the hut was open to the sun's warmth. A slant of light fell in a bright wedge across the table, and the instruments erected there. Manfred was bent over them. Suddenly his head shot up and his nose twitched, as though he could smell sound. He felt a strange vibration in the lining of his stomach.

'It sounds like an engine!' His voice rose because he was getting excited.

'I can't hear anything.' Dieter had skied to the door.

'My ears are fine-tuned and highly sensitive.' Manfred was adamant. 'I know what I heard.'

'I think you've fallen on your head too many times,' Dieter said, not taking him seriously. But Orff was suddenly alert.

'I don't understand what –' A violent rumbling cut Manfred off. All the cups in the cupboards jiggled (some cracked), then a mechanical cough tore through the ground and sent him flying. It steadied into a chugging – the chug, chug, chug of a river boat, which stopped with a final hiccup.

IDK had landed head first in the softer perimeter snow, Anne was again sliding on her stomach, and Georg was in the kitchen up to his knees in fallen pots. Even Ziggi was thrown to the ground by the vibrations and hurriedly wiped at the snow before it stained her metallic red ski suit.

Manfred stood and checked for damage, aware that Dieter was looking at him for answers. The inventor scratched his chin, worry and confusion in his eyes.

'Was that an earthquake?' Ziggi and IDK crowded in at the door.

'No, not an earthquake.' Manfred scanned his instruments, checking and re-checking 'Yes. Mmmm…interesting. Of course!'

'What!?!'

'It's all a matter of weight displacement.' Manfred was on a trail, like a bloodhound following a scent. 'I've just realised this planet must be hollow. If it wasn't, the Earth would have been pushed out of orbit when it crash-landed.' He stopped, expecting a response from the others, but they stared at him, their expressions blank. 'Which means it's not a planet at all!'

'I knew it.' Ziggi was triumphant.

'So what is it?' Dieter saw there was something else lurking behind Manfred's statement.

'It's a spaceship, an artificial planet. We just heard the motors.'

'Your imagination's out of control.' Ziggi glared at him, accusing.

'That's the absolute limit!' Anne didn't care who she shouted at. She was white from head to toe and stomped towards them, fists balled. 'I fall over enough as it is. What is going on?'

Manfred waited until Anne's temper had subsided.

'If it was a real planet,' he said, his words evenly spaced and well modulated, the way newsreaders sounded (a tone Manfred used to add weight and importance to what he had to say), 'it would have collided with Earth with the same impact as a meteor. Gravity would have seen to that.'

'So what happened?' Ziggi's voice had its sneer again.

'It floated in – like a zeppelin. It must have had motors or brakes to counteract the gravity.' Manfred paused for breath. 'It makes absolute sense. Once the planet was iced over, and couldn't travel like light travels, it had to have motors, or it could never have returned.'

'If it is a spaceship,' Georg's eyes became wide, 'it could fly away again, couldn't it?'

'Yes,' Manfred said.

'Oh Mei!'

'You mean kidnap us?' IDK asked, startled.

'If they can get the motors going.' Manfred nodded. 'So it's in our best interest to locate where the motors are and who is trying to start them. Before the spaceship takes off with us on it!'

'What a load of rubbish!' Ziggi accused him. 'Do you believe *everything* you're told?' she flared at the others and stalked off. Her eyes were smarting and she didn't want them to see that. She climbed the hill with ferocious steps, thrust ski-stocks into the snow, one after the other, a line of them dotting the hill, and then she climbed again, expending all her energy, anger and confusion.

'Spaceship. What rot! ROT!!!' she yelled into the valley.

'Well actually, it's not rot,' a voice said behind her. 'It's a clever supposition and it takes brains to work out.' Ziggi froze. The voice was cracked with age and came from the forest. A figure separated out from the trees and walked towards her, his beard wrapped around him as a scarf.

'Arggghhhhh!' Ziggi tipped forwards into the snow and slid down the hill far more spectacularly than Anne ever had.

Green lightning, starlight and peppermint

'I'm pleased you're safe.' The Weatherman smiled at them all in turn.

'For our sake?' Ziggi asked, sceptically.

'For the sake of the crystal,' the old man replied. 'It must not fall into the wrong hands.'

'Exactly how safe are we?' Manfred asked.

'A potent spell protects this valley.' The Weatherman rolled up his beard and secured it with a clip. 'As long as the trees survive, no Shadows are permitted entry – unless we carry them in, in our hearts.' He regarded each of them intently, but could find no Shadows playing in their eyes. 'So now it's time.' He pulled a cloth sack out from under his coat. A silver green light pulsed from beneath the coarse weave.

'Is that the Key?' the little boy whispered.

'Do you remember?' the old man asked softly.

IDK passed his hand across his mouth. He could hear that voice again. It had spoken to him recently, soft as birdsong. And there were other voices, too, from long ago. Voices on summer air, coming from dreams, speaking in words he couldn't comprehend.

'I…I…'

'He doesn't remember anything,' Manfred supplied. 'His mind's a sieve.'

'It'll come.' The Weatherman patted IDK's shoulder, then brought the tiny Key out of the sack. 'This is the last of the ancient light, captured and put into a crystal, so that it could be stored safely.' His hands were bathed in the warm glow.

'Green lightning,' Manfred said, in awe.

'Starlight.' Dieter's eyes were drawn to it.

'It's anything you want it to be,' the old man said.

'It makes me feel warm.' Anne followed the path of the beam. 'Happy.'

'Can I hold it?' Georg was the first to take up the crystal. He was hesitant, in case it might burn him, but it was cool to touch. He turned it, once, twice, losing the small disc in the folds of his palm. He sniffed it, as though it were something to eat.

'Mmm. Peppermint.'

IDK watched him closely, ferocious eyes guarding the crystal. Its glow had diminished as soon as Georg touched it. It was barely alight. Georg passed it to Anne.

Anne viewed it suspiciously. The disc glinted at her, a flash like a grin, then lay drab, a dull stone in her hand.

'It doesn't feel powerful,' she said out of politeness.

'How does it work?' Manfred asked.

'I've used it to burn away the cloud,' the Weatherman replied. 'But the light doesn't destroy the Shadows, not when I'm holding it.'

The littlest boy tugged at the Weatherman's sleeve,

waiting his turn. But Dieter took the crystal. He held it towards the firelight, and the flames reflected inside it and leapt tall.

Beside him, Epsilon jumped onto the table and growled. Her whiskers shivered, and her body shook with the effect of the vision before her.

'It doesn't look like a Key.' Ziggi snatched it before Epsilon could steal it. 'It's a stupid stone.'

'Give it to me.' IDK finally found his voice. 'It's mine.' He tried to wrest the disc out of Ziggi's hand.

'Rot.' Ziggi held her hand above her head. 'It doesn't belong to anyone.'

'It's mine.' Everything inside IDK told him so. He stamped hard on Ziggi's toe, a tactic he'd learned from Anne.

'Ouch!' Ziggi yelped. Annoyed, she pocketed the disc. It dragged heavily for its size. There was a sudden tinkle as the disc fell to the floor, having burned a hole through her pocket. Before IDK could retrieve it, Manfred swept it up.

'May I?' he said and, not waiting for permission, he went to the door to study it in daylight. The door flew open before he even reached for the handle. The crystal remained lifeless in his hand.

'Can I please have the Key?' IDK was at his side, his expression severe, his hand outstretched.

'Here.' Manfred pressed it into his palm, and suddenly the room lit up and they all felt a surge of happiness.

IDK turned the crystal this way and that, feeling the radiant warmth that flowed from it, making it hot to touch.

He held it high. A sunray passed through it and sheared out, hitting an old sleigh that stood under the eaves of the hut. The crystal pulsed in his hand, the pin-light growing into a beam wider than a street. It swept across the forest, strong as a searchlight, touching the snow-covered trees, then a snowdrift at the side of the hut, and finally exploding into a giant tree in the heart of the forest, sending a shower of green and silver sparks high into the air.

'That's enough!' The Weatherman had been watching the group huddled around the doorway. He took the crystal out of IDK's hand and threw the cloth over it. The light diminished immediately. 'This is not a toy.' He stared at each of them in turn. 'And you would be wise to remember that. You have been chosen, and with this Key you can save two worlds – or watch those worlds be destroyed.' He gave the Key to Dieter. 'It had best remain with you as you're the strongest skier.'

'I'm the best skier. Well, the fastest.' Ziggi pouted.

'Ability has many measuring sticks,' the Weatherman answered, kindly. And he wouldn't be drawn after that. He returned to his chair where he settled comfortably, and it wasn't long before he was snoring.

EIGHT

A GIFT OF MAGIC

The old sleigh

Sunbeams slid down tree trunks. Their bark was chocolate brown, damp where it had been beaten by snow, dry where the sun touched it. Two figures in woollen caps and jumpers stood under the trees like mushrooms in undergrowth. Unlike mushrooms they moved about, bending, straightening, collecting wood, which they threw into the old sleigh they had dragged with them.

'Aren't you homesick?' Anne asked as Dieter released his armful of wood.

'No. Why?'

'No reason.' She was sceptical.

'Are you?'

'No.' But she looked away as she said it. 'I'm often away from home.'

'What do your parents do?' Dieter asked before she could change the subject.

'Work.' Anne replied. 'They're always at work.'

'They must love it.'

'More than they love me,' Anne said softly. 'Don't we have enough wood yet?'

The light in the forest thinned the further they travelled into it.

'Me and my mum collect firewood every afternoon.' Dieter continued to forage. 'There's always work to do. It never stops.' For the first time, Anne noticed how worn his hands were. 'Maybe your parents work hard so you can have whatever you want. And go on holidays overseas.'

'My parents work hard for themselves. To do that they have to get rid of me. Can we change the subject, please?' But Dieter kept going.

'It must be good not to have to worry about money,' he said.

'Who wants to be like Ziggi?' Anne turned away derisively.

They had come to the centre of the forest. It was mostly fir trees, with here and there an oak, a larch, a birch and an elm, all without leaves during the winter months.

'They're like Earth's trees, only healthier.' Dieter ran his hand along tree stems. 'So many of our trees have been killed by salinity or acid rain. And we don't replenish what we use.'

'The black snow wouldn't do them any good either.'

'No. I wonder if that's what the Shadows plan to do? Choke our world to death.'

'We won't let them.' Anne's voice was iron. She pointed to a giant tree that stood blackened, freed from its burden of snow. 'What do you think happened to that one?'

'It must have been struck by lightning.' Dieter examined it, peeling off the charred strips of bark. 'Recently.' Underneath, the wood was still whole. He ran his hand along it. 'Is it my imagination or is it glowing?'

Anne peered at it too. The wood radiated a soft, green aura.

'It's the sun coming through the branches. The light's always green in a forest,' she said. 'What sort of tree is it?'

'A linden tree.' Dieter knocked against it with his knuckles. The wood was hard.

'We don't need anymore firewood,' Anne remarked when Dieter reached for his axe.

'This is different wood. Look how strong and supple it is. We might be able to use it.'

Soon rebounds of steel on wood rang through the forest. The tree shuddered as black flecks of charcoal fell onto the snow, until the shell of bark split and peeled off, revealing the kernel, like a tapering candle of golden wood, within. Dieter had to work hard for the wood to crack. He and Anne filled the sleigh with long pieces. Before they left, Dieter squatted down and pressed seeds into the cold earth.

'Maybe they'll grow when the snow thaws,' he said and took up the sleigh.

The valley was sunny when they broke out of the forest; the hut was below them, smoke rising from its chimney.

Anne took the rope out of Dieter's hands. 'My turn to steer.'

'It's okay, I can do it,' Dieter said, which as far as Anne was concerned implied she couldn't. She gave the sleigh a jerk to move it forwards.

'Be careful, it's steep here,' Dieter warned.

'I can handle it.' Anne sprang into the heavily laden sleigh. Here was an opportunity for a fast ride down a slope, instead of trudging knee-deep in snowdrifts. Dieter was soon left behind, watching her departure, shaking his head.

The sleigh gathered speed, heading straight for the hut. Anne grinned. Faster, faster, the blades sliced at the snow, the loosely stacked wood rattling. Sticks and twigs and kindling flew out behind. The hut came closer. Anne applied the brake. Nothing. She braked harder. Nothing, still; no dragging back, no resistance of wood on ice, no slowing at all. Anne tried one more time but there were no brakes.

'THE BRAKES!!!!' she screamed, bailing out: 'Agggggghhhhhh!!!!!'

The sleigh ought to have kept going, to land in a pile of splinters at the base of the hut. But there was no *thunk*, no wreckage, and worse still, no firewood. The sleigh had vanished without a trace. When Dieter and Anne ran to search for it and the others trooped out of the hut to see what the commotion was, they found the sleigh a little way away, on the other side of the hut. It was unscathed, with no sign of damage at all.

'But that's impossible!' Anne made up the tail end of the group. 'It was aiming straight for the hut.'

'It must have changed course.' Ziggi only ever believed what was in front of her eyes.

Georg turned to Dieter. 'What happened?'

'I have no idea.'

'Was it headed for the hut?'

'Yes. Straight at it,' Dieter verified.

Manfred immediately began a tour of inspection. 'There are no tracks that lead *around* the hut.' He backtracked. 'Look. The tracks stop before they reach the hut and start again on the other side.' He circled the sleigh. He touched this lever, tried the other one, said, 'Mmm. Hmm,' and, 'So that's it.' Not even the Calculator could understand. Finally he concluded: 'It must have flown over the hut.'

They looked at Manfred as if he'd taken leave of his senses.

'What! How?' Georg almost choked.

'I wouldn't have a clue. But I can tell you one thing. It's a highly technical contraption.' Anything Manfred didn't understand was highly technical.

'It's just a sleigh,' Dieter retorted. His father and his grandfather and the grandfathers before them had all used sleighs to bring wood out of the forests and hay from the alpine meadows.

Manfred unloaded the wood. Once the sleigh was empty, he climbed inside. The sleigh remained stationary. Under Manfred's instructions they swung it around so the nose pointed into the valley. It didn't move. Manfred checked the brakes. They worked perfectly. The sleigh stood fast.

'Great! This sleigh doesn't even go downhill now!' Dieter leaned on it from behind and then climbed in to add a little more weight. The others pushed.

'Primitive. If you want technical, you should fly in Daddy's learjet.' Ziggi slouched into the hut.

Inch by inch the sleigh slid forwards. Iron creaked; snow flowed coolly beneath its tracks and cold air eddied about the two boys' ears as it gathered speed.

'You'll drive us into a tree,' Dieter said, but he left the brakes untouched, so Manfred could complete his experiment.

They disappeared, hidden from those on the slope above by a bend. The world was still, peaceful as only a snow-world could be.

'It's phenomenal!' The boys had gone, but their voices could still be heard.

'I've always wanted to be an astronaut!'

Anne, Georg and IDK looked around.

'Where are you?'

'Up here.' Manfred's voice was really close now. The others surveyed the ridge-line and the trees. Nothing. They exchanged confused glances. 'Here.' Manfred repeated. 'Up here!'

Orff snapped his jaws as though a fly were buzzing around his head. The others looked up too. The sleigh cut an eagle's circle above them. Dieter and Manfred sat as kings in a carriage and waved, as if it were the most natural thing in the world to be sitting in a sleigh in the air.

'You fly it by thinking!' Manfred grinned at them. He circled once, twice more, floating on warm thermals, before putting it into a steep nose-dive, then reversing thrust and climbing again, tipping the sleigh from side to side, then finishing with a figure of eight.

'Hold on, Dieter!' They flew upside down and Manfred grabbed Anne's hat as they passed overhead.

'Hey!' Anne jumped to retrieve it, feeling the cold about her ears.

'Do you know what this means?' Manfred hovered the sleigh above the hut, letting it rock and buffet in the warm air rising from the hut's chimney. He didn't wait for Dieter's reply. 'We can get to the ice mountain now.' His face was red with excitement and cold air. 'We don't have to wait until Anne and IDK are good enough.'

'It's better we rely on ourselves.' Dieter remained cautious. 'And not on any contraptions.'

'I agree...up to a point. But we have to make the most of every opportunity and this...this is amazing!'

Manfred's excitement lurched the sleigh forward and the two boys disappeared.

'Ah, Manfred...do you know how to land?' Dieter's voice dragged behind.

They returned to the hut half an hour later, sound, although they looked a little like snowmen, covered from head to toe in snow. It was an emergency landing, Manfred explained, but he was sure he'd figure it out: as with everything, it required practice.

Christmas Eve

Later in the evening Dieter was examining the wood he'd chopped that morning. Carefully he pared away the outer layers, slowly cutting the kernel of the wood into long, even pieces, before shaving wood-curls from it.

'It cuts like butter,' he said, feeling the warmth of the wood in his hands.

IDK was close by, following his every movement with the fixed look of a dog watching its owner eat a meal. Dieter was making him a pair of skis. If – and Dieter was cautious with the promise – if he could get the bindings off Ziggi's broken skis and anchor them into the wood without splintering it, then he'd have a chance of success. So IDK kept the others away and flinched each time someone disturbed Dieter's concentration, in case his pocketknife slipped.

The fire spoke in tongues that leapt and fell, a fine layer of smoke rose into the ceiling branches; fir-scent seeped in from outside, and the aroma of baking bread lingered. Baking was a skill Georg had learned from his father, along with running a kitchen and organising menus. Georg took his job as chef seriously, knowing that all their strenuous activity needed healthy sustenance. But the Weatherman had insisted he take a break from the stove tonight, so Georg was soaking his feet in the thermal pool. Manfred was asleep over a book. Ziggi was lost in the wailings of her Discman. There was only the dip and stir of the Weatherman's spoon – nothing louder. Even Orff and Epsilon were in accord, which was a rare thing.

At that precise moment of absolute peace, the door flew open and Anne exploded into the room demanding everyone's attention immediately.

'Do you know what day it is?'

Manfred's head surfaced from behind the cover of the book, Georg slopped water all over the floor, and IDK checked on Dieter to see if there was any damage to his new skis.

'Tuesday?' Georg ventured.

'Shut the door,' Ziggi snapped. 'It's freezing.' But Anne had no intention of shutting the door. She went out again and returned with an armful of fir branches. One of Manfred's beakers was unceremoniously emptied, filled with water, and the branches arranged in it. Drops of moisture glittered like jewels in the firelight. Spiderwebs were tinsel, and Anne found a handful of nuts, which she strung onto thread, like beads, finally adorning the branches with a lit candle.

'It's Christmas Eve,' she announced solemnly.

'Christmas,' Georg sighed and added, 'gingerbread.'

'Sugared almonds.'

'Salmon,' Ziggi said wistfully.

'Roast goose.' Manfred's mouth watered.

'Turkey and ham.' Anne felt a stab of longing. 'Out by the pool.' And when the others responded oddly: 'Christmas is hot in Australia.'

'You don't have a pool,' Ziggi sneered. She was right – Anne didn't have a pool, but she wasn't going to admit it.

'Frankfurters,' the Weatherman placed his culinary achievement on the table.

But they'd lost their appetites. Even Georg. Thinking about Christmas meant thinking about home. They missed parents and brothers and sisters, and Manfred even missed his grandmother, which could only happen at this time of year. IDK couldn't remember who he should miss, but he missed them anyway.

'Ah, marzipan,' Georg said. Marzipan and the Christmas angel, myrrh and frankincense, and the giving of gifts on Christmas Eve. He remembered the duck his father always roasted, and the taste of the cinnamon stars his mother baked, and all the other taste sensations that came with Yuletide festivities. 'Everyone at home is celebrating and here we are…'

'Celebrating what?' Manfred asked, recalling images of black snow and the Darkness they had left behind. 'I doubt they'll even think of Christmas. They must be in a panic by now.' The candlelight in the hut flickered in a sudden draught. They all stared at it, glum.

'Well, we're going to celebrate anyway!' Anne thumped the table. 'This is my first white Christmas!' She fossicked in a bag. 'Here. Merry Christmas.' She handed Manfred a book.

Manfred glanced at it. 'That's my book. You can't give me my own book.'

'Have you read it?'

'No – that's why I brought it with me.'

'Good. It's my gift to you. I know you'll enjoy it.'

'You can't *give* me my – Oh forget it,' Manfred said, exasperated. Sometimes Anne's logic evaded him.

Anne turned to Georg. 'Merry Christmas.' She handed him a small piece of chocolate that was white with age. 'I kept it specially.'

'Thanks.' Georg took it, sniffed it, and the chocolate disappeared into his mouth. Anne turned and faced Ziggi.

'What do you give a girl who has everything?' Dieter asked her.

'Good advice.' Anne looked Ziggi straight in the eye.

'Don't want it.'

'Too bad. It doesn't hurt to be nice occasionally, Ziggi. Merry Christmas.'

'Bah!' Ziggi returned to her music and Anne pulled a face. She gave the Weatherman a kiss on the cheek, which made him blush. Her colourful woollen scarf she gave to IDK.

'That's my favourite, so don't lose it,' Anne threatened, and turned to Dieter. 'Here,' she said gruffly. 'These are for you. To plant healthy trees when you get home.' She poured the handful of seeds she had collected into Dieter's hands. 'Merry Christmas,' she said. 'Now it's your turn.'

Dieter considered the seeds in his hands, stunned. 'I haven't – I mean I don't –'

'What are you going to do with those?' Anne pointed to the skis, which were finished, the bindings fastened, the wood intact. 'They're handmade, and useful, and I think they'd make a very special Christmas present, don't you?'

Dieter blushed. 'I don't know how they'll go,' he said. He handed them to IDK. 'You'll have to try them out.'

'What else do you say?' Anne gave him a ferocious glare.

'Oh yeah, Merry Christmas.'

IDK looked as though he were the first child ever to receive a present.

'Thank you,' he said shyly. The wood glimmered faintly green, as if it were from a sapling. 'They're…magical!'

'Well done. Excellent.' The Weatherman acknowledged the work.

'Good craftsmanship.' It was high praise coming from Manfred.

'If you're making anymore…' Georg grinned. Ziggi refused to comment, and Anne was still on a mission.

'Right. Now we sing,' she said. No response. 'When it's Christmas you sing!' she encouraged them with force and volume. But they were used to Anne's 'force and volume' and it made no difference. So Anne started to sing. With a wobbly, uncertain voice that couldn't stick to a melody, no matter how hard Anne tried. She struggled through *Silent Night* then bravely attempted *Good King Wenceslaus*.

'Come on, sing!' she nagged, as she reached the second verse.

Manfred's eyes travelled all the way to the ceiling. Georg hummed in a deep bass, but didn't trust himself to open his mouth. The Weatherman joined in with a soft whistle.

'Louder!' Anne demanded.

Manfred took a deep breath and made noises that resembled a tune. Georg's humming turned to words, the Weatherman's whistle into a hum. IDK was so full of Christmas spirit he found his voice too, and it sounded like birds, his light warming them, making them feel carefree and happy, so that even Dieter, who was usually disdainful of emotion, joined in. Their voices wound around each other, grew harmonious and strong, and only Ziggi remained aloof, turning up the volume of her Discman.

'Come on, Ziggi,' Georg called between gulps of air. Ziggi pretended she didn't hear. 'Sing!'

Unhappy, Ziggi wouldn't look at them. She didn't want to admit she was feeling left out. She didn't fit. Didn't want to fit, anyway. Stupid song. She reclined further into her corner where the firelight couldn't reach her.

'Sing, Ziggi,' Anne called out.

'No!'

'Ziggi!'

'I don't sing.' And then in a small voice, 'I don't even want to be here.'

The Weatherman nodded at her and IDK smiled between mouthfuls of song. Even Georg and Manfred were smiling, though Georg's smile looked painful when he hit a high note. Dieter was concentrating on words he'd never bothered to learn properly. Then Orff jumped up and placed his front paw on Ziggi's knees and barked into her face. Epsilon's eyes glimmered and she gave Ziggi an encouraging lick. So Ziggi took a breath and sang.

Her glorious voice rose to the ceiling and through it, straight out into the night sky where the stars were. The night listened. The mountains, the moon, the trees listened. The wind stilled. The white snow lay deep; even the stream stopped splashing, letting the melody drift over it. And suddenly it really did feel like Christmas Eve. Nobody was sad or lonely anymore, or felt they didn't fit in. Not even Ziggi.

NINE

LEARNING TO FLY

Snow wings

'*Snow Wings!*' said IDK triumphantly, regarding his new skis.

'What's that supposed to mean?' Ziggi asked.

'*Snow Wings*,' repeated IDK as he rubbed off a snowflake that had settled on the new wood. 'That's what they're called.'

'What!?' Ziggi suddenly understood. 'You can't give skis a name!'

'They give racehorses names,' Manfred interrupted. 'It's very apt.'

IDK laid the skis flat on the snow. Then he looked Ziggi square in the eye. But Ziggi wouldn't be intimidated by IDK's stern look.

'Racehorses – yes. Boats – yes. Skis – no. They're not even proper skis. They're pieces of wood.' Final.

'They're not just pieces of wood!' IDK thumped his boots together to knock the snow off them. He stepped onto his skis and secured the bindings. 'They're my skis and they can fly.'

To Ziggi's annoyance, IDK was absolutely right. His skis were faster than hers and they could fly! They quivered in anticipation when he placed them on the snow, and floated above the ground, until he stood on them and fastened the bindings. With him on board, they sank down and followed the fall of the land, gathering speed. When they turned, they remained in parallel position, and forced IDK to, too. When they jumped, he sailed high, shooting through the air, before landing softly in the snow, where they ice-skated over the flat ground. In places where the hill was steep they made a stop-swing by turning across the slope, their upper edges cutting deep into the snow to halt their fast progress. There was nothing they couldn't do – those skis had a will of their own. It was IDK's ability to stay on them that was in question. Oh, he stayed upright, and didn't fall out of the bindings, but he had to learn to shift his weight and throw himself forwards, and not lag behind. The skis *were* magical, but it would take time for him to master them.

Dieter wasn't surprised by the speed of the skis, or that they'd transformed IDK's ability. He was learning to accept that things happened here that weren't possible on Earth. The wood had been unusual. He'd felt it in the tingling of his hands when he touched it, and in the energy he'd had when he formed the skis. He noticed the faint green glimmer of the wood now, and the pale green glint of the tracks the skis cut.

Gradually, IDK was able to find his balance and gain control, applying enough pressure on the inside edges to bend his knees more and bring his weight over his skis so that he wasn't dragging behind. He worked out where he wanted to get to on the slope, and arrived there soon after, with fewer spills. Dieter noted that Anne was improving too, not because of magical skis but because she applied herself for hours to one particular exercise, until she'd mastered it, before going onto the next. Even Georg was growing in confidence. The swish of wood on snow, the sound of their laughter, the confident speed each one of them was achieving, made Dieter think that IDK was right when he'd said skiing was like flying.

After being on the slope all morning, IDK grew tired and misjudged his speed. His skis screeched, snow gnashed and sprayed up, and he collected Ziggi. They toppled over.

Ziggi untangled herself and rocketed off, passing the Weatherman, who was climbing onto his Nordic skis. They were designed to ski cross-country over the slopes and not sing down them. The Weatherman had his anorak zipped up, and his rucksack was bulging (with goodies Georg had insisted he take). He'd unhooked his beard and wrapped it around his neck, a sure sign he was leaving.

'Are you coming back?'

Everyone except Ziggi gathered around him.

'First I have to find the missing animals.' He contemplated them with far-away eyes. 'Our world can't survive without them.'

'Do you think you could also look for the engine room?' Manfred suggested politely. 'We don't want them to fix the motors and fly off before we find the king.'

'I will search for it,' the Weatherman nodded.

'Why are they stealing the animals?' Anne asked, worried.

'Animals can't be tricked or flattered or deceived. They have a strong survival instinct, which the Shadows can't weaken,' the Weatherman replied. 'They can't bind them with thoughts, so they trap them instead.'

'Why can they bind us with their thoughts, and not animals?' Anne wanted to know.

'Humans have cluttered their lives with so many doubts. "I'm not good enough," "No one likes me," "I'm not the best." People worry about what they aren't. Animals simply are what they are. The Shadows can't manipulate them.'

'Do you think Violette was stolen?'

'Yes, Anne. She may well have been stolen. But that doesn't mean we won't find her.' He leaned closer to Anne and spoke only to her. 'Hope will always give you more energy than sadness, and the Shadows can't steal it.' He waited until Anne nodded, and knew she understood.

'Don't go.' IDK tugged at his sleeve. 'Please. I'm hearing things. Things that don't make sense. It's making me nervous.' An image of angel curls seared IDK's memory, before disappearing again.

'I can't stay, little one,' the Weatherman bowed. 'I have my job to do, and so do you.' His voice grew sonorous, 'The Dark cannot live unless it captures the light. The Shadows are cruel and powerful, and if we let them, they will destroy two worlds. But they can be overcome. That is the hope we have, to cling onto. The power is within us.' He left them with a smile and a wave.

Moments later, Ziggi came charging out of the forest.

'Epsilon! Stop! Drop it!'

Epsilon streaked past. She had something white in her mouth, squealing and flapping like a fish out of water. The cat raced into the hut. She still had hold of the white thing when they crowded in after her. It twisted and turned, trying to get out of the cat-tooth trap.

Manfred gingerly caught hold of Epsilon. He juggled her, trying to extract whatever it was from between her teeth. Epsilon spat and struggled, protecting her catch, and before Manfred could get a firm grip of it, the creature she held in her mouth melted. Within moments it was a puddle of water on the floor.

'What happened? Was I dreaming?' Georg stared with surprise-opened eyes.

'Your dream resembles a lizard,' Manfred replied.

'I must have dreamt it too,' said Anne.

'Is it dangerous?' asked IDK.

'A little thing like that isn't dangerous.' Ziggi's answer was slammed down, a queen's decree. 'And water certainly isn't.' She grabbed a cloth to wipe away the small puddle.

'Don't touch it!' Manfred said abruptly. He located a syringe in his instrument box and used it to draw up a drop of water from the puddle. He placed it on a glass slide under his microscope, put another drop into a test tube to boil, and added a third drop to one of four beakers filled with snow. Manfred became absorbed, opening his books, pushing up his glasses, which were threatening to slip off his nose (because his nose was pointed down), while the others stood around, helpless in the midst of all that scientific activity.

It was a long time before Manfred spoke.

'There's a peculiar substance here. If it's mixed with snow, it...well...it seems to cause the snow to come alive, to build life-forms.'

'Like a lizard?' Georg asked through crumbs, which he hastily wiped from his mouth.

'Like a lizard,' Manfred confirmed. 'It's a substance I've never encountered before. In fact, it's more like an energy...the life-form it creates seems to be dependent on the snow-type.' He paused, trying to find the right words to explain what he meant. 'The lizard was made from new snow, which is fine-grained, so the lizard was small.' He put the last droplets from the puddle into another test tube. 'It's impossible to measure the amount of energy generated, or how long it takes. Maybe if I reduce it by boiling...' Manfred increased the flame of his portable Bunsen burner. The melting snow shimmered slightly green. He left the table, rubbed bleary eyes and stretched again.

'Man, am I hungry.' He veered to the kitchen area of the hut. 'I made a ham roll earlier.'

No ham roll. A smear of mustard on Georg's face. Manfred glared. Georg looked away, and in two steps was at the door.

'OH MEI!'

The Snowman (part one)

'Oh Mei!' Manfred stormed outside. 'Where did he go?'

No Georg. Anne and IDK were building a snowman, using the snow that was piled behind the hut. It had a greenish glow to it, barely noticeable in the daylight.

'Have you seen Oh Mei?'

'I'm here.' Georg appeared from behind the snowman's torso. 'I was hungry,' he complained. 'I didn't know it was your roll.'

'You're always hungry,' Manfred snapped. 'One day you'll be as big as a house!' Then Manfred was distracted by the snowman construction and wanted to take over immediately. He'd built thousands of snowmen and knew all about balance, perspective, rolling snowballs and keeping them in place; if you wanted to build a snowman, Manfred was your man. He suggested scaffolding straightaway. Anne was indignant. The snowman was going to be life-size, not high-rise. But Manfred was adamant; he'd have scaffolding erected in no time.

'We want a snowman *now*, not next Wednesday!' Anne continued to roll big snowballs.

'He should be bigger.' Ziggi eyed the snow-creation as if it were a work of art in a gallery.

'What would you know?' Anne snapped.

'His head's too small.'

'Not like yours.'

'You need a model.' Ziggi stood her ground.

'Yes.' Manfred agreed. 'A prototype. And there he is. Perfecto.' He pointed to Georg. 'You're so nice and, and – round.' Manfred really could be spiteful when crossed.

Georg let out a sigh that suggested he didn't want his image to be that of a round snowman; but what he wanted wasn't taken into consideration. Manfred and Ziggi pushed Anne and IDK out of the way and operations began in earnest.

'His head has to be larger. Larger…bigger than that…'

'Build up his cheeks.'

'Stop it,' Georg said weakly.

'As though he's stuffed food in them… Hamsterish! Better! And the torso has to be like a barrel.' The two architects cast appraising eyes at their creation, and then worked on.

'You've forgotten his feet.' Anne was still critical.

'Snowmen don't have feet,' Ziggi said confidently.

'Why not? Is he going to stand on his stomach?'

'I think he should have feet!' Manfred's Calculator said with feeling, having none itself.

Dieter came out of the hut. 'I thought you were practising your skiing.'

'We've been practising all morning. A few hours off won't hurt.' Manfred continued adding snow to the snow-body. 'Even the greatest sportsmen have time out – so should we. Have you forgotten how much fun snow can be?'

'It doesn't sound like you're having fun.' Dieter remained uneasy.

'We're letting off steam.' Manfred suddenly noticed Anne had built a pair of snow feet and was adding them to the snowman, 'Hey! What are you doing?'

'Why can't it be a snow-woman?' Anne demanded.

'Don't be stupid!'

'What would you know?'

'More than you!'

'Then why don't you do it better?'

'I would if you let me!'

And so it went. Squabbling voices filled the afternoon as the snowman was completed. Snow was moulded like clay, buttons from Ziggi's coat pockets were used for eyes, and a banana skin served as a mouth. It was a crooked mouth that sagged at the corners – they couldn't get it to smile.

'Oh!' The 'Mei' was left out. Georg reached for the nearest piece of food and bit into it.

'Broom!' Manfred held out his hand, a surgeon expecting a scalpel. Ziggi handed him the broom from the kitchen. Manfred removed his twirling bow tie and pinned it under the snowman's chin so he had the air of a waiter.

'Now for the nose,' Ziggi said as she reached for the carrot she'd put aside for the job. No carrot.

Georg stealthily left the circle of action. Manfred found carrot crumbs on the windowsill.

'OH MEI!!!!' But Georg had disappeared.

'We can't have a snowman without a nose.' Disappointed, Ziggi wanted to tear the whole thing down.

'Leave him, he's sweet.' Anne ran her eyes over the snowman. 'But I think he's cold.'

'Snowmen don't feel the cold, stupid.' Ziggi again.

'You would if you had nothing on,' Anne insisted and hastily made a skirt of fir-needles. It had the effect of an apron tied around the snowman's corpulent middle.

'No self-respecting snowman would ever wear that!' Ziggi was contemptuous.

'Who made you the fashion police?' Anne roared back.

'You spoil everything.' Ziggi turned towards the hut. One by one the others followed her in.

Snow-lizards

Tempers were slightly better the next day. The rest had done them good, and Anne, Georg and IDK were practising their skiing again. Manfred, whose mind was still on the curious substance Epsilon had brought into the hut, was consulting his Calculator. They were submerged in scientific study and enveloped by green clouds of steam that came from bubbling test tubes.

Dieter stood in the doorway of the hut, watching his friend working. 'It'll be New Year's Eve soon.'

'I know.' Manfred noted a new equation. 'But this might be relevant. I think I'm on the trail of something.'

'While you're doing that, Ziggi and I'll work out the best route up the ice mountain.'

'Good idea.' But Manfred wasn't listening.

'If we get high enough we might be able to see what's on the summit.'

Manfred made no sign that he'd heard.

'Can I come?' IDK asked Dieter.

'We'll be travelling really fast,' Dieter replied. 'Wait until tomorrow, when we all go.'

IDK nodded, unhappy.

'We have to hurry,' he said softly, and although Dieter was looking at him, he wasn't sure if his mouth had moved.

'Are we going?' An impatient Ziggi skied to the door. Giving IDK a perplexed glance, Dieter hurried out.

They set off and were nearing the edge of the Green Valley, when IDK's alarmed voice reached them. 'My ski!'

A runaway ski hissed between them and disappeared in the trees at the bottom of the hill.

Ziggi's reaction time was quick. She leaned into racing position, eyes fixed on the departing ski. Dieter followed. At the same time, inside the hut, Manfred ripped his eye away from the microscope and sprang up from the wooden chair, knocking it over.

'Oh no!' His expression was horrified. 'Dieter! Ziggi! Anne!' He raced to the door.

'They've gone,' said Anne. Manfred leaned weakly against the doorframe.

'Oh no!' he repeated again and again.

Ziggi's long, fluid racing skis flew over the snow, her knees absorbing the shock of the rough terrain, like the shock absorbers of a car. Muscles straining, she whipped through trees, ducked under branches, jumped over small mounds of snow to land further down the slope. Ziggi the racer was pitted against the lone ski that seemed to have a life of its own.

Bit by bit she inched closer to the ski, her skill keeping her on course. Bending even further, her shins pushing into the top edges of her boots, she drew parallel to the ski, transferred her right stock to her left hand, and reached for the ski with her right hand. When she had it, she held it up, triumphant. Then she swung around and stopped.

Dieter was following Ziggi, a considerable distance behind. He grinned, and Ziggi grinned too. Skiing was a language they both understood well. The exhilaration of it. Testing the body's strength and flexibility. And for Ziggi, winning the trophy was an important part of the sport.

'Not bad.' It was high praise, coming from Dieter.

'I have my own personal trainer in the States.' For once Ziggi wasn't skiting.

'Wow! That's good, isn't it?' Dieter sensed uncertainty mixed with Ziggi's pride.

'I suppose so,' Ziggi replied. 'My father wants me to be a champion, doesn't matter what it costs.'

'What do you want?'

'To be a champion, I guess.' Ziggi shook the snow off one of her skis. 'I do love skiing.' She hoisted IDK's runaway ski onto her shoulder and turned up the slope, suddenly seeing how far they'd come, and how thick the forest was here.

'We'll be right if we follow our tracks.' Dieter realised it too. 'The Weatherman did say the Shadows can't penetrate the forest.' They began the slower journey back, climbing up the slope sideways.

'Too tight a curve here.' Ziggi assessed her performance by the shape of the tracks. It was easy to see where they weren't clearly cut into the snow, where they were blurry and crumbly, with ill-defined edges. 'Ski slipped there,' she said, pointing out a fault in her own technique. 'You can improve too.' She analysed Dieter's tracks next. 'See here – your skis have slipped, you put your weight over both of them, instead of on the outside ski.' This was so unlike Ziggi, full of knowledge *and* helpful. 'Especially in your left-hand curve.' She pointed at Dieter's left-hand curves, which weren't the clear sweeps the right-hand curves were, and which were not nearly as sharply cut as Ziggi's.

After that they didn't talk. It was hard work, climbing the slope, one step at a time. Their breath came in short gasps. Around them, trees groaned, like doors with creaky hinges.

'Look!' Ziggi pointed to tracks, thick as logs, that cut across theirs. 'What would make tracks like that?' They stood listening. Whip-cracks sounded, branches broke and they heard a slithering and slipping, then the dull thud of a heavy body landing.

Lizards – great, heavy-bellied ice-dragons – surrounded them. The biggest lay on the lowest branches of the trees, the smallest in the crowns. They usually slept all winter, blanketing the trees, and melted in the spring, but something had woken them. One by one the snow-lizards slithered down and crawled towards them.

Ziggi searched the slopes for any possible avenue of escape. A path to the right was their only hope. It was steep, relatively free of trees, and it was downhill.

'We have to get out of here. Let's go!' Pushing hard on her stock, Ziggi jumped in midair and landed metres away. Dieter did the same, and they were soon rattling over corrugations of ice that made their skis sound like rapid gunfire. They leapt over small shrubs, wending and bending their way through the taller timber, but no matter how fast they skied, the snow-lizards were closing in, belly-sliding after them, using stout legs to push off, scrabbling claws in the snow, chasing them. Nothing slowed them, they ploughed through everything in their path, leaving behind an icy wake.

Dieter tripped. He missed a tree, re-balanced, skied over an out-jutting rock, and fell. Further down, Ziggi turned.

'Get up! Hurry!' She waited long enough to see Dieter regain his footing. 'Don't look behind you! Go!'

Dieter leaned further forward and concentrated on Ziggi.

His curves were as tight as Ziggi's, his balance was as good – for the first few curves – but he was losing ground. He hadn't been in training for speed the way Ziggi had. Dieter skied precisely, was the better skier, but precision didn't count here. Speed meant everything.

The forest was never-ending. The lizards were getting closer. Splinters of ice from their spittle lodged in Dieter's clothes. He couldn't get away. His muscles were giving in. He was running out of breath, his legs had no more strength and threatened to buckle, and he was skiing without control. A rock loomed. He tried to slow to avoid it, but clipped it. He rolled, limped up, went on.

Ziggi could see a snowfield, clean and smooth as silk, glimmering through the trees. She reached inside herself and asked her body for extra strength, for the energy that would propel her to the finishing line first, ahead of the snapping jaws and dragon teeth.

'Ski *schuss*, Dieter!' Ziggi yelled. But Dieter couldn't. He had already spent his energy. A giant lizard slid towards him, unfurled its ice-veined tongue and wrapped it around his waist, pulling him off his feet. Ziggi cut across the slope to stop and side-stepped back, quickly.

The lizard's skin was green-tinged, like fish-scales, but each scale was a flake of ice. It lashed its tail angrily to ward Ziggi off. Its tongue was wrapped around Dieter's leg now. He tried to kick out but couldn't reach it, and was slowly, surely being pulled towards the needle-sharp teeth in its gaping mouth.

'Use your stocks! Cut its tongue off.' Ziggi lunged her own stock at the lizard's tongue. Thick blood, green and ice-choked, squirted onto the snow, and coagulated. 'Use your skis!' Ziggi continued to stab, her voice hardly heard over the roaring.

Dieter lifted his skis so they were cross-wise against the lizard's mouth and its jaws couldn't close on him. The ice-dragon grew wilder. It used its tail as a club, thumping the ground, making it shudder, lifting its small stubby legs, clawing at Dieter, hissing. Ziggi continued to stab at it, finally hitting its tongue which snapped, and Dieter rolled free.

'Quick!' Ziggi continued stabbing it, aiming for its head. 'I'll finish it off. You go!'

Shaking, Dieter stood and skied away, swinging his stocks at the smaller lizards teeming on the forest floor, while Ziggi stayed to fight the ice-dragon. She stabbed the lizard so hard a chunk of its jaw flew off, and a yellow-green liquid emptied out onto the snow. A final stab and the head blasted into fragments of ice that sprayed through the air.

Ziggi scooped up IDK's ski, assumed a racer's position and shot off after Dieter. She took hold of one of his stocks to steady him and together they skied away as fast as he could manage. Behind them a mountain of lizards wriggled and squealed and slid to where the large lizard lay.

Yellow droplets glistened on Ziggi's racing goggles and stained her red ski-suit. Green-brown spots of blood soaked into her gloves. She skied a wide curve and halted, facing the mountain.

'Are you hurt? Will you be able to climb up there?' she asked.

'I'm okay. I'll make it as long as there aren't any lizards on this side.' Dieter threw a glance at the forest where the lizards had attacked. They were far away now, wriggling worms that glowed a poisoned green. The little lizards were devouring the ice-dragon Ziggi had killed.

Ziggi fished around in her pockets and held out a cube of glucose.

'Take it,' she said. 'You need it.' Dieter's face was pale and he was supporting himself on his stocks.

'Thanks,' he replied. For the glucose. And for saving his life.

'Just returning the favour,' Ziggi said. 'I could still be under an avalanche.' They both grinned, a half-earnest, crooked and totally exhausted grin.

The Snowman (part two)

The sun disappeared fast, and was replaced by the moon.

'I'm going to wrap this ski around IDK's neck!' It was slow work side-stepping across the steep ridges and hills. 'What if we're going in the wrong direction?'

Dieter studied the stars. 'No, we're right.'

'It's freezing.' Ziggi's teeth chattered. 'Brrrr.'

'Grrrr!'

'Oh no. What was that?' Ziggi wailed. 'Bears!'

'Grrrr! Orff orff…'

'It's Orff!' Ziggi was hugely relieved. 'Hey! Orff! Over here! We're here!'

A cold nose was thrust at Ziggi; firelight approached them.

'Dieter? Ziggi?' Anne's voice posed their names as questions, and then the glow embraced them. Ziggi and Dieter grinned with relief. So did IDK and Orff. Manfred's worried and strained features broke into a smile.

'Where have you two been?' Anne glanced at them sharply.

'Ease up, Anne. You sound like my mother,' Dieter replied softly.

'We were worried.' Manfred swung the sleigh around and, thankful, Dieter and Ziggi climbed in. 'You didn't notice anything strange, did you?' Manfred whispered it. As usual he didn't want anyone other than Dieter to hear.

'Strange?' Dieter didn't keep his voice low, and Manfred winced.

'Yes. Epsilon's lizard…you know, the one that melted? They can grow…'

'I know. We encountered them.' Dieter said, shivering as he recalled the fierce attack. 'How do you explain it?'

'If the snow's old, coarse snow, and the crystal's light touches it, the monsters that are created can be huge!'

'So it was the light?' Dieter eased his sore muscles.

'I think so. I don't know what else it could be.'

Manfred guided the sleigh through the air with his

thoughts, following the sweep of the valley and pulled in at the front of the hut. The shutters were drawn. Firelight seeped from under the door.

'Oh Mei said he'd cook.' Manfred scratched his head perplexed. There was no Georg to welcome them, no pot on the stove, no table laid, no food in sight.

'He's probably eaten it,' Ziggi said, derisive.

'Oh Mei?'

'Where is he?' Manfred grew worried.

'Oh Mei?' they all yelled.

No answer. Only Epsilon complaining, fur on end, her green eyes as round as saucers. In two leaps she was in Ziggi's arms, burying her whiskers in Ziggi's jacket.

'What's wrong with her?' Manfred scanned the dark trees beyond the hut, then the black hills beyond the trees. Orff was howling, the eerie tone lifting high, his hackles standing on end. He bared his teeth and growled, angry, vicious, fearful.

'What's the matter, Orff?' Anne bent to pat him.

'Shhh,' Manfred said suddenly.

Steps in the snow quickened, coming at them. The five stayed close together as Dieter led them cautiously around the corner of the hut, where they ran smack bang into Georg, whose momentum nearly bowled them over.

'There you are! Thank goodness. Oh Mei!' Georg jumped and jiggled on the spot, first on one leg, then the other, trying to articulate, getting nothing out but another, 'Oh Mei.'

Anne peered into the darkness where he was pointing. In two seconds she was as inarticulate as Georg.

'Oh dear, oh my, oh, oh, oh!'

A moon-shadow fell over them. Snow dropped in clods, though it was a clear night. Huge button eyes glowered at them.

'Silence that dog!' Banana-skin lips grimaced. Then a snow finger pointed to Anne and Georg. 'Do they have to behave so hysterically? Haven't they seen a snowman before?' The apron of branches, big as trees now, shook, the bow-tie twirled like helicopter blades, and more snow fell in clumps.

'Oh, oh, oh!!!' They stared at the Snowman, lifting their flaming torches for a better view.

'You're as big as a house!' Manfred said in awe. 'Bigger!' The Snowman was so tall the flickering light from their flares didn't reach high enough to see his face properly.

'Take that fire away from me, it's hot!' His voice boomed. They did what he said, promptly, not wanting to argue with a snowman who was fifty metres high. The torches were thrust into the snow where they extinguished.

'Tell that stupid dog to be quiet!' the Snowman ordered.

'Orff isn't – oh, Orff, shhh!'

Orff stopped howling, and lay at Anne's feet, eyeing the Snowman mistrustfully. There was silence now – they were all open-mouthed, and disbelieving.

'Don't stand there gawping. Oh Mei,' he said, more forcefully than Georg ever did. He looked sulky and grumbled, the way Manfred did, lips moving, no words coming out. Because he was annoyed, more snow fell.

'Ah...good evening.' Manfred carefully approached the

Snowman, hoping good manners would make a better impression.

'What's good about it?' The Snowman was holding his head. 'My cheeks are hamsterish, and because I have such a big head, I have a huge headache,' he complained. 'Who's fault is that?' Ziggi and Manfred coughed discreetly and blushed.

'And *WHO* gave me this ridiculous apron?' the Snowman glared like Anne glared. 'No self-respecting snowman would ever wear *this*!' They all recognised Ziggi's sneering tone.

'A snow-woman would have had better manners.' Anne was blushing too.

The Snowman's hands lifted to the flat spot in the middle of his face.

'Well, that's the last straw! *The Last Straw!*' he bellowed and a heap of snow landed on them all. 'I suppose you think that's funny? I don't see anything even slightly amusing about it. A nose isn't too much to ask for!'

The others cast furtive glances at Georg, whose face was now as red as Manfred's, Anne's and Ziggi's. The Snowman bent, broke off an icicle from the roof of the hut and screwed it into his face. It was long and hooked, a Roman nose in a balloon face, and it started dripping immediately.

'I'm hungry.' The Snowman's tone of voice wasn't unlike Georg's. 'What's for dinner?'

'Chilli peppers,' said Ziggi. 'Nice and hot.'

'Ah – there isn't anything as yet, actually. We've been busy skiing,' Georg quickly jumped in. The Snowman's mouth tightened into a tight, thin, banana-skin line.

'This is a wonderful state of affairs,' he said, completely sour. 'You get invited out and they don't even feed you.' He was as sensitive as he was tall.

More snow fell as he stomped off. The ground shook, the shutters rattled, then the valley grew quiet.

'I hope you two are satisfied,' Anne said. She glared at Ziggi and Manfred. The 'engineers' said nothing, eyes glued to the ground.

'It's your fault, you know,' Dieter said tersely to them all. 'He's in a bad mood because you were all grumpy when you built him. Let's hope he has our positive qualities as well.'

'At least he has feet.' Anne wouldn't be cowed.

'What does that have to do with it?'

'If he didn't have feet he'd still be here!'

Stars of ice

The next morning, as he attempted to leave the hut, Georg encountered an eye. The Snowman had pressed it against the doorway (a tricky thing for someone of that height), and was peering in.

'Good morning, it's me,' he said in tones friendlier than the night before. His face filled the entire doorframe, the visible eye twinkled and the banana-skin mouth tried to smile, but didn't quite succeed. 'I've been waiting for you to wake up.' He stood stiffly and hit his head on the eaves. Icicles tinkled, the Snowman cursed, and his good mood vanished.

'Don't be frightened,' he said, as they eyed him suspiciously. 'I won't hurt you.' Then he saw IDK and bowed low. IDK bowed in return. 'What do you want, my young friend?' The Snowman sat in the snow, crossed his stubby legs, made himself comfortable and focussed his attention on IDK.

'Why would we want anything?' Georg was the first to speak.

'Because you brought me to life. I am the consequence of your actions.' A hurt expression settled on the Snowman's face.

'There is a reason!' IDK said quickly, surprising the others. 'We thought you might help us out...' He paused, thinking: '*with snow!*'

'Yes.' The Snowman was pleased. 'I can help with snow – I'm made of it.' He reached into the clouds and plucked out several unfallen snowflakes, which he brought to ground level for the group to inspect. They didn't melt in his cold hands. 'Have you ever analysed a snowflake?' he asked. 'Can you tell me anything about it?'

'It's wet?' IDK said hopefully.

'Not necessarily,' said the Snowman.

'Snow. A large snowflake has approximately 3000 snow-crystals,' the Calculator boasted. Manfred tapped it hurriedly, to keep it quiet.

'They're such small, delicate things.' The Snowman took no notice of the mechanical interruption.

'May I?' Carefully, with a pair of tweezers, Manfred placed the snowflakes on a glass slide, which he inserted underneath one section of the Calculator. He switched on the tiny light of the projection unit and an enlargement of the snowflakes was cast onto the snow-covered ground. Manfred adjusted the lighting so the snowflakes were visible against the white background. They could all see the snow crystals clearly now, tiny stars of ice.

The Snowman was impressed. 'See how thousands of snow crystals hooked together make one snowflake.' He pointed to the edges of the crystals, to where the spokes had broken off. 'But they damage easily. Even while they fall, when they knock into one another. In warmer weather they ball together.' He held one out to Manfred. 'Blow on it,' he directed. Manfred's warm breath transformed the crystals.

'Temperature changes cause different kinds of snow formations, because the shapes of the crystals change,' the Snowman continued. 'Think of all the different types of snow. Hard, fresh, new snow is light, like whipped egg-white. Soggy spring snow is heavy and wet, like cold porridge. Ice, of course, is a different proposition altogether – it's hard and slippery and dangerous.'

'As per the snow-lizards?' Manfred couldn't contain his curiosity.

'Yes, there's a fair bit of ice in them.'

'And you?' Anne chipped in. 'How –'

'How did I come to life? You did that.' They stared at him. 'You have the Key.'

They continued to stare. The Snowman grew suspicious. 'You *do* have the Key, don't you?'

'Yes,' said Dieter and fumbled in his pockets for the green disc. The king's crystal lay dull and lifeless in his hands.

'You should be more careful where you hide that,' the Snowman said, critically.

'It's so small.' Dieter sounded apologetic. 'We don't exactly know what it is.'

IDK took it from Dieter. Suddenly the sun caught it and a green beam of light formed, strong and powerful, brighter than the daylight. The Snowman jumped out of the way.

'Keep it away from me!' he bellowed. IDK dropped the Key in surprise, and the snow around it melted. 'You don't know how to use it, do you?' The Snowman looked disappointed. 'It brings to life anything its beam touches. Anything that isn't already alive.' He cast around for an example. 'Look at those trees. The king didn't want a white world anymore, so he made these. Turned this valley into his special garden.'

'I thought he planted them as seeds?' Manfred had to be exact.

'He did. But the planet was already growing very cold, so he used the crystal's light to warm them and help them grow.' The Snowman sniffed, suspicious. 'You haven't been very well informed,' he said. 'Are you sure the Wise Man sent you?'

'About this king?' Ziggi asked. 'You seem to know a lot about him. Do you think there might be a reward?'

'If you're doing this for money…' The Snowman glared at Ziggi.

'No,' Manfred said quickly. 'It's more a matter of scientific curiosity, really.' The Snowman wasn't reassured.

'We want to return the Key to the king. We want to do what's right.' IDK frowned at Ziggi and Manfred.

'Good. I was getting worried.' The Snowman's glance lingered longest on Ziggi.

'Could I ask about the king's magic?' Manfred turned the Calculator off. 'What kind of spell makes the Green Valley safe?'

'The trees are protected by an aura of light,' said the Snowman, his ruffled mood settled. 'Light is the Shadow's enemy. As long as you have the light, you'll be safe.'

'How does this Key work?' Manfred hated to admit he didn't understand.

'When the light of the Key touches snow, it hooks the crystals together in such a way as to release their energy. It's the same principle with every substance.'

'And the type of life-form it creates depends on the type of substance!' Manfred continued to speak carefully, containing his excitement. It's what his experiments had been leading to. 'The energy of the snow crystals coupled with the light of the king's crystal not only creates a particular life form, but also determines whether it's good or evil and how complex it is.'

'That's right. The lizards have hard natures, because they were created from icy snow.'

'And the sleigh flies because of the crystal's light?' Manfred's eyes gleamed.

'Yes,' the Snowman nodded. 'But the real power comes when natural light and the crystal's light combine.'

'And why are you so knowledgeable?' Ziggi pushed her way into the conversation.

'I know about snow because I'm made of it. I know about light for the same reason,' the Snowman replied. 'And because the trees are protected by light, I know about them as well.' He scooped up a handful of snow and gave it to Georg. 'Here. Make something,' he said. Georg looked unsure. 'Go on.'

Whenever Georg was asked to think on the spot, he grew flustered, then embarrassed, and his mind remained blank. He didn't want that to happen now, so he quickly clumped the snow together into a snowball and handed it back.

'Not very creative,' the Snowman humphed, 'but under the circumstances it will do.' He glanced at IDK critically. 'Your glow is too weak.' He sounded mournful. 'You'll have to use sunlight until your own light returns.' He gave the Key to IDK, careful that it wasn't pointed at him, and showed him how to pass a beam of sunlight through it, forming a green ray, which he focussed onto the snowball. 'Look out!'

The snowball suddenly jumped high and rolled a wide circle on its shoulders. The movement was so unexpected, they all laughed out loud. Orff barked and frightened it – and it leapt in the air and onto Orff's nose, where it disintegrated. Orff backed away, shaking his head and licking his nose.

'Snowballs are flighty creatures,' said the Snowman. 'But you can see what I mean.' They did. The new knowledge weighed on them.

'You must be careful. Anything the Key's light touches, anything that is alive, dies. The Key is a powerful weapon. If it falls into the wrong hands.'

'Is that why the Shadows want it?' Manfred asked. 'To kill things?'

'Yes.' The Snowman shuddered. 'But not only to kill. The Darkness itself is dead, but should it capture the Key, it will come to life.' His words were grave. 'And if that happens, nothing will save us.' He brandished the Key. 'You must promise to guard this with your lives. It's why you have been chosen.' He gave it back to Dieter, and stood. The sun was high in the sky and he was dripping.

'I must go,' he said, wiping his brow. 'I have to preserve my energy for when it's needed. The Shadows are getting stronger and we must beware.' He bowed to IDK, who bowed too. 'If you need me, think about me,' he said, the banana-skin mouth finally lifting into a faint smile, then he lumbered away.

TEN

BEYOND THE GREEN VALLEY

The ice mountain

No one wanted to leave the hut, or the safety of the Green Valley. But time was running out and after another long day of ski practice they knew they must search for the king. Georg was in charge of the provisions: food, water, warm clothes, first aid; the others collected maps, compasses, tools and Manfred's instruments, which were carefully packed into the sleigh and secured. As soon as the sun rose, skis were waxed and their edges filed so they were sharp and could slice into the snow cleanly. Boots were thoroughly dried so their feet would stay warm. They worked in silence, each of them focussing on their immediate task to keep their minds off the uncertainty ahead.

But when they hooked their stocks into the sleigh, expecting it to rise, the old sleigh stood fast. They repacked it, leaving half their supplies behind.

'It still won't fly if it has to pull all of us,' Manfred said.

'I don't have to hook on,' IDK's skis floated above the snow. 'See!'

'We'll never make it in time,' Manfred's voice was starting to sound stressed. 'In two days it will be New Year's Eve.'

Manfred and Dieter conferred, calling Ziggi over to join them. They returned moments later, to face Anne, Georg and IDK.

'We've been thinking...' Manfred said ominously.

Anne guessed what that meant and her answer was emphatic. 'No!'

'It'll be faster if only three of us go,' said Dieter.

'But we have to stay together,' Georg argued.

'It's too dangerous,' Manfred countered.

'I'm not scared,' IDK exclaimed.

'Neither am I.' Anne's jaw stuck out obstinately.

'Look Anne.' Ziggi tried a conciliatory tone.

'No, you look. We're coming too. We're a team, and we're sticking together.'

'We *are* a team,' Dieter agreed. 'And we need to play to our strengths. Ziggi and I are the strongest skiers, and we need Manfred's expertise. We also need you and Georg to stay here and protect IDK and the Key.' Dieter handed the green disc to Anne for safekeeping. 'It won't be safe, on the mountain.'

'It's not fair.' Anne knew she was losing ground.

'You've proven you're courageous Anne.'

'And if we get into trouble – you're our back-up,' Ziggi added.

'How would we be able to help from here?' Georg asked, unconvinced.

'It's simply a reconnaissance mission.' Manfred tried to make it sound as unimportant as he could. 'I have to see what's on the summit of the mountain.'

'No.'

'Be reasonable…' The argument could have gone on all day but Dieter held firm. 'You're staying!' he said, and the discussion was over.

'Look after my cat!' Ziggi called to Anne as the three skiers hooked their stocks onto the sleigh. It lifted into the air, pulling them along behind it.

'Be careful!' Sour faces watched them go.

'Don't do anything stupid!' The resentment gave way to worry, as the sleigh wound along the valley, and Dieter, Manfred and Ziggi disappeared among the trees.

*

As soon as Dieter, Manfred and Ziggi were out of the Green Valley, they could feel the Darkness. The black cloud had thickened; its ragged edges, where the Weatherman had ripped it apart with the Key's light, were being woven together again. In the growing gloom, Shadows darted furtively across the snow and circled around them, gathering in places where the sun didn't reach. Dieter was careful to guide the sleigh on a course that kept them in the sunlight, where he knew they would be safe; but when they skirted the shaded areas, they could feel a cold breath, dark and menacing, and could see the yellow gleam of watchful eyes.

'We have to return by mid-afternoon.' Dieter glanced around uncertainly as they continued to climb the steepening slope. The ice mountain reared in front of them, needle-sharp and milky white, snowfields like the wings of a moth folded around it.

'It's so hot,' Manfred said suddenly. He unzipped his anorak.

'Yes.' Dieter loosened his collar. Ziggi did the same.

'I'm thirsty,' Manfred said five minutes later. They stopped and drank from their water bottles. Above them the sun burned fiercely. Manfred searched for his sunglasses. 'It's very glary all of a sudden.'

'Got anything else to complain about?'

'I'll think of something.' Manfred threw his woollen jumper on the growing pile of discarded clothes in the sleigh.

They found another hut two hours later. Unlike the Green Valley hut, this one sagged, a tumbledown shack that leaned precariously against the rock-face behind it. It wasn't marked on the Calculator's map.

'Deserted.' Ziggi walked around it.

'Derelict.' Manfred retraced the path she had taken.

'We have to keep going if we want to make it to the top.'

Dieter urged them on. They hooked into the sleigh again, and continued to rise towards the summit.

'That's strange,' Dieter said suddenly. 'I just felt a raindrop.' He borrowed Manfred's binoculars. The cloud was like a huge feather quilt, shaken, discolouring the sun with its dark taint. 'We have to go back to that hut!' He turned the sleigh as the sun was extinguished. The Dark pressed in closer, the silence deepening, until the cloud burst open. It rained. Huge, heavy drops splashed onto the snow, spearing it from all directions.

They crossed the rain-whipped snow with difficulty and entered the old hut. It was damp inside, unkempt and rancid; old wood, old smoke, ashes in the grate. Three wooden walls were built against a cliff, which made the fourth wall. Droplets of water flowed like snails' trails to the floor. Hammers of iron pounded the roof, which leaked, and a sheet of water soon cascaded down the face of the cliff, so it was almost as wet inside as out.

Manfred scrutinised the cliff-face wall. 'Does this look like natural rock to you?' He scratched away the flaky lichen that grew on the rock. 'Look at this – it's hewn, these are bricks.' Manfred chewed his lips. 'Why would there be bricks halfway up a mountain?' He kicked at the base of the wall, then used his stock to dig. The bricks went a long way into the ground, which perplexed Manfred even more.

The others found a place to sit, watching Manfred work, waiting out the deluge. Curtains of water flooded drainpipes, falling onto the rain-trammelled earth. It stopped suddenly, ten minutes later, as though a tap had been turned off. Almost immediately the overflowing water stiffened into icicles, a thick row stabbing into the ground, surrounding the hut. A cold settled, so overpowering it knocked the breath out of their lungs. Hands, noses, ears were pinched in its malicious fingers. Manfred reached for his woollen cap.

'Ouch!' He let it drop. It was stiff as a board and smashed as it hit the ground. 'What's happening – it's freezing!'

'Warning, minus 15 degrees Celsius,' croaked the Calculator.

They put on one layer of clothing after the other but it didn't help. Dieter went to the door. He could hardly open it. His gloves were wooden, his fingers stiff and clumsy.

'I've been thinking,' Manfred's voice sounded frightened. 'If this is a spaceship, it might have a thermostat. The Shadows could be controlling the weather.'

'But they couldn't switch off the light, could they?' Ziggi said it half-jokingly, until she realised Manfred was serious.

'I'd say that's exactly what they intend to do. They've been repairing the black cloud pretty fast.'

'Warning, warning, minus 30.'

'They're certainly trying to stop us from reaching the top of the mountain,' Manfred added, thoughtful.

Dieter managed to kick through the ice bars of their prison. The sky was still grey outside, hard steel. There was no sun, just a weak, diffuse light. The water, which only seconds ago had run fast down the mountain, lay in sheets of solid ice.

'We can't stay here till nightfall.' Dieter peered into the gloom. 'We need to go back.'

'You mean give in?' cried Ziggi, disgusted.

'For today,' Dieter replied. 'If we stay here any longer we'll never get down.' He took up his skis and precariously slid out the door. It took all his strength to stand on the slippery ice.

'But these bricks –' Manfred had remained at the door of the hut. 'I'm sure they're important. I need time to work out why. If we light a fire we can keep the Dark away.'

'There isn't any wood.' Dieter handed Manfred his skis. 'Our clothes are wet. If we stay here we'll freeze.'

'Minus 40,' said the Calculator in a slurred voice. 'Minus 50.' The voice broke off, the machine shut down.

'Come on!' Dieter waited until they had all put on their skis.

They tried to move the sleigh but it was glued to the ground and nothing they could do would budge it. Every path looked treacherous, no matter which way they turned. They stared at the harsh ice as if hypnotised by a cobra rising in front of them, and fear coiled itself tightly around their hearts.

'I can't ski that,' said Manfred quietly. He held his breath, for even the act of breathing threatened to dislodge his skis, and if he should begin to slide then he'd never be able to stop. 'This slope is perpendicular!'

'Think about soft snow.' Dieter tried to subdue his own fear. 'Soft, new snow is easy to ski on.'

'This is *not* soft snow!'

'No, but you can ski on ice – if you know how,' Dieter continued. 'Manfred, you've skied ice before.'

'Not like this! You know how clumsy I am!' It was almost a wail.

'Ziggi and I will help you. It's no different than any other slope. The trick is not to tense your body and remember the rules of ice-skiing. As long as the edges of your skis grip you'll control the speed.'

'I'll go first,' said Ziggi. She faced across the slope, leaving Manfred cramped in uncertainty.

'You go after Ziggi, Manfred. I'll be right behind you.'

Ziggi pushed off. She stopped metres away so she wouldn't get too fast and out of control.

'Come on, it is manageable!' Ziggi pushed off again. Her fear made her cautious.

'Throw yourself forwards,' Dieter called out. 'Don't look up the mountain, look immediately where you're going. Bend your knees into the slope so the edges will grip.'

Ziggi needed all her strength to cut a hold into the ice with the edges of her skis. For the first time in her life she took heed of another person, and it showed in her skiing. Her confident style returned, but the tempo was controlled. She stopped again and waited for Manfred.

'We'll ski around the mountain,' Dieter called to her. 'Gradual curves like bangles around an arm.' Ziggi nodded.

Dieter didn't need to add that they had to avoid the Shadows, that their curves must always follow the light.

'Go on, Manfred,' he said. 'It's not as bad as you think.'

Manfred cramped his will and his body together. He wanted to push off; he wanted to have the courage.

'The ice is too hard, the mountain is too steep.' His voice was shaking. He glanced towards the Green Valley, which was too far away. The ice glittered clear and held him in its stare.

'Forget the ice!' But Manfred didn't hear Dieter. 'Trust yourself.' No response. 'Trust me.'

'I want to, but –' Manfred couldn't move.

'Then I'll carry you,' said Dieter in despair.

'Don't be stupid. I'm far too heavy, you'll kill us both!'

'I'm strong.'

'Go without me, Dieter. I'll stay in the hut. I'll light a fire.' But Dieter wouldn't leave him. He turned his skis so he was face to face with his friend.

'You can do this,' he said and reached for Manfred's hand. His skis didn't grip the ice and Dieter slipped away with an awful ripping sound, backwards, down the slope.

'Dieter!' Without thinking, Manfred pushed off after him.

Dieter had to use all his skill and strength to retain his balance and bring the tips of his skis around so they faced across the slope. His thighs and his knees were shaking by the time the edges bit into the ice, and he stopped. Manfred caught up with him and slowed too, and together they carefully skied towards Ziggi.

'See. That's ten metres.' Dieter managed a grin. 'How long will it take if we're going at this rate?'

'Forever.' Without waiting for them, Ziggi pushed off again. Dieter smiled at his friend.

'Coming?' He pushed off too. Manfred reined in his fear and knew it wouldn't return.

Fear of pain

It took the rest of the afternoon and many stops, for breath and to ease their shaking muscles and the vice-like grip of their boots around their ankles. The sun was about to set when they reached the ridge from where they could see the first of the king's trees. They were about to re-enter the Green Valley at last, and were filled with a huge wave of relief and pride for having conquered the mountain. The ice wasn't as hard or slippery here and they kept up a steady pace. Ziggi even skied backwards in a circle around them, knelt on one knee and 'played the violin' with her stocks, though it was a wobbly tune. They were nearly at the hut, nearly safe.

Ziggi stopped to adjust her boots. Manfred and Dieter skied past. She pushed off to follow; Ziggi the racer with opponents ahead. She ducked, held her stocks up and behind her, and shot off. The slope was icier than she realised and Ziggi skied too fast – so fast she could only ski in a straight line, with no curves to control her tempo.

'Whoaaaa!' she screamed as she cannoned towards Dieter and Manfred. Dieter saw her at the last moment, turned to avoid her, and Ziggi skied over the ends of his skis. Dieter fell, hitting his knee on the ice at an awkward angle, so it buckled. When he tried to stand, he couldn't. Further down Ziggi managed to come to a breathless halt.

'Sorry,' she called sheepishly.

'Zttch! How many times have we told you?' Manfred said, annoyed. He climbed back to Dieter, collecting the ski that had come off in his fall. Dieter lay on the icy slope, his breath knocked out of him, a stabbing pain in his knee.

'I'm sorry. I didn't mean it. Are you hurt?' Ziggi had also returned.

'You don't think!' Manfred snapped. 'Are you all right?' he asked Dieter.

'I'm okay.' In all his life Dieter had never shown anyone he felt pain, and he wasn't going to start now. 'Give me a minute,' he said, his hand massaging his knee, his face obscured. Manfred hesitated. 'You two get going, go on.' He was aware of the approaching evening, and the Shadows creeping closer. Manfred placed Dieter's ski beside him and gave Ziggi another black look.

'Come on,' he said abruptly and pushed off. Ziggi stayed a moment longer, wanting to help Dieter, but not knowing how. Then she went too. Dieter was alone.

'You know the rules of the slope, but you're so careless…' Manfred's voice drifted through the fading light, and then trailed off.

Dieter tried to stand, but his knee wouldn't support him. He was sweating, aware of the watching eyes of the

Shadows, their shape and form growing more solid as the sun sank to the horizon. The mountains crowded around him and for the first time in a long while he remembered the mountains at home – constant, familiar as family. He'd skied all his life; he couldn't imagine winter without gliding across the slopes, and now, as he lowered himself onto the snow again, he wondered what it would be like never to ski again. Quickly he pushed that thought away. He'd fallen before, it was part of the sport – the sprained and torn muscles, the bruises, and the weeks it took to heal. But he didn't have weeks. He concentrated on stretching out his hurt leg. The pain made the breath in his lungs freeze. He slowly let it out, determined not to give in, bending, stretching, pressing snow against the swelling, before cautiously trying to stand again. He collapsed, sinking into the snow.

Ziggi. It was always Ziggi's fault, whenever something went wrong. The bitter resentment gnawed at him. And yet Ziggi never hurt herself, it was others who suffered the consequences of her thoughtless acts. She had a natural talent, a graceful flair, all the tuition, all the opportunities – she'd never had to work hard for what she had. It wasn't fair. Ziggi didn't want to be here, she didn't care about their quest. She...Dieter stopped, ashamed, recognising the force of his jealousy.

Angry with himself now, he tried to stand for a third time, using his stocks as crutches, slowly easing his weight onto the injured foot. The shock of the blood-flow electrified his toes, but his knee held. He bent it, straightened it, bent it, and it was easier this time. He righted his ski, ready to cautiously continue towards the safety of the valley.

Suddenly the misty figure of a man stood in the snow in front of him, wearing a cloak that blotted out the day. The dark form deadened the atmosphere, exuding a flat, blank dread. The evening sun was feeble now and the Shadow wasn't afraid of it.

So we meet again – one to one. The thought, soft as snake's breath, pushed into Dieter's mind, and he could feel himself breathe the mist in. He turned his head away. Held his breath. But the mist was everywhere and seeped into him, so that his skin felt clammy and cold.

You can't escape me. The voice drew Dieter's gaze towards its own. Shadow and boy were locked together, yellow eyes and cool, grey eyes, motionless.

Do you know what fear is?

Dieter didn't answer. But slowly a thought caught in his mind and his eyes clouded, as doubt was mirrored in them. He wondered again how it would be, never to ski, to always feel pain, to be sick and weak and unable to do all the things he took for granted, and he realised the one thing he feared most of all – to be away from his mountains.

You do know what fear is. The Darkness had his answer. Dieter hadn't spoken a word, but he had replied. His eyes had spoken.

The Shadow flickered and was gone in an instant; its Dark form momentarily passed across the face of the evening sun, and vanished, leaving a lingering thought.

And now there are five.

*

Ziggi and Manfred hadn't skied far. They stopped to wait, but when they sensed something was wrong, they clambered back again. They found Dieter standing where they had left him, pale as the snow, and as cold, and they couldn't get him to take a step.

'We're staying here,' he answered their impatience.

'What?' Ziggi couldn't believe her ears. 'The Valley's only ten minutes away.'

'We're staying here,' Dieter repeated. He didn't sound like the Dieter they knew. His inner strength was missing. His voice wavered, and his eyes didn't focus on them when he spoke. They tried every argument they could think of: it was too cold, their clothes were wet; the Shadows could come for them at any moment; it was simply ridiculous to even stand here and argue! Then Ziggi grew mad.

'Don't be so stupid!' she blustered. 'You're coming and you're coming *now*!'

'Is it your leg?' Manfred tried a more gentle approach, but Dieter wouldn't say. 'Dieter, please!'

Finally Dieter spoke again. He'd stay the night, no problem; he said it as though it were the most natural thing in the world. He'd catch up with them in the morning, when they'd all had a good night's rest.

Ziggi stared at him in shock. 'Have you lost your marbles?'

'What's got into you?' Manfred asked. 'We're not leaving you here!'

'Stop fooling around – let's go!'

'No.' No. The most unbending word there is.

'Dieter? Ziggi?' Torch-flames glowed golden in the dark. 'Manfred?'

'Anne?'

'Where are you?'

'Here! We're over here!' Relief washed over their fear.

'Where?' Anne, Georg and IDK arrived, peering through the gloom as though they were short-sighted.

'What are you doing?' Georg asked. 'We have to get to the Green Valley. It's almost dark.' But he could see the difference in Dieter. Georg approached him. 'Accident?' he asked. Ziggi and Manfred nodded. Dieter shielded his eyes from the torch light. 'Are you injured, Dieter?' Georg addressed Dieter directly. Still Dieter didn't reply.

'He fell, but he's all right now.' Manfred answered for his friend.

'Doesn't seem like it.' Georg checked Dieter more closely. 'He could be in shock.'

'He won't come,' Ziggi said, miserable. 'I think he's scared. Something's switched off in his brain.'

They all crowded around Dieter. Orff snuffled his hand. Dieter pulled it away, and a look of fear crossed his face.

'Where's the sleigh?' Anne asked.

'We had to leave it.'

'Put your skis on. Let's go!' Anne commanded. Dieter didn't react. They were outside, and he was inside, and he couldn't get out or they in. 'Dieter!' Anne's voice jolted him.

His eyes flickered; he bent over, became an old man, tightening his boots, touching his bindings.

'They're iced over,' he said feebly.

'Tsst!' Anne scrubbed the ice off the bindings, kicked his foot into the ski and fastened it.

'Are we ready?' Ziggi prepared to lead the way.

Dieter's face was grey in the torchlight. 'It's too dark.'

'You've skied in the dark a thousand times before.' Even Georg was losing his patience.

'I might fall.'

'So you'll stand up again.'

'But I might get hurt.'

'Pull yourself together, Dieter! You're a great skier. If you stay here, you'll freeze.'

Ziggi skied out of the circle of the light. IDK skied after her, holding the flame of the torch high. Manfred and Anne positioned themselves on each side of Dieter, and Georg stood behind. The torchlight beamed across the snow in front of them.

'You go.' Toneless voice.

'Not without you.' But Dieter didn't move.

'We don't have time for this!' Ziggi, tired as she was, had retraced her steps. 'Stand on my skis and I'll dink you.'

'No! I can't!'

'I know!' Anne said suddenly.

'Yes!' Georg jumped in, ahead of her. 'We need help. So let's ask for it.'

Anne brought her hands to her lips.

'Snowman! Snow–man!' She listened. Nothing moved. 'Snowman?' She tried again, louder this time, more persistent. Only her echo answered. 'SNOWMAN!' Anne yelled at full strength.

'I don't think you gave him ears,' said Georg.

'He said he'd come if we called him! I heard him.'

'No he didn't.' Manfred stroked his chin thoughtfully. 'He said "think about me". He said it to IDK, if I recall correctly.'

'Yes.' IDK nodded, remembering. He wrinkled his brow and thought, 'Snowman?' Then a little more concentrated, turning up the volume of his thoughts. 'Please come, Snowman. We need help.' Until he reached full volume, and snow fell from the towering Snowman who appeared suddenly, noiselessly in the gloom.

'What is it?' he asked. Then he saw Dieter. 'Oh yes, I see.' He placed the cowering boy gently onto his shoulder. 'I'll give you a lift,' he said in fatherly tones. Orff barked at him. 'I suppose you all want to come.'

'If that isn't too much to ask,' said Ziggi. 'I'm exhausted.'

The Snowman lifted them all, so they were perched like sparrows on his massive shoulders. In two steps he was outside their hut in the Green Valley, where he lowered them again.

'I suggest a good night's sleep,' he told them. 'Though I doubt it will help him.'

'What should we do?' Anne asked him.

'Don't let Dieter out of your sight.' The Snowman bowed to IDK, and left.

The left-hand curve

Dieter sat cross-legged, an Indian in his blankets, and stared into the dark. His hands were still, almost lifeless, as though he were holding a heavy weight he couldn't lift. The fire flickered, the flames leaping tall, then shrinking, playing shadows across his face. They paled in the morning, and then only one Shadow remained.

'Good morning.' Anne had been watching over Dieter for most of the night. 'Beautiful day.' Dieter didn't reply.

'Bread roll?' Georg asked. Still Dieter didn't reply.

Manfred had been sitting with Ziggi, making plans.

'I'm going to get the sleigh,' he announced to the others. 'Tomorrow is New Year's Eve. It's our last chance to get to the top of the mountain.'

'We're *all* going this time,' Anne said in a tone set against contradiction.

'All of us,' Manfred agreed with a sigh. 'Tomorrow.' He turned to Dieter. 'Are you coming with me today?'

'I'm tired,' Dieter replied. His face was pale, dark circles discoloured the skin beneath his eyes.

'What happened on the mountain, Dieter?' IDK asked gravely. 'Did you speak to anyone else?'

'There wasn't anyone there,' Ziggi said impatiently. 'Otherwise we would have seen them too.'

'Yes there was.' IDK turned to her. 'Can't you see it? In his eyes. That's what they do – they take away your power, your light.'

'So you're an expert all of a sudden?'

'Yes! It happened to my –' IDK stopped suddenly. He'd come to a blank part in his memory; the word wasn't there.

'To who?' Manfred prompted him softly.

IDK shook his head, and pointed to Dieter. 'He's brought a Shadow into the Green Valley.'

They all turned to Dieter. In the morning light they could see the faint outline of the Shadow in Dieter's eyes.

You can't get rid of me, it grinned at them, and although they tried to pull Dieter free, it wouldn't release its grip.

'Do something, Manfred,' Anne implored her cousin. 'You're his best friend.'

'Nothing works.'

'But Dieter helped you.' She glared at them. 'He helps everybody.'

'That's different – *he* was different then.' Ziggi shook her head.

'There's nothing we can do, until we find the king,' Manfred agreed. He adjusted his sunglasses, and pulled his cap well over his face. 'If Dieter can't ski, then we have to leave him here. Today. Tomorrow. We can't take him if he's a liability. And if anything happens to me today,' Manfred continued, 'there's still enough of you to go on tomorrow.'

'But you don't desert a friend,' Anne persisted.

'We don't have time to discuss it.' Manfred crossed to the door. 'I'll be back before dark.' The bright sun crashed in, and he strode out into it.

'Come on.' Ziggi urged the others outside. 'We have more training to do.' Uncertain, Georg and IDK followed her.

'I'm not leaving him.' Anne stayed indoors.

*

Dieter wasn't aware the others had gone. The dark veil across his eyes discoloured what he saw. Nothing was beautiful anymore, everything was meaningless and drab. Most of all he felt a dark constriction around his heart, as though the fear had tightened, so he couldn't breathe. He had to get away, they were better off without him. He stood and put on his boots. The sudden movement alerted Anne.

'Where are you going?'

'For a walk.'

'No!' Anne protested, but Dieter insisted on going outside. 'You're staying here!' If Dieter went out now he'd never come back. He'd simply walk out of the hut and wouldn't return. She used all her might to force him onto a chair.

Dieter defended himself but Anne wouldn't give in: she was a warrior – she'd proven herself lots of times, and there had never been as much at stake as there was now. Dieter and the chair fell over. Anne threw herself onto him, ready to throttle him if she had to.

'Let me go!' With one hand he brushed her off and she landed in the corner. But she came straight back at him and grabbed hold of his leg. 'Anne!' He shook her loose and ran to the door.

'My goodness,' said an old voice. 'Do you two always behave like this?' The Weatherman stood in the doorway blocking Dieter's way out. 'It seems to me we have a problem,' he added, seeing the Shadow in Dieter.

'I don't know what to do.' Anne had to admit defeat.

'We'll see about that. Look at me, little one.' The Weatherman tilted Dieter's chin, forcing him to lift his eyes. 'Everybody gets scared,' he said, 'but they don't give up, and I know you won't, either.' He took a step outside. 'So come on, don't dawdle. We have a job to do.' He wended his smile to Anne. 'We'll get him back,' he said, and took Dieter into the bright light.

Dieter stood on the slope, surrounded by the Weatherman, Anne, Georg, Ziggi and IDK. His skis on, his stocks poised, he was stiff, hunched over, regarding the gentle slope as if it were a black ski run – the steepest descent.

'Ziggi, you're in charge,' the Weatherman said. Hearing Anne's intake of breath, he quickly added, 'but I need all of you to help. We have to give Dieter back his skiing. It's been stolen.'

'Why do the Shadows need to ski?' IDK looked up sharply.

'The same reason you do.'

'How can we help?' Georg asked.

'With knowledge,' the Weatherman prompted. 'We can each give him a piece of knowledge about skiing.'

'I'll do balance and the left-hand curve first,' Ziggi said immediately. 'Balance is crucial and his left turns are weaker than his right.'

'Good choice.' The Weatherman nodded. 'What's Dieter taught you, Georg?'

‘A lot of things,’ Georg replied thoughtfully. ‘But mainly climbing.’

‘Then that’s what you’ll give him.’

‘I can teach him the stop-swing!’ IDK had thought about his contribution.

‘Anne?’

‘I can’t teach him anything,’ Anne admitted, downcast.

‘Yes you can,’ the Weatherman corrected her. ‘We all have knowledge we can impart.’

‘Not me,’ Anne’s eyes burned. ‘I’m still learning. Besides,’ she added, uncertainly. ‘I’m nowhere near as good as Dieter…or Ziggi.’ The Weatherman immediately understood.

‘It’s not a competition, Anne,’ he said patiently. ‘It’s about helping a friend, and Dieter needs his friends right now.’

‘Ziggi is the best skier. She can teach him everything.’ Anne turned away from them and would not be drawn.

The Weatherman sighed. ‘Teaching him will require patience, Ziggi.’

Ziggi nodded and tried to mimic the calm, thoughtful tones of the Weatherman’s voice.

‘We’re going to look at your curves, Dieter.’ Ziggi drew a curved line in the snow with her stock. ‘The principle behind curves is that you continuously change your weight from one ski to the other, in order to get a change in direction. Are you following me?’

Dieter nodded unhappily.

‘Now, when we were chased by those lizards…’

Dieter shuddered and Ziggi had to think fast.

'No – there are no lizards here, Dieter. I just want you to think back to your left-hand curve.' Ziggi's voice was shaking with the effort of being patient. She swallowed and continued. 'Do you remember what I said?'

Dieter nodded again, his lips too dry to speak.

'Okay. So let's take a look at the big picture and break it into segments.' Ziggi added a parallel line to the drawn curve in the snow, to resemble Dieter's tracks. 'Even if there's the tiniest fault in your technique, it can get incorporated into your individual style. If you start off with a fault, it causes other faults to happen. Imagine the building blocks of a house. Or a building on sand. It's not stable.'

Dieter fidgeted uncomfortably.

'What I want to do is pinpoint that first fault of yours and then work out the others, because they're built into and around each other. If we can change the first one, we have a good chance of finding, and changing, the others as well.'

Dieter still didn't lift his gaze from the slope.

'Are you listening?' Ziggi's patience was ebbing. 'Come on, give me a hand. It's really hard finding faults in experienced skiers like you. Dieter!' She finally stamped on his toe to get his attention.

'Hmm!' The Weatherman gave Ziggi a keen glance, forcing her to rein in her wayward temper. 'Why don't you show him, Ziggi?' he suggested.

'No,' Dieter replied flatly.

'I don't know the meaning of the word.' Ziggi grabbed hold of Dieter's hand. 'Let's go.' She pushed off so that they both slipped down the slope slowly, as she forced him to ski a left-hand curve. When they came to the end of the run, they stopped.

'Right Dieter, can you give me a hand?' The Weatherman had followed them, and now took over. 'I've had a memory lapse. How do I turn around and face the other way, when I'm standing here?'

Dieter glanced a question at the Weatherman, who returned his gaze calmly.

'The bones aren't as young as they used to be.'

'I can't help you,' Dieter whispered.

'Yes you can,' the Weatherman replied. 'Show me how to do it.'

Dieter looked at his skis as if they would move of their own accord, but they remained motionless on the snow.

'To turn around,' he said at last, slowly, trying to remember forgotten secrets. 'To turn…' He lifted his stocks cautiously and pushed them into the snow behind the upper ski. 'You put your weight on your stocks, and lift one ski upright.' He stood the lower ski up straight and turned it 180 degrees so its tip faced the other way when he laid it back onto the snow.

'I see,' the Weatherman said.

Dieter stood with one ski tip in each direction. He swung his other ski around so that both tips now faced the new direction, his skis still angled across the slope and not down it. He did it again. This time the movement came more easily. He positioned the old man's stocks, and then bent to place his ski, guiding the wood up and then onto the snow, forgetting about himself completely. The Weatherman followed Dieter's directions, his joints creaky, his movements slow, but he succeeded. He smiled his thanks.

'Georg?' The Weatherman motioned to Georg, who was on the slope above them.

Georg skied to the end of the run and it was his turn to be the teacher now. He showed Dieter how to side-step up the slope, an activity he'd grown familiar with, ever since they arrived in the Green Valley. Then he demonstrated walking straight up, with his ski tips apart and the ends together.

'You waddle like a duck.' He laughed, then advised, 'Always use your stocks for balance.'

Once they reached the top, it was IDK's turn.

'The stop-swing,' he said importantly. 'Is vital to…to…'

'Stop,' the Weatherman supplied.

'If you're skiing straight down the slope, bend forward, so your knees face the tips of your skis. Then turn the skis across the slope so your knees face up the hill and your heels point down into the valley. That's where you have to be looking too. Down, not up.' IDK showed Dieter how, and grinned. 'See. Nothing to it.'

Ziggi took over again, monitoring Dieter's fear, knowing it had returned, but glad to see that the Shadow had grown paler. She studied the way Dieter stood on his skis.

'When you're turning left, you have your weight on both skis instead of on the lower valley ski. That's your initial fault. Because of it, your lower shoulder is too far forward, which is fault two. This upsets your balance: fault three. Once your balance is wrong, the position of your knees changes, so you don't have maximum strength or support…it goes on and on.'

❋

From the hut door, Anne watched Ziggi push Dieter again so that they skied the same curve, a little more easily this time. And so it went all morning, Ziggi forcing Dieter to ski the left-hand curve, IDK adding the stop-swing, the Weatherman needing help to change direction, Georg helping them climb, to start all over again. Occasionally the old man beckoned to Anne, indicating she should join them, but she pretended she hadn't seen. Throughout that long day, Anne remained at a distance looking, not participating; feeling alone.

❋

Dieter slowly found his rhythm of snow and skis, muscle, will and ability. He felt the air brushing past, saw the sun again and the snow gleaming in it, and remembered what it was he loved about skiing. With every curve he skied, his ability grew stronger, and the fear grew smaller. Because Ziggi had found the original fault and helped him adjust it, his balance improved and he made fewer mistakes. Now there was nothing to be scared of. The next time he pushed off, it was with such force he painted his curves into the snow as deftly as an artist's brush stroking canvas, and as his trail foamed snow, his fear was finally jolted backwards and shaken from his body. He arrived at the hut breathless.

'Anne!' he called out. 'What a day. This snow's super.' He was distracted by a dark shape flitting away. 'What's that?'

'Nothing important.' Anne knew she should be happy. The old Dieter had returned. But her heart was leaden. It was Ziggi who had rescued him. Ziggi was a better skier, and had more in common with the mountain boy. Anne had thought Dieter was her friend, but now she realised she had been mistaken.

ELEVEN

THE ICE WAR

Museum of ice

That evening at dusk, Anne thought she heard her cockatoo. *Kookaburra sits in the old gum tree,* it sang throatily. Anne ran towards it, but each time she came near, the sound shifted, calling to her from further away, and so Anne kept going, although Orff tried to stop her. She finally emerged from the trees at the edge of the Valley, but there was no sign of Violette. Instead, she found a small, dark child-like form sobbing, huddled against an old wall.

No one loves me, its cries were plaintive. *They push me away.* It whimpered in a voice so soft Anne had to move closer to hear it. Orff growled. He circled, nudging her, trying to convince her to retrace her steps, but Anne didn't listen.

'Please don't cry.'

Feel sorry for me, the child hiccupped pathetically, then sat up suddenly, and Anne saw it had no face, no features, just the pitiless, yellow eyes of the Shadow that had possessed Dieter.

'No!' Caught off guard, Anne took a step backwards, but the Shadow giggled gleefully and sprang at her with the agility of a cat. *You're not wanted here,* its voice hissed in her ear. *You're an outsider.* It laughed at her. *You'll never fit in.* Laughing and laughing until Anne couldn't hear anything else.

*

When Anne woke it was daylight again. She didn't know where she was. Icy white walls surrounded her. The sun's feeble light radiated through the icy ceiling; blue, thick and watery, it bounced around the walls, poisonous. Anne tried to get her bearings. She immediately saw a familiar red eye. It stared at her.

'Violette!' She sat upright. Small flakes of ice that had formed on her body splintered with silvery cracks as fine as spider webs. Anne shook them off. 'Violette!' she said again. Violette continued to stare with red eyes that didn't wink. She was motionless, trapped in a cage of ice.

'Violette!' Anne reached into the ice cage, stroking the stiffened feathers. 'Here. Wattle seeds, your favourite.' The bird remained silent. 'Violette. What's wrong? Don't you remember me? Kookaburra sits in the old gum tree…' Anne sang in her crooked, froggy voice. The cockatoo did not join in. 'I thought you loved me, Violette.' Anne was close to tears. 'Do you remember the bush, the sun in Australia, what fun we had? Violette! It's me – Anne.' Violette didn't move. Finally Anne realised her cockatoo was frozen.

She looked about her and saw animals in ice cages everywhere – chickens, foxes, rabbits, deer, wild geese, a guinea pig, dogs, cats, eagles, sparrows, pigeons. All the winter birds from Wintersheim, all the herds of deer and cattle, and the old horses that had pulled the even older sleighs through the cobblestone streets. There were animals as far as Anne could see, turned into statues, on display in the sterile hall of this ice museum.

Anne's toes nudged Orff who was lying at her feet. The dog lay on the ground, his head on his paws, eyes shut, his ears like paper corners, folded over.

'Orff!' He didn't move. Ice pearled off his fur. 'Orff! No! Not you too.' Anne pressed her face into him. 'Orff.'

Orff squirmed, then sneezed. He managed to wag his tail and whimper. Relieved, Anne rubbed his ears.

'Don't you fall asleep,' she commanded. Orff sneezed again, shook the ice clear, and began an investigation of scents. Anne did not let him out of her sight. Placing Violette under her anorak, next to her heart, Anne followed the dog.

The museum was huge. The floor, walls, ceilings were marbled ice, milky and blue-veined, alive with the sound of splashing, trickling and dripping. She could hear the sighing of running water as if every stream and every river on the planetary spaceship had been diverted to form the walls of the museum and flowed behind the surface of the ice.

Anne stopped at a pedestal. A large cage stood on it, its door, and the ice of its walls, were as transparent as glass. It was empty. Beside it were five similar cages, with names at the bottom of each cage. Manfred Decker, Dieter Pfeiffer, Georg Woerndle, Ziggi Twigg, IDK. Anne's name was on the plaque of the first cage – the door was open to receive her.

'Oh no,' Anne said, understanding what the Shadows had planned for them. And again, more forcefully. 'No!'

She backed away from the ice cage and ran through the corridors of frozen animals. She reached the exterior walls of the mausoleum and hammered her fists against them. She could see the world outside, distorted by the texture of the ice walls. There was the white of the snow and the darkness of the cloud, and a faint blur that was the sun. Colours ran into each other, but they were unreachable. The ice wouldn't break under her blows, and Anne was so blue with cold and with bruises, she had to stop.

'Let me out!' she yelled. 'Somebody help me!' But her words echoed, bounced from the walls and returned unanswered. 'Help! Please help!' It was useless. There was no one to hear.

Further along, Orff barked and scratched at the wall.

'What? What is it?' Anne could feel a draught at her feet and knelt to investigate. There was a small hole in the ice. 'A mouse couldn't get through that, Orff.' Her fear turned to resignation. 'We'll never get out. Nobody cares.'

Orff nudged Anne with his nose. He barked at her. She had to listen. But Anne's eyes were filled with tears and she wouldn't move.

*

As dusk was settling on the evening Anne disappeared, Manfred returned, flying in the old sleigh, to find a happy group waiting for him.

'Dieter can ski again!' A chorus of voices greeted him.

'Thanks to my friends.' Dieter was almost shy, the way he said that, his gaze resting on Ziggi in particular. But their happiness was short-lived.

'Where's Anne?' Manfred asked.

'Anne!' No Anne. 'ANNNNNNE!' No answer.

'Orff's gone too,' IDK exclaimed, after they had searched the immediate area thoroughly.

With the night arriving it was growing colder; they could sense the presence of the Shadows at the boundaries of the Valley and knew that wherever Anne had gone, they couldn't follow.

'She hasn't been herself all day.' Dieter looked miserable. 'And there's something else. I gave her the Key to look after, when we climbed the ice mountain yesterday. If the Shadows have taken her, they'll also have the Key.'

'If they know she has it.' Manfred refused to lose hope, although his logic – and his heart – told him it was forlorn. Tomorrow was New Year's Eve.

*

They left the Valley at dawn. They carried only the essentials:

food, warm clothes and Manfred's instruments. Even so, with four of them and the Weatherman hooked on, the sleigh could barely lift off the ground and it could only tow them slowly. IDK skied alongside them, on his Snow Wings, floating higher and faster than the sleigh could. As no snow had fallen overnight, they could follow Anne and Orff's tracks, but they took them in the wrong direction, away from the ice mountain.

'She has to be here, somewhere,' said Georg in a tone of voice that hoped as much. 'Did she take her anorak?' He was clearly worried. 'What would the Shadows want from…?' He trailed off, not wanting to name the danger Anne was in.

'I know why they've taken her,' Manfred said quietly, skiing beside Dieter. 'They want to keep us from the top of the mountain. Every time we try to get there, we're side-tracked. It's significant.'

'We can't leave her,' Dieter replied.

'I'm not suggesting that,' Manfred said. 'But I do want to know what's up there.'

Their speculations ended with Anne's tracks, which stopped at an old wall where the markings of a snowcat clearly began.

'Tyre tracks!' Dieter examined the snowcat markings. 'Whoever took Anne used a snowmobile.'

'Snowcats were stolen from the Mountain Station,' the Weatherman verified. 'As well as snow-dozers.'

'That's funny…' Manfred trudged around the wall,

poking it with his stock. 'Another brick wall. It doesn't make sense.'

'These tracks are our only lead,' Dieter said. 'We'll follow them.' They hooked their stocks into the sleigh again. It rose slowly, inches off the ground, like an old car in heavy traffic, as if their leaden hopes weighed it down.

The tracks of the snowcat stopped at an ice wall that stretched endlessly in front of them and was so high they had to crane their necks to see to the top of its battlements. There were no doors and no windows, but neither the snowcat nor Anne were anywhere to be seen.

'What sort of building is this?' Manfred tapped it with his stock.

'Is it a building?' Georg pressed his nose flat against the ice, trying to peer in. 'Do you think Anne's in there?'

'If you ask me, we've lost her.'

'No one asked you, Ziggi.'

'We'll have to fan out. See if there's a way in.' They each investigated a section of the ice wall, Manfred flying over the roof on the sleigh, but after half an hour they hadn't located an entrance.

'Maybe it's melted shut,' Manfred grumbled.

'Hey, listen!' Georg pointed to a small hole in the ice.

'Orff, orff.'

'That stupid dog!' Ziggi said in relief.

Georg bent to look. 'Orff,' he called.

The dog barked again.

Georg scrabbled up and rummaged in his rucksack. 'I

knew it would come in handy,' he mumbled. He took out an old battery and the iron they had used to wax their skis, brandishing it like a trophy. They stared at it, then at the enormous wall. 'I can turn up the heat,' Georg quickly added. He held the iron against the wall. 'It'll be faster if you clear the snow away.'

'This'll take a hundred years!' said Ziggi, but Georg continued and managed to increase the size of the hole.

'A few more minutes.' He didn't take his eyes off his work. Tears of water dripped off the wall, seeping into the snow on the ground, making it porous. From inside they could hear Orff barking louder now, more urgently.

'Get a move on,' Dieter urged Georg. 'He's with Anne.' Georg adjusted the iron, causing small clouds of steam to drift off the ice.

Suddenly there was a flash, followed by a cracking sound, and the magic sleigh was in pieces, bits flying high, hitting the snow like hail. Another flash and another crack, this time hitting the wall. Flash followed flash, the thunderous storm growing louder, closer.

'They're attacking us with heatbolts!' Manfred's voice could barely be heard above the noise. The bombardment intensified, hailstones larger than goose eggs striking them. But Georg didn't leave the hole he was melting in the wall.

'I can fit through!' Before anyone else could reply, IDK disappeared into the hole.

'We have to get away from here.' Ziggi threw herself to

one side, narrowly escaping a cascade of ice that came crashing to the ground.

'We can't leave Anne and IDK,' Dieter replied. He and Manfred remained at Georg's side.

'They'll kill us! Can't you see – the whole place is disintegrating.' But Ziggi stayed too.

'Anne's asleep. I can't wake her.' IDK crawled backwards out of the opening.

'Wait a minute. I have something.' Manfred ran in a zigzag to his rucksack. He brought back the first-aid kit and handed a bottle of ammonia to IDK, who disappeared again.

The flashes of heat came continuously now, turning the walls into sorbet, the ice-slush oozing around their feet. Once the steam dissipated, they could see inside to where IDK was holding the ammonia under Anne's nose. She suddenly sprang up and knocked IDK over.

'That stinks!'

IDK dragged Anne away as another section of the wall crumbled. Splinters of ice fell like glass shards. In places ice burst open, hairline fissures running along its surface then yawning wide and splitting in two. A fine drizzle started, and one after another the frozen streams that had been harnessed into building the museum were freed. Their sound, swollen now, was added to the thunder.

'This way.' IDK tugged at Anne's hand again, but Anne stood motionless.

'You came for me?' she asked IDK.

'Yes.'

'You risked your lives?' Anne could feel the weight of the hurtful thoughts in her heart growing lighter. 'Why?'

'You're our friend.'

'I am?'

'Yes. You're important to us. Can we talk about this later? Hurry up!' As IDK tugged at her hand again, he saw a Shadow dissolve from Anne's body. It hung in the air above her head, flickering in the harsh light and, when Anne smiled, it faded. IDK understood at last.

'Let's go,' Anne said, but instead of running to safety, she ran into the crumbling museum.

'Where are you going?' IDK asked increduously. 'It's this way.'

Anne ignored IDK and kept running. She could feel the warmth in the air, could see all the cages around her melting. Pedestals toppled under the force of the heat-waves, ice glowed hot as coal where they struck.

'Anne – what are you doing?' Dieter climbed over the rubble to reach her.

'The animals.' Anne pointed at the swaying cages and the stirrings of life within. 'We have to save them!'

A pink head suddenly appeared from underneath Anne's anorak. A red eye winked at them. Once, twice, not a blank stare now, but with the touch of a laugh in it, as though Violette had just played a prank. The cockatoo's beak tugged at the zipper, her pink-and-white-feathered body fluttered into the air, landing on an ice ledge, and she heftily shook herself.

'Kook...' Violette squawked. 'Kooka...' She tried again but she couldn't get any further. 'Kooka... I've forgotten! D... D...' (She had also forgotten how to swear.) 'Brrrr, who turned the heater off? HATCHOOOO!!!' Cockatoos don't often sneeze and Violette fell off her perch, landing in Anne's outstretched hands.

'Lucky catch.' Anne smoothed the ice-spiked feathers and placed the cockatoo on her shoulder, where she belonged.

Zzzzppppp! Bullets of heat crashed into the centre of the museum. The walls shook. All around them the cages leant in, swayed, fell, and crashed to the floor, splintering the icy prisons. The heat was reviving the animals, and barking, neighing, stamping of feet, cackles and clucks, baaing and whistling – a waking circus of animal noises – sounded from one end of the great hall to the other.

'Anne! Dieter!' Georg waved at them, frantically.

'Over here! Orff!' Anne whistled and Orff wheeled around. With a snapping at ankles and a bossing of barks, he rounded up the animals as they broke free of their cages. Around them the floor was tilting as if it were an iceberg floating in water.

'We'll never get them out.' Ziggi was all for a quick exit – now!

'We will if you help. Get the ice out of the way so they'll have a clear path. Hurry, the roof's collapsing!'

Already Violette was flying low circles, directing the growing herd with whistles and pecks. Georg and Manfred,

Ziggi, IDK and the Weatherman tackled the rubble from outside. Dieter and Anne shifted blocks of ice, aware that the animals had grown fearful, crowding around so closely they could hardly move.

With tactical dive-bombs Violette shepherded a small flock of sheep through an opening in the wall. The cows and deer followed, the stags clearing the hurdles of ice in great leaps, as squirrels, foxes, mice, chamois, moles, hedgehogs and marmots streamed out after them, the birds fluttering above, navigating through the airborne debris.

'I think they've made it.' Dieter reached for Anne's hand. 'But *we* won't if we stay here a second longer.'

Shielding their heads and faces, ducking the falling columns, nearly being squashed as one wall after another fell in a spray of ice chips, they struggled through, pushing the herd away from the chaos and confusion.

World in a cloud

'I was afraid they were all extinct.' The Weatherman beamed as the large herd of animals surged away from the museum. 'I'm beginning to see the Shadows' strategy.' His face grew serious. 'They stole the animals and were going to appropriate their souls.'

'Why?' asked Ziggi.

'Camouflage maybe. To master their environment, the way animals have. Certainly to discover why animals can't be manipulated by thoughts, the way humans can.'

'They were going to freeze us as well,' Anne added.

'To steal everything you know.'

'Like they tried to steal my skiing?' Dieter asked.

'Yes. So they can use it themselves.'

'Well, I'm glad you're safe,' Dieter said to Anne. 'And I'm glad they didn't find the Key.'

'Why would they?' Anne looked perplexed.

'Because if they'd imprisoned you…'

'The Key would still be safe.' Anne sounded annoyed. 'You didn't think I'd keep it, after what the Weatherman said? It's precisely because we can be caught… Tsst!' She crossed to Ziggi and stroked Epsilon, who was perched on Ziggi's shoulder.

'Hey!' Ziggi protested.

Epsilon sprang off and immediately disappeared, white fur on the white snow.

'She has perfect camouflage.' Anne parted the cat's thick fur and unclasped the small sack from the diamante collar. 'No Shadow would think about messing with her,' Anne said triumphantly, as the silver-green light lapped around them.

The ice museum glowed a deep, fiery red, pulsating with the heatbolts that had been pumped into it. Suddenly it burst, exploding into a million splinters that fell in a glimmering rainbow, down, down, to be extinguished in the snow. Now nothing but the grey-blue fog remained, thick, soupy and cold.

Dieter returned the Key to Epsilon's collar. 'Let's go.'

'Where?' Georg blurted out.

'To the ice mountain.' Manfred pointed in what he hoped was the right direction.

'Which way? Where is it? Where is anything?' Georg asked.

'Watch out!' Dieter said as Georg bumped into him and ski on ski clashed like swords in a duel.

'Watch out!' Ziggi protested as Violette landed on her shoulder, squawked, lifted off and found Anne after two more tries. 'So your fleabag's back.' But Ziggi was pleased.

'Shouldn't we stay here until the fog clears?' Anne asked, knowing it wasn't safe to ski in fog.

'It's good cover,' Dieter said. 'As long as there's fog, we can't be seen.'

'And direction's not a problem,' Manfred smiled. 'The Calculator has a compass.'

'But *I* can't see,' Georg said, plaintive.

'Trust your skis.' Dieter swung around in the direction Manfred was pointing. 'Let them be your eyes.'

It was an uncanny feeling – skiing in fog. They couldn't tell where the snow ended and the fog began. The slightest sound, even the hiss of skis on snow, was out of proportion because their sense of sight had been taken away. They were in a different world. Everything that slipped by was nameless, formless; ghosts in this grey-blue place.

Anne was behind Dieter, skiing where he skied. She couldn't see his tracks in the snow – the fog washed them away – so she kept her concentration on the dark blur in front of her. It felt as though her skis watched the slope for her, curving with the drop; her knees were springs that absorbed the ground's undulations, lightly reacting to its rise and fall. But it was difficult controlling speed when there were no points of reference; no trees or rocks to show her how fast she was passing them by.

The quick pace Dieter set frightened IDK most of all, so he skied carefully, losing ground and eventually ploughing into an out-jutting rock. He fell hard, for a moment losing consciousness. When he came to, he could feel a bump the size of a pigeon egg on his forehead.

'Wait!' He rubbed his head, dazed. 'Where is everyone?'

Orff barked, jumped off the sled and doubled back. Soon the little boy was surrounded by his friends and by a circle of animals that blew softly through their noses and waited for him to stand. Orff licked his cheek.

'No! Stop!' cried IDK. 'Leave me alone.' He flinched in fright.

'It's Orff,' Anne said. 'He's trying to help.'

Orff nuzzled IDK, to encourage him to get up out of the snow. The boy cowered against the rock.

'What is it? Stop.'

'It's Orff,' Anne said again. 'What's wrong? Don't you remember him?'

'Orff?' And then, in a flood, IDK recalled other things, from a long, long time ago. He sailed lightly to his feet.

'We know!' he said, wildly. 'We know!'

'We don't know any more than we did five minutes ago.' Ziggi peered at him. 'And you probably know even less because you would've killed quite a few brain cells with that bump.'

'We have not given you permission to speak.' IDK said it so firmly Ziggi's mouth snapped shut in surprise. 'Six hundred years,' he said. 'It's been six hundred years.' Light flickered within him, glowing like golden candle-flame.

'Six hundred years since what?' Manfred was on instant alert.

'Since I was left behind.' IDK didn't give them a chance to interrupt him again. 'What day is it? When was Christmas?' Without waiting for an answer he counted on his fingers. 'Two, four, six, seven days ago! It's New Year's Eve! It's too late.'

'No!' Anne cut in.

'You don't understand.' IDK fixed Anne with a regal stare. 'If the Key does not reach my father...' The light surrounding IDK flared ominously.

'IDK! What's happening? Are you all right?' Anne cried out in surprise.

'Our little friend is strong enough to remember the truth. He is heir to the king's throne.' The Weatherman smiled at IDK. 'Welcome, Your Highness.' And the old man bowed low, tousling the boy's duck-down hair.

Blanc-mange

'We must save the king, my father.' IDK bowed in return and faced the others. 'If we can reach him.'

'The day hasn't ended.' The Weatherman edged towards Dieter. 'Has it?' He held his hand out. 'Now it's time for the rightful owner to have his Key.'

Dieter lifted Epsilon from Ziggi's shoulder. The cat growled, not wanting to relinquish her prize. Undeterred, Dieter stroked her, and undid the crystal from around her collar. He handed it to IDK.

'I told you it was mine.' IDK gave Ziggi a cheeky grin. 'I hope I can remember.' His brow puckered. He peered into the sky and saw the fog had cleared. 'The sun is very feeble.'

He focussed the crystal into the weak sunlight pushing through the cloud. A pencil-thin beam of light formed, which he directed into a dark puddle on the ground. For a moment the water slid along the path, trying to elude the green-white light, but IDK kept the beam trained steadily. The light shivered as the water in the puddle boiled, small black bubbles bursting sulphur fumes that made everyone else wrinkle their noses. Clouds of black steam rose, hanging momentarily in the air until the breeze dispersed them. The puddle shrank until nothing but a black stain remained.

'Good,' the Weatherman beamed.

'But will it be enough?' IDK had assumed a new authority. 'Is there time to wipe out all the Shadows?'

'We shall see,' the Weatherman remained calm.

'What's the worst that could happen?' asked Ziggi. 'What if we don't get to the king in time? What will become of his lordship or whatever he wants to be called?' She nodded in IDK's direction.

The Weatherman looked grave. 'If the Light Star is destroyed the host planet will be too.'

'What?' They all looked at him, shocked.

'As you've discovered, it's in their power to influence the weather. If they meddle with that, then Earth, as we know it, is history.'

'Why didn't you tell us that before?' Ziggi asked, incensed.

'Didn't want you to get cold feet. Figuratively speaking.' The Weatherman indicated his surroundings. 'The battle can only be won from here.'

'And are we really the only ones who can do it?' Georg asked.

'Yes,' said the Weatherman.

'Are you able to help us with the directions, Your, um, Majesty?' Manfred showed the maps to IDK.

'The whole place has changed since I was here. It's all iced over.'

'Not a clue?' Manfred persevered.

'Sorry.'

'He was too young,' the Weatherman interceded. He skied ahead, then turned to face them. 'Now it's time I left you.'

'WHAT?!'

'I've done what I was meant to do. You must finish the quest.'

'BUT…'

'The Queen's Prophecy says six will save our worlds.'

'You can't abandon us!' Ziggi's voice rose sharply.

'I'm not. But these animals have to be returned, or Earth's ecology will be destroyed.' The Weatherman's voice, though mild, was decisive.

'Maybe we should come with –'

'We have a job to do.' Ziggi was primly cut off by IDK.

The Weatherman rounded up the animals and slowly skied behind the flock, moving them along the slope. The others skied with him until they came to a fork in the path. It was time to say goodbye.

'Look at you.' The Weatherman regarded them all fondly. 'Look at how you've changed. No one could be better prepared.' He shook hands all round. 'Should anyone ever need looking after, I'll recommend you as shepherds,' he smiled.

'Will we see you again?' Anne asked in a small voice.

'I'm sure you will.' The Weatherman's eyes had a faraway look in them. 'I'm always there, at the top of the mountain.' He turned and placed his hand on IDK's shoulder. 'I doubt we'll meet again.' Though his eyes twinkled, his words were sad. He bent over, so his eyes were level with the prince. 'Goodbye little one. Take good care. If you don't know, ask for advice, for you will always find people to help you.' He bowed low one last time. 'Give my regards to the king.'

'Thank you,' IDK's voice quavered. 'Do you think we'll find him in time?'

'I don't have any doubts.' The Weatherman urged the animals ahead of him. There was a flicker of light where the sun caught gleaming hides; they could hear the snort of a deer, the cough of a fox, and the soft, sweet warble of a nightingale. At the crest of a hill the Weatherman turned and smiled, and in the afternoon sun he looked like a young man again. He gave a final wave, and shouted, 'I'm proud of you all!' And then he, and the caravan of creatures, were gone.

The six stood waving, before turning and taking the other fork, to battle their way up the steep slopes again. They could see the ice mountain caught in the rays of the sun. It glowed golden, the crown of this small world, but its tip was still shrouded by cloud.

'He's right, you know.' Georg skied alongside Anne. 'We have changed.' He held out his arm. 'Look.'

'It's an arm.'

'No, look!' Georg flexed. 'See. There.' He was grinning broadly. 'Muscle. I have muscles all over.'

'So?' Anne didn't see the significance.

'Don't you get it?' Georg executed a perfectly co-ordinated turn, snow fizzed, crystallised cappuccino foam. 'Never in a million years,' he chortled, 'did I think this was possible.'

Laughing, the agile Georg practically ran up the slope on his skis, ahead of her. Anne had to smile. She too, felt the ropiness of her muscles, and the strength in her legs. They had been skiing for hours and she wasn't tired. She glanced around. Manfred wasn't tired. Ziggi. Dieter. IDK. Maybe the Weatherman was right to be proud of them. Maybe they did stand a chance. She was starting to believe they would, and having that certainty made her feel stronger still.

Manfred stopped suddenly, the abrupt movement bringing them all to a halt.

'I don't believe this,' he murmured, stabbing the snow in front of him with his stock. There was a dull thud as the spike met with resistance. In an instant Manfred was on his knees digging, using both hands to shovel snow until he revealed an old, crumbling brick wall.

'Another one.' Georg kicked at it with the toe of his boot. 'I don't know why you've developed such an interest in stone masonry.'

'Because…' Manfred didn't elaborate, but pressed figures and formulas into the Calculator. And then: 'Because I'm beginning to suspect we're not on a mountain at all.'

'It looks like a mountain to me,' Georg said.

'Not if you view it from another perspective.' Using his Calculator as an electronic sketchpad, Manfred drew lines across the screen. 'There was a brick wall we climbed over, where Anne disappeared at the end of the Green Valley. And if you think about the walls of the chasm as a buttress, and you draw a line from there to the wall we discovered in the old hut on the ice mountain – which is around and to the right – and then you add this wall…' Deftly Manfred finished his drawing. 'I think the mountain is a castle that has been iced over.'

'Right.' Ziggi had to work hard at not raising her voice. 'First we're on a planet that turns out to have motors, and now we're climbing a mountain that's a castle in disguise. Make up your mind!'

'I will. Once I've collected and collated all the facts.' Manfred turned towards IDK. 'Do you remember living in a castle?' he asked hopefully. IDK thought for a long moment.

'Maybe if we give him another bump on the head,' Ziggi offered, unhelpful.

'I don't remember,' IDK finally said, sadly. Ziggi let out an exaggerated sigh.

'Manfred, do you really expect me to –'

'I expect you to trust me.' Manfred cut her short.

'Why should I?'

'Because...' Manfred considered his words carefully. 'Because under certain conditions I'd trust you.'

Ziggi blinked at Manfred as if she hadn't heard him right, and then her face turned so red it matched her hair. She was flabbergasted. No one had ever said that to her before.

'So would I,' Dieter said softly.

'Me three,' Georg said.

'I trust you, Ziggi,' IDK chimed in. Which left only Anne.

'I suppose I would, too,' she said ungraciously. 'But only under exceptional circumstances.' Then she softened. 'No, that's not true. You're an excellent skier – and a good teacher.'

'But...but...' Ziggi stammered.

'I think it's about time we trusted each other.' Manfred was still looking at Ziggi. 'After all, we've come this far together and survived.'

There were no more arguments after that. A subdued Ziggi agreed the ice mountain could be an enormous castle

– depending on how you viewed it (she tried looking at it backwards and upside down), and she had to admit that if the planet was a spaceship, the inhabitants would have had to live somewhere. And it might not be too far fetched to suppose that if they copied the idea of trees, on their last visit to Earth (when castles were fashionable), they may have pinched the idea of castles too. And if the spaceship was subjected to years of cold and piles of snow with no sun, then it could be possible that the castle they'd built had frozen over. It was something to think about as she kept going, and it took her focus off aching muscles that were straining with the climb.

After hours of independent thinking, Ziggi reached a conclusion which differed markedly from Manfred's calculations. They had stopped to get their breath. Manfred huddled over his instruments, Georg dispensed food, Anne and Dieter climbed a little further to the crest of the hill for a better view of what lay ahead.

'Psst.' Ziggi offered a bottle of water to the young prince. 'This is useless,' she whispered in IDK's ear. 'If this king we're looking for – your dad,' (she still found that hard to say), 'was kidnapped and this is a castle, where do you think he'd be?' IDK wrinkled his brow. 'Think. Where do they keep prisoners in castles?'

'In dungeons?' The image of a dark tunnel tugged at IDK's memory.

'Spot on. And where do they keep dungeons?' Before IDK could reply, Ziggi supplied the answer herself. 'In the basement. So how come we're climbing?' Ziggi whipped around and faced downhill. 'I'm telling you – this is a wild goose-chase!'

IDK hesitated – he had an inkling where this was leading.

'They won't miss us.' Ziggi steam-rolled on. 'And if I'm right and we find him, we might still have time to save him.'

'But I've never skied on new snow.' The snow on the slope Ziggi pointed to was deep and soft.

'Nothing to it,' said Ziggi breezily, and then added, 'Trust me. Everyone else does.'

IDK didn't move. There was a great deal he didn't know, but he was certain of one thing: he shouldn't ski slopes that were above his abilities. Dieter always took great pains to avoid difficult slopes – for his sake. There had to be a reason for that.

'I don't know if I can.' But he was wilting under Ziggi's impatient stare.

'That's right. Live up to your name. How are you ever going to learn anything if you're too scared to try?' Ziggi spoke loudly to reassure IDK. And when that didn't work she simply said, 'You can do it!' and pushed off, without further consideration for IDK's capabilities.

*

'Hang her by the thumbs,' said pacifist Georg.

'By the ears,' Manfred added.

'By the toenails,' Anne put in forcefully. 'Why is it always Ziggi?'

‘Well, actually it isn’t always Ziggi.’ Manfred was about to go into a lengthy discourse about how certain other members of the party didn’t always follow instructions, when Dieter interrupted him. ‘They’ve gone that way.’

Ziggi’s tracks were clearly marked in the snow. So were IDK’s. Dieter cast a worried look at the darkening sky.

‘The wrong way.’

‘Typical.’

Unlike IDK, they didn’t have a choice, they had to follow Ziggi and IDK’s tracks, which soon led them into fine powder snow that reached to their shoulders. But Dieter kept going, cutting through it, and they found its softness opened to them.

They skied down unfamiliar slopes and found IDK buried in the snow, one ski pointing into the sky, the other in the opposite direction. Ziggi was bent over him trying to get him on his feet, but IDK didn’t want to move. Ziggi’s voice was quite hoarse, trying to convince him.

‘Come on, IDK, get a move on!’ Her temper was inflamed, but it didn’t help. IDK was scared, and he’d rolled himself into a ball. He wouldn’t say a word (which only infuriated Ziggi more); he wouldn’t open his eyes when the others arrived; he wouldn’t unwind.

‘Just as I thought,’ Dieter said crossly, and turned on Ziggi. ‘He can’t ski new snow. What did you think you were doing, Ziggi?’

‘We were wasting time,’ Ziggi yelled, and poked IDK. ‘Come on, it’s easy.’

'It's easy if you know how to do it properly.' Dieter untangled IDK's skis.

'Idiot,' added Anne, and then through gritted teeth, 'I knew we couldn't trust you, Ziggi.'

'We have to keep going, IDK,' Dieter said. He grabbed him under one arm. Manfred grabbed IDK under the other arm and they stood him upright, so he was forced to uncurl. Dieter scanned him. 'Your *Snow Wings* are okay and so are you.'

'I can't see anything in this snow,' IDK said half-heartedly. Which was true – the snow reached over his ears.

'It parts when you ski through it,' Dieter explained. 'You couldn't see anything in the fog, either.'

'That's right, and I skied into a rock.'

'Lucky for you, or you wouldn't have regained your memory. Come on.' Dieter tugged at his hand.

Orff barked encouragingly, Violette landed on IDK's head and swung sideways to look him in the eye.

'Hurry up, hurry up,' she twittered, not as gently as Dieter, but IDK didn't react.

'I'm scared,' he said at last.

'But don't you see,' Ziggi leaned forward, 'that's what happened to Dieter. And we helped him through it.'

'I know,' the little boy mumbled, but still didn't move.

'Everyone's scared – at one time or another.' Dieter tried again. 'Especially when we're unsure. You're scared of new snow because you don't know how to deal with it, and that's good, because it makes you cautious.' He glanced at Ziggi, who'd never been cautious, and then waved the others ahead. Anne, Manfred and Ziggi pushed off. Then Georg, who didn't feel confident in new snow either. Dieter stayed with IDK.

'Once you know how to do something, you won't be scared of it anymore.' He waited until IDK had stepped onto his skis and fastened the bindings. 'Okay? Hold your skis parallel. They have to slice through the snow. If you ski a plough it anchors you. So no V-formation, okay? It's slimline from here on in. Skis side by side, close together.' Dieter talked as though his voice were a lead IDK could hold onto. 'Nothing can happen to you. It's the safest snow to ski in. Relax...bend your knees, weight back, not forward.' And when IDK still hesitated, he added, 'Trust your *Snow Wings*, IDK.'

IDK was slow at first, frightened to do what Dieter said, frightened of applying a new technique to a new situation. The others, who were ahead, seemed to be swimming. Then they disappeared completely in the snow, which surrounded them like blanc-mange. He cramped at the thought. Snow around his ears was alien to him. It should be underfoot.

But the more he listened to Dieter, and allowed his body to move with, rather than resist, the flight of his *Snow Wings*, the easier it became. It felt strange at first, and then from strange and restricted, his skiing eased into an effortless sweeping through the layers of white that crackled in his ears. Powder touched his cheeks, crystals rolled off his clothes; the snow was harmless, frozen froth. His pace became faster, his movements free, so that the snow felt silken and IDK's skis whispered through it. Nothing resisted him; it was oiled, silent motion.

'Not hard, is it? Once you get the hang of it.' Dieter grinned.

'It's the easiest thing in the world!' IDK laughed out loud, and could hear the others laughing too. Sometimes only a red woollen cap, or a striped green, blue, yellow or orange cap bobbed out of the snow, showing where they were and who was who.

'Turn left here.' Manfred had been keeping an eye on his compass.

Dieter left IDK's side, taking the lead again. IDK could keep pace now. Everyone could. Everyone except Georg, who had been skiing as close to Dieter as he could, so that he too could listen to the words of encouragement aimed at IDK. He had been concentrating hard, searching for that sensation of flight they had all found – but he hadn't quite achieved it yet. They all turned left. Georg skied straight ahead.

TWELVE

TEAM PLAY

Georg in trouble

Georg suddenly realised he'd parted company – there were no voices and no coloured caps bobbing. He could feel the ground slope away beneath his feet. He was speeding up, following a natural curve of a valley, into a gully, where the evening light was cut off and pools of night lay underneath overhanging rocks.

Georg sensed he was skiing into danger. Instinctively he brought the tips of his skis together into a V-shaped plough to slow his lonely journey through the white mass. The plough hooked into the snow and Georg fell. He landed head first in the snow and was not be able to get up again. Skis at all angles, stocks buried out of his reach. His goggles, his cap, everything was full of fine, white grains. Georg brushed the snow off his goggles. There was no sound here, in this dank place, no light. Grey shadows discoloured the snow.

Then a voice hissed: *Georg Woerndle. Look at me.*

A large predatory bird drifted in the air above him, staining it a deep, impenetrable black. Georg's eyes were drawn to its poisoned yellow eyes and he was snared. And then, beak opened, talons bared, the Shadow swooped at him, wrapped its cloak around him like vulture's wings.

Where is the Key? demanded the voice, which had grown flat and metallic.

Georg tried desperately to not be afraid, but his brain had gone blank. He was sweating even though he was shivering with cold and fear. Awful images danced in his mind. The thing that Georg was most afraid of was coming true. He could see himself shrink in size, his flesh wasting away, the muscles he had recently discovered turning to jelly. He was alone and sick, starving in a strange place. Georg could hear the rumble of hunger in his stomach, he could feel the weakness of it in his knees, and in the way his saliva gathered in globs at the back of his throat, and he could do nothing except tremble, swallowing, staring into the merciless yellow eyes.

'Lemon meringue.' He tried to resist but his voice was weak. 'For lemon meringue you need eggwhite and sugar and lemon and you beat, you beat, you beat…' But it was no good. Georg could see himself getting thinner and weaker, and hungrier. 'Mockingbird...' he tried again. 'No, Hummingbird cake. Black Forest. Apple Strudel, Bee-sting and Gugelhupf...'

Where is the Key?

'Raspberry Tart,' but the strain was too much. Georg's resistance was crumbling.

Who has the Key? The thought-question screeched at Georg, who was shaking so violently now, he couldn't speak. He didn't want to betray his friend – he mustn't – but the Shadow was emptying his brain of any resistance, so the answer simply tumbled out.

'I Don't Know,' Georg said.

You do know. The force of the Shadow's anger brought Georg to his knees. *Who has the Key?*

'I Don't Know.' Tears of shame mixed with his sweat and ran rivers down Georg's face into the collar of his ski suit. He pressed his white knuckles into his mouth to stop the answer coming out. 'I Don't Know.' And with that he passed out.

*

'Five,' said Manfred when they had stopped again. 'Someone's missing.'

'If you're not here, say so,' Ziggi piped up.

'Not funny.' Manfred counted again. 'Five.'

'Can't you count?' Ziggi taunted him.

'I can't count to six when there's only five here.' Manfred was worried now.

'Where's Oh Mei?' Anne asked.

'He was with me a minute ago.' Dieter checked behind

him and to either side. At that moment Orff growled in the distance.

'Oh Mei?'

They found Georg lying on his back, feet in the air. The Shadow was bent over him, pecking at him, its beak coming closer to his eyes.

'Hide,' Anne hissed, pushing IDK behind her. 'Epsilon. Look! A bird.'

Epsilon crouched long and low. With a guttural miaow she streaked forward and dug her claws into the Shadow's cloak. The Dark bird flew up with a shriek, beating its wings to dislodge the cat, lifting her into the air. Suddenly Epsilon plummeted into the snow. The bird had evaporated. The Shadow's hold on Georg had broken. He groaned. Manfred and Dieter each grabbed a foot and dragged him away.

'Oh Mei, are you all right?'

Georg flexed his limbs painfully, slowly getting to his feet. His eyes were blank, dazed.

'I told it,' he said, his voice miserable. 'It made me feel hungry and thin.' He still trembled at the memory. 'I thought I was dying, and I gave in. When it asked me who has the Key, I told it. I said, "I Don't Know."' Georg's body shook with relieved laughter. 'But it didn't believe me!'

The storm of the Shadows

'There's only half an hour of daylight left.' The worried expression had returned to Dieter's face. 'We're not going to make it.' They were nowhere near the pinnacle of the ice mountain.

'This is all your fault!' Anne accused Ziggi.

'Let's not blame anyone,' Manfred said, reasonably. 'We did what we could. And there was no guarantee the king would be at the top of the mountain. It was all guesswork on my part.'

'But you're certain something's on that mountain.' Ziggi's face was burning. 'And I could get there if I had IDK's *Snow Wings*. Let me go.'

'Thanks, Ziggi, but no.' Dieter's voice was final. 'We're stronger as a group.' He scanned the smooth, white slopes. 'So let's keep going for as long as we can.'

'I…ah…' Manfred cleared his throat. 'I thought I'd try to increase our chances.' He dipped his hand into his rucksack and brought out six sets of lights, with battery packs attached. 'They work on the principle of miners' lights,' he explained, and fitted his to his woollen cap. 'So we won't be completely in the dark.'

IDK was near despair. 'It's not enough.'

'We have other sources of light. Torches, flares.' Manfred handed them around.

'Candles, matches.' Georg added what he had. 'We can form a circle of light.'

'And we have you, Your Highness.' Anne made her voice sound brave.

'My light's almost gone.' IDK's expression remained distraught.

'Good. Then they won't see you,' Dieter replied.

'I don't want you to risk your lives for me anymore.' IDK faced his friends. 'Find somewhere safe. I'll go the rest of the way alone.'

'I haven't come this far to quit now,' Georg stated.

'I'm no quitter either,' Ziggi added, annoyed at the suggestion.

'I'm certainly one to see quests through to their conclusion,' Manfred agreed.

'And you're not getting rid of me,' said Anne.

'Looks like you're outvoted, because I'm not going anywhere without you, either.' Dieter put his hand on IDK's shoulder.

'If only we could find my father.' IDK looked forlorn.

'His light will be weak as well,' Manfred said gently. 'Sitting in the dark for six hundred years with no sun to boost his energy.'

'Don't worry, IDK. We'll find him,' Ziggi said, and she meant it.

Slowly, around them, the air changed; shades of blue rubbed night into the sky, as the sun set on the last day of the year. The clouds, the snow and the mountains disappeared. They were now climbing into a vacuum, no moon, no stars; everything was black.

'Hats,' Manfred commanded, and they turned on the pinlights on their caps.

'Keep your eyes peeled,' Dieter warned. 'Stay together

and keep moving.' In the curtaining darkness they could hear the arrival of the dark things.

'What are they doing?' Georg asked, after minutes had passed.

'They're trying to scare us.' Anne remembered what the Weatherman had said outside Manfred's house. That it was only their own fears that would stop them, not the Shadows. 'They can't get to us if we don't let them. We've all thrown them off once before.'

'But they're stronger now.'

'So are we. If we keep our minds focussed. Don't think about them. Keep going.'

There was a movement above them. A huge spider had crawled onto the cloud. It was so large it filled the sky, and hung from a web thick as rope, its legs stretching from horizon to horizon.

'It's an illusion.' Manfred swallowed. 'They're trying to trick us.'

'Don't look at the eyes!' Anne yelled. They could feel the spider's eyes burning into them. 'It can't touch us. They can't do anything until the king's light dies. And that's not going to happen!' She faced the spider defiantly. 'I'm not scared of you!' she shouted at it. 'Do you hear me? I'm not scared!'

Anne could feel the same defiance in Dieter and in Ziggi, saw the hesitant courage in Manfred. Georg was determined to be as brave as they were. Only the little prince was shaking like a leaf.

'I'm frightened,' he whispered. 'It's going to eat us. It's eaten all my people.'

'No.' Anne said decisively. 'It hasn't eaten your father.'

'How do you know?'

'Don't give in now.' She took hold of his hand. 'We'll protect you.'

'I'm tired of fighting them.'

'I'm not.' Anne pushed and prodded the others until they had formed a circle around IDK as they climbed. 'Shut your mind to it. Don't let the Dark come in. It feeds on fear. We need to show it we aren't afraid. IDK – please!'

'If I can survive an avalanche,' said Ziggi, digging IDK in the ribs, 'then we can survive anything.' And as she struggled up the slope, Ziggi started to sing. 'Kookaburra sits in the old gum tree…'

'Kookaburra sits in the old gum tree…' Anne joined in. 'Manfred!' The way she said it, Manfred had no choice, his voice coming in underneath, wobbling and one phrase behind.

'Merry, merry king of the bush is he.'

'Kookaburra sits in the old gum tree…' Georg echoed. Then Dieter and Violette (Orff howled his version). The words twined around each other, their voices strengthening as they repeated the verses, shouting at the sky until finally IDK joined in.

'Laugh, kookaburra, laugh, kookaburra… Look, it's working.' The outline of the spider was fading. 'Gay your life must be.' Again and again, their voices rose full throttle and bounced off the spider, the force of their will pushing it out of the sky.

As they were singing, Anne listened, watching their faces – the way IDK fought hard to be unafraid, how Georg closed his eyes to concentrate, the way Manfred tripped over the melody and reddened, and the way Dieter smiled at her. Ziggi's eyes caught hers and she pulled a face, making her laugh. Anne felt the sting of tears. They were all being so courageous, singing their hearts out, not knowing what lay in wait.

'Whatever happens, I'm not sorry I came,' Anne said. It sounded as though she was saying goodbye, so she began the song again.

They continued to move up the slope in a tight group, shielding IDK. The small lights that crowned their hats were weakening, the power in the batteries giving out. Only the soft, green light of the Key warmed them in its glow and showed the way. The spider had gone, but the Darkness around them had thickened and they could feel the presence of the Dark things crowding around them. Waiting.

'My skin feels funny.' IDK's voice didn't sound quite right, as though it were being pushed through metallic air. The feeling wouldn't leave him alone. It was as though an army of ants were running all over him.

'My skin feels funny too,' Georg admitted.

'So does mine.' Manfred scratched.

They all felt 'funny' now. A tickling sensation swept over their skin. The fine hairs on their faces and hands and the nape of their necks stood to attention. It felt like fleas. Alive.

Everything metal hummed. Wristwatches, spectacle frames, hairclips, zippers, pins. Manfred's Calculator, the money in Ziggi's pockets, even the tags on Orff's collar. Then the air about them began to pulsate. Softly at first. It bent and stretched and pulled taut. Blue lights, little tongues licked the rocks. The snow turned blue. Small currents of light danced between the layers of air.

'They're playing with the weather again.' Manfred didn't need his instruments to tell him that.

'This isn't a game.' Dieter's voice was deadly serious. 'It's an electrical storm.'

'Run!' Ziggi was the first to scatter.

'No! They're trying to separate us. We have to stay together!' As Dieter said that, a flash of light crashed into the rocks above them, followed by thunder that pushed between the ground and the sky and squeezed all else out. Clouds spat out one lightning bolt after another. Hot sheets of light illuminated the snow; rain, thick as whiplashes pounded into them. Smaller bolts of lightning leapt from one raindrop to another and joined in one vast wave of electrical currents that hissed past the children, biting at their feet and nipping their hands.

'We need to find shelter!' Dieter yelled above the tumult. They linked arms, and strained against the strength of the wind, searching behind mounds of snow, exploring bare rock-faces that slanted against the weakening light. They searched everywhere but couldn't find an opening, not even one the size of a mouse-hole.

A rumbling began above their heads and deep at their feet; a growl that boomed and reverberated through all the veined passages of the planet. The shock of the vibrations slipped up their spines and clutched their hearts. The roar intensified, as though the planet were crumbling and crying out in pain.

The sound hung dark and foreboding in the sky, as an army of snow-dozers and snowcats lumbered onto the horizon like great prehistoric beasts, blades gnashing, orange lights revolving, a wall of steel coming towards them. Snow-lizards, bellies dragging, ice tongues lashing, rose out of the snow. Small creatures with bat-wings and teeth of fire flew at them, blindworms wriggled from beneath the ground. And all around them yellow eyes blinked, and dark thought-voices called their names.

The Key, the Key. A black mist seeped from fissures in the earth, a column of it rising from the wormholes. The Shadows had united to become a wall of darkness that towered over the children. Forks of lightning struck from above, electrified snakes writhed from the depths below; eyes blazed fiercely, directed at IDK. The little boy trembled, his own light growing weaker.

Who are you, the voice spoke from a deep pit, *to stand against me, who has power over all Dark things?*

'Who are you to stand against me, future king of the Light Beings?' IDK's young voice hung on the air as clear as morning. The Key's glow spilled from beneath his garment and fell onto the snow; its glitter stole out and illuminated him.

'Use it like a hockey stick,' Manfred hissed at him. 'Belt the lightning back at them!'

IDK reached into his pocket, took out the crystal and held it up, but it didn't catch the light. With a harsh, cruel laugh the Shadow broke into the group and snatched the little boy; tipped him upside down, shaking him with such violent strength it dislodged the Key from his hand. The Key fell, and the Shadow cast the boy aside. It swooped to grasp the crystal at last, to close its fingers on the prized possession that would give it power for all time.

The last race

'Violette!' Anne's voice rang out. Violette reacted immediately. She darted through the air and, screeching, flew at the Shadow. Epsilon sank her claws into it. Orff pulled at the grasping hands. The Shadow tried to shake the animals off, swatting at them as though they were annoying flies, but they would not let go. The crafty eye of the cockatoo caught sight of the crystal in the depth of the Shadow's hand. She renewed her attack, darting into the dank, black mist and ripped the glimmering disc from it. Soaring away, she dropped it out of the sky. IDK caught the disc, slipped past the Shadow and disappeared into the dips and waves of the snowfields that lay, a frozen sea, in front of him.

Howling, the Shadows broke into a maelstrom of bullets that flew after IDK, their feet elongating into great black boards – becoming skis. They had mastered the art of skiing, with Dieter's dexterity and skill, and came flooding down the mountain after the prince and the Key.

IDK brought his skis together, his weight on the valley ski, and leaned forward, the position Dieter had shown him was the most balanced. Trusting his Snow Wings, he jumped over moguls, screeched over ice, hid in drifts of new snow, eluding the reaching arms and the sharp nails that flicked past him. He could feel his fear return, hammering in his temples; he could hear his breath, gasping, and the slicing of the boards behind him.

'Faster!' Anne squealed.

'Faster!' His Snow Wings reacted on command. He felt their power, as they lifted into the air, and the ground's undulations fell away. He was flying, soaring high above his friends, but when he turned his head he saw the Shadows leap up effortlessly to follow.

'This way.' Dieter was skiing directly beneath him.

IDK threw the Key. Dieter caught it, took on a racer's position, the way Ziggi had taught him, and shot off. The dark army peeled away from the young prince and chased the mountain boy instead. Dieter continued straight ahead. He could sense his friends fanning out, following him.

'They're cutting you off,' Manfred cried out. 'Go left.' So Dieter skied a tight left-hand curve.

'They're coming from all sides,' Georg called to him from the slope above.

'Oh Mei!' Dieter threw the Key. The disc sailed through the air as Georg pushed off, moving fast. Georg caught the disc and skied with it. He held his own for half the slope, his curves tight, his knees absorbing the corrugations, his hands clenched around the disc. But he couldn't ski as fast as Dieter, and so the Shadows hunted him, three to the right of him, two on the other side, one behind, edging him towards a patch of ice.

Georg spotted the danger and stopped. Shadows behind him, beside him; in front of him ice. He hastily pushed off again, unsure this time.

'Oh Mei!' Ziggi was parallel.

'Yes!'

Shroud hands gripped Georg's wrist, the cold shearing into him, but his hands were empty. The Key flew in a glittering arc.

Ziggi had it. Ziggi hurled it to Dieter. Dieter caught it. A black hand reached for him. He threw the Key to Manfred who immediately threw it on to Georg. Backwards and forwards, illuminated like a firefly, it passed between them. Until two dark skiers attached themselves to each of the children, mirroring their every move. They recognised the tactics – they could see how the team worked, and reformed to come between them.

Ziggi had the Key. She knew she couldn't throw it again, not with the Shadows tagging each of her friends. It was up to her now. This was the race she was destined to win. Her chance to show how strong she was, and how fast. She pushed off with all her might. Her speed was reckless and she outdistanced the Shadows chasing her, aware that

Dieter, Manfred, Anne and Georg were skiing behind her, trying to keep pace.

'Watch out for the snowcats in the dip, below you.' IDK was flying high in the air above her, keeping a lookout. Instinctively, Ziggi skied to her left. She could see the line of snow-dozers and snowcats forming a solid barrier below her. Her path was blocked, and she saw that she had been wrong; she would not win this race alone, she needed the others.

'Dieter?'

'Here!' He called to her from behind.

The Shadows turned to him the instant he replied, so Ziggi threw the Key straight at IDK, who caught it and veered away, his skis singing through the air. He cleared the snowcats and the dozers and continued to sail on, following the curvature of the slope, leaving Ziggi to ski around the vehicles, aiming to meet him further down.

Anne had managed to elude her Shadows by skirting around them. Now the slope in front of her was open, and she went into racer's position, knees supple, body tucked tight, the way she'd done countless times in the last week.

'IDK, I'm here!' Anne reached him ahead of Ziggi. IDK threw the Key. The Shadows turned, flying across the slope to converge on Anne. Anne ducked further and pushed harder.

'Anne – look out!' IDK yelled. Anne screamed past a Shadow.

'I'm right behind you!' Ziggi followed in Anne's tracks,

mirroring her turns. She stabbed at the trailing Shadow with her stocks and knocked it flying, then lunged at two others. But more and more dark forms were streaming in from all sides.

'They're surrounding us!' Ziggi could see that every avenue was blocked off. 'Hand it to me, but don't let them see you,' Ziggi whispered fiercely, still skiing a short distance behind Anne.

'They're coming in underneath you.' Georg signalled with his stock.

'Please Anne, give me the Key,' Ziggi whispered again.

Still Anne hesitated. At the last moment she pushed it into Ziggi's hand and called loudly, 'Here I am!' She raced down the slope, drawing the Shadows with her.

Ziggi knew with certainty that this time she was their only hope. She had to ski fast. She had to elude them and hide. She held the Key tight and pushed everything she had into this last race. Snow flew up behind her like seaspray, her skis hissed with speed; the air around her, cold, singed her, and all the vile and debased creatures slid and slithered in her wake. Ziggi saw nothing, heard nothing, but the roar of her own heart in her ears. For the first time in her life she felt fear, not for herself, but for the prize she was carrying. It spurred her on, she excelled herself, but it wasn't enough. There were too many Shadows, a heinous wall of dark intentions that bore down on her. She couldn't shake them, and if she couldn't, no one could and, with that realisation, her hope and her strength finally ebbed. With one final spurt of energy, the last she possessed, Ziggi lunged forward, outward, but a wall of snow suddenly blocked her; she couldn't avoid it and skied into it. Huge white fingers closed around her. She was lifted into the air, and found herself staring into button eyes.

'I really must protest,' said the familiar voice. 'If you had called me earlier, you wouldn't be in this mess.' Snow fell because the Snowman was annoyed. He brought Ziggi to safety and kicked at the Shadows, swept aside the snowcats rolling towards him, stood on two dozers and squashed them. He smashed two more into one another, and pulverised the lizards so the slopes were soon littered with ice and metal and dark pools of shade. But where Shadows fell, more rose up, attacking the Snowman. More dozers drove forward, rearing up on their chains, scraping at him with their blades, dislodging huge chunks of snow from his legs. He didn't notice. He kept batting at the Shadows and catching the dozers and throwing them so their tank-shells cracked open like nuts.

Suddenly a Shadow wrenched the Key from Ziggi's hand. A lightning bolt caught the crystal and fused with it – fire growing out of night, rays building, striking into the snow and opening a deep chasm on the slope. Then the Shadow directed the green light at the white giant.

The Snowman turned, feeling the heat in the nape of his neck. He let the last of the dozers fall, and took a step backwards, surprised. His button eyes clouded. With one hand he tried to ward off the light, but his hand melted. His movements became heavy, as the snow he was made of grew sodden. The ray of light continued to bore into him, and what was left of the black army threw itself at his feet, toppling him.

'We have to stop them!' Anne cried out.

'We can't.' Dieter held her back. They couldn't do anything but watch their friend fall to his knees, watch his head roll forwards and his other arm fall off. With a groan the man of snow became a soggy mountain of mush.

'I won't let you do this! I won't let you beat us!' Anne's white face was lit by the Key's glow. The Shadows had risen above them, wailing with malignant laughter, one holding the Key high.

With the last strength she possessed, and summoning all her sadness and fury, Anne pushed at the dark form. She was a small being at his feet, but she wouldn't be cowed. Beside her Dieter pushed; Ziggi, Manfred, and IDK pushed too. Georg pushed until his muscles were tight as steel, but the black wall held against them.

'Save yourself,' Anne whispered to IDK, who was straining beside her.

'No!' IDK continued to heave. 'I won't give up.'

'Our only chance is the Key,' Manfred said, on the other side of him. IDK nodded. He knew. He tilted the magic skis skyward, and lifted off, until he was level with the Shadow's hand. He hovered for a moment, then the skis lunged forward and he was enveloped by the Darkness. Closing his eyes, holding his breath, he sought the heat of the light. The

Shadow's hand drew away, the laughter that had howled in triumph was suddenly cut off. IDK lifted his stock and plunged it into the Shadow's yellow eyes, felt the being shudder and stumble. He twisted and dived for the Key, which was falling. He felt it in his hand, and it gave his Snow Wings power. He darted out of the mist, and landed on the snow. His light and the Key's light fused and he directed it at the Darkness and its army. The radiance thrust them into the chasm. With screams of fear and a fever pitch of voices, the evil and the wickedness were swallowed. Rocks flew like comets, and the mountain groaned, leaned and fell in an avalanche that continued until the seam of the chasm closed, finally, and the snow that had once been the Snowman covered it. Nothing Dark remained, nothing at all, but mounds of churned, broken snow, boulders of ice, two buttons, a bow tie and a banana mouth that tried for a smile.

THIRTEEN

RETURN OF THE KING

Georg and the king

The tears they hadn't had time to cry, fell now. Despite the chaos around them, they stood bent double in the unrelenting wind, mourning the Snowman. Tired and stiff, Manfred stooped to retrieve the buttons and his bow tie. In the bright flashes of lightning he saw the naked cliffs above them and recognised the base of the ice mountain again.

'What time is it?' IDK asked.

'We have less than two hours,' Manfred said heavily. 'Should we keep going?'

'It's too far and too dangerous.' There was panic in Dieter's voice. 'We have to stay here.' He looked around desperately. 'Over there.' He pushed off towards a gully.

Hurly burly, they scrambled after him, until they reached an overhanging rock.

'Squat down,' Dieter called out, pushing his way along a ledge under the rock. He threw his arms around his knees and brought his head forward, rolling his body into a tight ball. The others did the same. 'Water conducts electricity – find a piece of dry ground,' Dieter shouted in the gap between crashes of thunder and crumbling rock.

Black clouds meeting head-on, over, beside, below the mountain, were soldered together by forked lightning, so that they became one solid mass. The wind screamed; the hail was as hard as diamonds; the rain attacked the slopes with needles and spears. It was an army of soldiers that scratched and bit and ripped across the planet with weapons far worse than those of the Shadows, tearing it with shocks and jolts so strong they threatened to pulverise it. And in a shallow cave beneath the surface, where the scent of earth was moist and the touch of stone cold, sat the bedraggled little group, wet and totally exhausted, but safe from the blue-tongued light.

'Dieter.' Anne had to raise her voice to make herself heard above the wind. 'For some reason I feel really happy and warm.' She blinked into the flashing light. 'Can you feel it too?'

'What?' It was hard to hear her above the noise.

'The Light Beings. I think they're here!' Anne was scratching at the snow and rocks that lay in piles around her. 'It can't hurt to look, can it?' she called to Ziggi and Manfred.

The ledge they were under ran along the side of the gully, and soon they were all searching under rocks, probing fissures, knocking, listening, digging.

Georg could smell peppermint. It made him ravenous, and he followed his nose. He crawled away from the others, his hands groping for anything that resembled a handle, feeling for the shape of a door, pushing at every indentation. The aroma intensified and every now and then he thought he saw a soft, golden light seeping through a crevice. Stooping, he swept away the snow and pushed hard against the wall, again and again, in case there was an opening. Suddenly he fell through a door, down three steps and unrolled on the floor. He lay dazed, on cold, hard ground. Only when he heard a sneeze did he sit up – and he couldn't believe his eyes.

He had landed in an ice-cave, where a pale ice-light gleamed. Icicles reached down from the ceiling into the ground where others grew up to meet them. The cave echoed with dripping water and smelt of damp fur.

'Aaaah…haaaa…haaaa…haaaa…HATCHOOOO! A row of sneezes, neat, alike, chased the first sneeze, precise in imitation.

'Bless your Highness,' peeped a thought-voice.

'Bless your Highness,' a twitter of echoes in unison, then silence, until a third sneeze, well mannered, restrained – an apology of a sneeze – sounded. A chorus of well-mannered, restrained, apologetic sneezes was followed by a rustling movement of furry bodies and soft clothes, and the thud and scurrying that spoke of warm beings huddled close together.

Georg couldn't see anything, nor was he sure of what he'd heard. He squinted in the direction of the sounds, rubbed his bruises and hollered, 'Hey!' His voice echoed through the warren of passages beneath the earth.

'Ssssshhhh!' It was a thought, more than a voice.

'Where am I?' Georg looked around wildly.

'Sssshhhhh!' the thought sighed again. 'His Majesty is unwell.'

'We are not unwell! We have simply never grown accustomed to the cold,' said another voice, feeble, but more imperial in tone.

Georg scrambled to his feet. He fished around in his anorak pockets for matches. He found an apple core…no…a piece of string…no…a piece of chocolate…not now…a piece of chocolate? Well, maybe…glove…matches…wet matchbox. Wood scratched against sodden cardboard. The matchstick broke.

Again, renewed scrapings, with more vigour this time. A little flame finally licked the darkness and cast a weak circle of light around Georg. He held the match high and reeled as a group of small beings, milky white, materialised, blinking because they'd been in the dark for so long.

The Light Beings were stout, almost portly. Icicles were intertwined in the locks of their beards. Their eyes glowed luminous green – friendly eyes in gentle faces that smiled, but showed fright easily. Their noses twitched ceaselessly. In the small, flickering light, they radiated a soft, subtle glow of their own and it made Georg feel at peace.

'Ahhh...ahhhh...ttttt...sssssshhhhhhhhh!' The being in the middle of the huddle sneezed again.

'Ahhh...ahhhh...ttttt...sssssshhhhhhhhh!' The loyal subjects surrounding the king rocked slightly with each sneeze and fell open, the petals of a flower, to reveal their golden centre.

'Sssshhhhh! We're frightening him.'

Georg's eyes travelled from one face to the other, for no one had spoken, and yet he'd heard the voice. The beings shuffled into a semicircle surrounding him.

'Oh Mei,' Georg said, and his mouth snapped shut. The match went out, but a soft golden glow hung in the air, coming from the beings themselves. 'Oh Mei!' Georg said again. 'DIETER! MANFRED!' Georg roared and the cave amplified his voice.

'What is it?' Manfred muttered from his cramped position further along the ledge. His back hurt and his knees were stiff, and he hadn't found the slightest evidence of what was causing Anne's happiness. He certainly didn't need Georg's voice yelling in his ear. But Georg didn't shut up.

'DIETER! MANFRED!'

'All right!' Manfred yelled, and groped his way towards the sound.

Ziggi and Anne reached the open door at the same time as Manfred, with Dieter and IDK not far behind. They all tumbled down the three steps in their hurry to get through it. When their eyes grew used to the dim light (and Manfred had turned on his torch) they discovered Georg shivering in the furthest corner of the cave. He was surrounded by a group of beings who were regarding him solemnly.

'Oh Mei?' Dieter asked and the Light Being closest to him almost fell over with fear. A small, regal figure separated from the others. The king drew his cloak about him and straightened his crown. His subjects fell into line to the left and to the right of him in an imperial welcome.

'Who has come?' His voice was difficult to distinguish, for the Light Beings had strange, tiny voices. 'What is it you want?' He chirped one octave higher and a fraction louder.

'We have come to return the Key, as you requested.' IDK was glowing again, as the little beings in front of him glowed.

Tentative, the king walked forward to meet him, his people moving with him to keep him upright. He had a large forehead and his fair duck-down hair nestled in the nape of his neck. He stopped in front of IDK, who held out his hand. The Key sparkled in his palm. The king touched the boy's fingers with his own hand, which was as white as milk and covered in thick, blond curls. IDK was the same height. He looked placidly at the king.

'Who are you?' said the king in an uncertain tone.

'I am your son,' IDK said without hesitation, and handed over the Key.

They all talked at once then. The Light Beings had to

compete with Georg's deep bass voice, Ziggi's exuberance, Manfred's stream of questions and Violette's excited squawking. They sighed (and sometimes sneezed), and their bodies flowed in a movement that expressed joy. It continued for minutes, this babble of voices, laughter, the barking of a dog, screech of a cockatoo and Epsilon's miaow. Everyone spoke at once, without pausing for breath, happily chaotic and universally understood.

The children discovered that the thought-voices of the Light Beings were feelings that they also expressed in the way they moved. In this case of overexcitement and joy, they heaved like an incoming tide, their bodies flowing as one group, one feeling, not individuals at all. The light they exuded grew stronger by the second.

'Ahh…' Manfred had been checking his watch surreptitiously. 'Attention please!' He had to shout to be heard. 'I hate to interrupt the celebrations, but we have half an hour. If we're going to save a planet…' It silenced them immediately. Manfred bowed to the king. 'What do we do?'

'It's a task only kings can complete,' the old being said. 'The Key must be brought to the Keyhole and turned at the midnight hour.'

'Where is the Keyhole?' Manfred asked. He followed the king, who squeezed through the cave's opening and pointed to the top of the ice mountain.

'It was built high, to reçeive the light,' said the king.

'There's no way we can get there now.' Manfred's voice was hoarse with frustration.

'Yes we can.' IDK stepped forward. 'I can take you. On my Snow Wings.'

He left the cave, snapped on his skis and reached for his stocks. The king remained at the cave, uncertain.

'Come on, Your Majesty!' IDK pointed to his skis. 'They'll carry us. Someone help him, please.'

Georg and Dieter positioned the king on the back of IDK's skis. IDK was about to lift off.

'Wait!' Manfred rummaged in his rucksack. 'Here. Take this.' He brought out Violette's old cage, the floor dismantled, the bars smoothed round, like a helmet.

'I'm not wearing a funny hat!' IDK said, severe.

'It's not a hat.'

'It's a Faraday cage,' the Calculator boasted its knowledge. 'Farad, unit of electrical capacity. Named after Faraday, the scientist.'

'Put it on – it'll stop you being electrocuted,' Manfred insisted.

'Twenty minutes,' Ziggi intervened.

So IDK put on the Faraday cage and, giving his father a reassuring smile, closed his eyes and concentrated, willing his skis to rise. For a moment nothing happened – they were planks of wood, lying on snow, radiating a faint green light. Then slowly, haltingly, they lifted off the ground.

'Hold on tight,' IDK called over his shoulder, and together they sailed into the gale of all weathers as the wind hurled its weight against them.

Soon IDK and the king were so far away that those left behind could barely see them. But each time the lightning slashed into the dark, they could see the two tiny specks on IDK's Snow Wings, in stark contrast against the mountain's ice.

'What's happening?' Anne, Dieter, Ziggi and Georg crowded Manfred, who had his binoculars pressed firmly to his eyes.

'They've nearly made it to the summit,' Manfred reported. 'They're disappearing through the cloud.'

'What IS up there?' Ziggi's demand was forthright and she grabbed the binoculars to study the sky. 'Nothing. Nothing but cloud.'

'Eight minutes to midnight,' announced the Calculator.

An eerie green glow diffused the sky. Silver tears appeared in the underside of the cloud, through which the green light streamed.

'He's tearing a hole in the cloud.' Ziggi handed the binoculars back to Manfred.

The cloud was turning into black steam, then evaporating. Behind it lay the summit of the mountain, and beyond that they could see the star-studded sky. Built on the mountain peak was a needle, fashioned out of crystal and ice. It reared high into the sky and ended in a circular loophole. The king and the prince stood at the base of the needle.

'One minute to midnight,' said the Calculator.

'The Keyhole!' Manfred examined the structure on the mountain. 'It's a portal! Now I understand.'

‘Thirty seconds to midnight,’ said the Calculator.

‘They’re cutting things mighty fine,’ Manfred muttered.

‘Twenty-eight seconds.’ Beside him Ziggi checked her digital watch.

‘What are they doing?’ Anne asked.

‘I don’t know.’ Manfred’s eyes strained as he tried to see what was happening.

*

‘There they are!’ The king’s watery eyes had been searching the sky. Three stars formed a line, their light as silver-green as the crystal’s light. He held the Key high. Nothing happened. The disc lay cold and lifeless in his shaking hands.

Nineteen seconds, eighteen seconds.

IDK’s heart pounded.

‘I can’t do it, my hands are too cold.’ The king’s thoughts were quaking.

‘May I try?’ IDK saw the stars move into the frame of the Keyhole.

The old king didn’t hear him. ‘It always works for me.’

Gently IDK reached for his father’s hand and together they guided the Key’s light through the portal. Lightning split the sky, running fissures and sparks into the Key. The bolts danced around the boy, warded off by the cage he wore. They hit again and again; it did not seem possible that he could stem such a force. But he continued to hold the Key high, so that the crystal sang, and with each hit, his own glow grew stronger. Until the last bolt slashed through the air and found its goal, as the midnight hour struck. The light and the Key united, streaming through the portal, where its strong green beam met and fused with the light that rained down from the three stars.

The flickering in the sky suddenly died, the roar of the thunder stopped, the trembling of earth and ice subsided. The last of the clouds parted and, with soft hands, a hue as strong as morning reached into the sky and coloured it gold. The snow gleamed apricot and pink, delicate hues. The rocks reddened, then glowed gold too, as a ball of light lifted above the distant peaks. The planet had its own sun at last.

Setting the light free

The children, the Light Beings, the cat, bird and dog streamed out onto the snow to welcome the king and the prince, as the Snow Wings brought them back.

'Only kings could do what you have done.' The king addressed IDK in a clear, birdsong voice. 'You have returned our light to us.' He unclasped his cloak and put it around his son's shoulders.

'Please,' IDK blushed. 'I only did what anyone else would have done.'

But IDK didn't look like 'anyone else' in the newborn light. He had a new, regal bearing, and there was a strong resemblance – no one could miss it now – between him and his father. The old king was ancient, as ancient as the mountains they were standing on. IDK was fresh. Both were wise.

'You must finish what you have begun,' the king said. They all looked out onto the ruins of the night. There was no trace of darkness, only the chasm into which the Shadows had fallen, where the ruptured snow showed that they had ever been.

IDK held the Key high once again. It caught the new sun this time, and a wide river of light was born, a greenish gold issuing from the crystal. He swung it to the remains of the strange, black cloud and the cloud vanished. Then he directed it at the broken ice and rubble that lay on the snow. It shivered and formed shapes. Sticks and twigs rose to their knees, grew towards the light, became branches and trunks, hoary with bark, lifting, standing; trees stretching into the sky. Icy leaves hung on the fingertips of every branch, the drops of a chandelier. In the light breeze they chimed like bells, a tinkle of sound, a forest of glass and ice and crystal, shimmering. Suddenly, as if each of the leaves were a butterfly, they detached themselves and, in a glittering cloud, flew away. In their place stood living trees, and all around the snow was smoothed and healed and the mountain stood untroubled.

'You have saved two worlds,' the king addressed the gathering. 'And we are beholden to you.'

'You're welcome,' the three boys, Anne and Ziggi murmured.

'But we're not quite sure what happens next,' said Manfred, always a stickler for procedure.

'The Key will be returned to its vault in the heart of our

world,' the king said firmly, 'to be used when the king needs to use it, and all will be well.'

'Will it?' It was Anne who dared to speak. 'I don't think it's right for one person to have all that power.' Her serious face was turned towards the assembly. 'I think that's missing the point.'

'Which *you've* been known to do.' The Calculator had switched itself on. Anne took no notice. She held the gaze of the king and IDK.

'The thing is,' she said quietly, 'I have this hunch.'

'What!?!' Manfred nearly choked. 'This is not a time for hunches! It's imperative we rely on scientific calculation.' Beside him, the Calculator flashed a red warning light.

'I... I'm not sure that keys in themselves are all that important,' Anne stammered, her voice quieter than it had ever been before. 'I think what's more important are the people who hold the keys.'

'You're saying whoever has the Key determines its use?' Georg took up Anne's train of thought.

'Yes. Think about it. What if the Shadows had captured it?'

'Totally different scenario,' Ziggi chimed in. 'But we stopped them, didn't we?'

'Remember what the Weatherman said. Where there's light there's darkness.' Dieter spoke in support of Anne.

'What if they come back and are successful next time?' said Anne, and they were all looking at her now, her face so very serious, her hands trembling.

'I see what you mean.' IDK nodded.

'There is an alternative,' she went on, and they suddenly all recognised what Anne had in mind. 'The thing is – do you trust me?'

'What? Trust *you?*' Ziggi couldn't help herself and Anne glared, until Ziggi added, 'Only in exceptional circumstances.'

'In our world it is the king who makes the important decisions.' The old king's words, light and clear, broke into their heavy thoughts. 'And as my son is to be the new king, it is for him to decide.'

'Yes.' IDK studied the faces of his friends, then turned his gaze to his father. 'We usually discuss the options and then decide,' he said at last. 'At least that's what we've tried to do,' he added, remembering. 'Lately.'

The Calculator coughed impolitely.

'Shhh!' Georg hissed, and if the Calculator had any ribs, he would have dug his elbow into them.

'You may proceed,' the king said heavily. It was the hardest thing he'd ever had to say.

'The Key has done what it was meant to do.' Anne turned to the others. 'If we destroy it and set the light free, no Shadow will ever be able to claim it. It would never cause another war.'

One after the other they thought about it. Dieter was the first to nod his head. Then Georg. Then Ziggi (Anne could hardly believe it), until only Manfred and IDK were left.

'Manfred?' Anne felt her eyes burning.

'I don't know,' Manfred said, shaking his head. 'There's very little supporting evidence.'

'But don't you *feel* it's the right thing to do?'

'Feel it?' Manfred always had trouble with feelings.

'Try.'

So Manfred closed his eyes and tried to turn his brain off so that he would only hear his heart. It hammered in his chest, and his thoughts, intrusive, clamoured about in his head. But gradually his face cleared, and the furrow in the middle of his forehead disappeared.

'Yes,' he said, and a grin replaced his frown. 'I think I can.'

'But what if you're wrong?' IDK faced them all, wavering. 'My people…'

'I'm not wrong,' Anne said with certainty.

IDK sighed. And then he smiled.

'Okay,' he said. 'Go ahead.'

Anne stepped away from the group and held the Key high. But unlike IDK, who had sought the light, she snapped it in two. A snowflake fluttered out of its crystal encasing, a bird freed from its cage and, in its release, they could feel a sudden warmth stroke their cheeks. The snowflake glided above them, buoyed by the breeze, drifting in larger and larger circles, higher and higher, until it was so small they could no longer see it. Its light fused with the new sun's light and encircled them.

'Now it's where it belongs,' Anne said, her eyes moist. 'Everywhere. Protecting everything.'

'I see what your problem is.' Manfred stroked his chin. He was standing in the control room of the spaceship, examining the motors, with the king and the king's technical advisers standing beside him. 'You've run out of fuel.'

'Yes,' the king sighed. 'The Shadows destroyed our supply, once we were captured by Earth's gravity. We can't pull ourselves free.'

'And it's not your typical run-of-the-mill fuel, is it?' Manfred said, and activated the Calculator.

'These rockets require a key substance,' the Calculator advised him. 'They won't fire without it.'

Consternation enveloped the room. The planet might be stuck on the highest mountain for some time to come. So they argued among themselves while Manfred focussed his concentration on the motors. His eyes glazed over, his mouth hovered on a smile, he remained motionless while he thought, then he whirled into action.

'I have an idea!' he said, riffling through his rucksack. He re-emerged, glasses askew, waving a tattered and burnt-around-the-edges formula. You take Formula A, and you take Formula B – six drops of each, not five, not seven, but six. Manfred's Calculator hurriedly turned itself off and hid deep in Manfred's pocket.

Manfred evacuated everyone else from the control room, in case of an explosion. But he seldom made the same mistake twice (not when there were so many other mistakes to be made) and besides, Grandma was safe in Wintersheim, he didn't have to meet his cousin at the station (she was standing worriedly outside the door) and he had made absolutely sure there were no distractions. Nevertheless, tense moments followed. Everyone was waiting on the mountain face, expecting a boom and a crash and clouds of billowing green smoke.

But it was jubilation that flew out the door; and following that, Manfred. The motors ignited, sounding clear as bells. They coughed once, hiccupped once, paused and then sprang into life. The spaceship was in business! Manfred rushed into the snow towards his friends, who surrounded him and hugged him. He'd made it: Manfred Decker had become an Inventor First Grade.

'They are wise, your friends.' The king took IDK aside. 'You have done well to choose them.'

'We keep telling him that!' said Georg, who had overheard. Everyone grinned.

While Manfred had been experimenting, the ice and snow on the little planet was melting. It crackled now, and fizzed, and the most delicious breath of warmth was carried in the wind, to touch them gently on the cheek. Around them water ran off the mountain slopes in rivulets, waterfalls foamed and a blue lake was filling an entire valley. Behind them, as the ice on the mountain grew more transparent, the turrets and towers of a great stone castle emerged. When at last the ice cracked open, like the shell of an egg, the castle was freed, and rose majestically into the cornflower-blue sky.

'See? What did I tell you?' Manfred turned to Ziggi. 'I'm usually right 99 per cent of the time.'

'And 100 per cent humble,' Ziggi muttered under her breath.

'It's a nifty piece of architecture,' Georg said.

'Yes.' IDK grinned. 'I remember now. That's where I live!'

'It's where we'll all live,' the king said, proudly, 'after renovations.' He turned to the children, 'You will stay, will you not?'

They studied one another to confirm what they were each thinking.

'It will be different now,' the king added hastily. 'Peaceful without the Shadows.' He looked towards IDK. 'But my son will still need his friends.' There was a long, drawn-out silence, made worse by the unconditional trust that glowed in the Light Beings' eyes.

'I'm afraid we can't.' Manfred's voice was shaky. 'Although personally I'd love to,' he added. 'It'd be a buzz to live on a spaceship.'

'It isn't home,' Georg agreed.

'Stay for a while.' The king was adamant. 'For a holiday. Five hundred years is nothing, and then we'll return you to your homes.'

They shook their heads.

'I have to go back to my mountains,' Dieter said.

'Now's a critical time on Earth,' Georg added huskily.

'That's right,' Anne agreed. 'There's so much to do.' The way she said it, she meant to do everything she planned to. She hugged the little prince. 'I won't ever forget you.'

'What about you, IDK?' Dieter said softly.

'Of course I'm going to stay,' the little boy said staunchly, but the wobble in his voice betrayed him. He turned to his friends. 'Please change your minds. Georg? You could teach my people how to cook. And Dieter, you can teach them how to ski when the white weather falls. Anne, you know how to be brave – I'm not sure my people are good at that.'

'But you've learned all those things yourself,' Dieter reminded him.

'I suppose I have,' IDK sighed. It crossed his mind to lock them all up until the planet was well and truly away from Earth. Luckily that thought flew out the window.

The motors idled steadily, the little planet was ready to lift off; the king's technicians were awaiting the king's orders. IDK faced his friends and found the weight of his decision to stay a heavy one. He watched as they gathered the remains of what they'd come with: tattered rucksacks, and skis, and the bibs and bobs of Manfred's inventions.

'Here.' Manfred pressed the Calculator into IDK's hand. 'You'll need him more than I do,' he said thickly and turned away before he could change his mind.

Sniffling, IDK turned to Ziggi, who was last in line, and who pumped the little prince's hand vigorously. There was a curious glimmer in Ziggi's eyes. The way she held her head showed she'd been thinking. She had momentarily forgotten about the races and the trophies she'd planned to win. She was thinking how exciting it would be to stay on a planet and fly around the Universe. Of course they'd have to make her a baroness or a duchess, at the very least.

And what would Ziggi have to teach the Light Beings? Certainly to be fit and how to ski fast. Independent thinking, how to limber up and be disciplined about their sport. Yes, she'd probably instruct them on taking short cuts that could only lead to trouble, but she knew how to get out of trouble, too. The Ziggi Twigg Diploma of Impatient Self-confidence, Risk-taking and Recklessness. The Light Beings (who knew what Ziggi was thinking) held their breath while she made her mind up. But she decided to go home after all, to enter all those races and win them too.

'Keep practising.' Ziggi grinned.

'Every day,' IDK assured her. Ziggi handed over her racing suit.

'I can buy a new one,' she said. 'My father –' But there was no time to hear about Ziggi's father. The motors increased in pitch, the spaceship gave a small shudder as it pulled away from Earth's gravity.

'Hurry.' Manfred knew what those sounds meant. 'The pilot has selected reverse gear.'

'We'll take you to the threshold,' the king said. 'My son and I.'

It didn't take them long to get to the border of the two worlds. In the distance were familiar mountains, and beyond that lay the world they knew. Earth's powdery clouds shot out of the valleys, no trace of the dark cloud remaining. The king had taken them to the top of an enormous ski-jump that bridged the gap between one world and the other, a giant slide, its runway made of hard packed ice.

'We have to ski down that?' Even Anne the Brave swallowed. The ski-jump jutted out into the space between this world and theirs. Looking over the edge was like peering into a crevasse.

The motors quickened, the planet strained.

'It's high time,' Manfred said, but he wasn't game to go first. Another shudder and the two frontiers drew apart. Mountains separated from mountains, rocks creaked and fell.

'Georg. You go first.'

'Oh no! Not me!' Georg turned around to climb back again, but the others blocked his way.

'I'll go.' Anne's voice wasn't trembling, but she was.

'Let me go.' Ziggi swept up her unwilling cat. 'I've ski-jumped before, there's nothing to it,' she added. She clipped on her skis and positioned herself at the top of the jump. 'Hold your skis parallel, not too close together. When you land, let your knees absorb the jolt. See you there!' She hurtled down the slide, leaping across the borderline of the planet and Earth, and continued sailing through the air. Anne followed immediately, holding Orff, Violette gliding beside her.

'Manfred?' Dieter asked.

'Why not?' his friend said. They pushed off together, slid and jumped high and far.

Only Georg was left, clinging to the ledge, quaking.

'Jump, Oh Mei.' But Georg hesitated still. The two worlds grew further apart. 'If you don't jump, you'll be stuck here.'

The motors were screaming, pulling the planet away from its anchor of gravity. Steel screeched and rock crumbs slid into the widening abyss.

'Jump!!!!' IDK roared.

Georg jumped as he'd often seen ski-jumpers dive. He rocketed into the air, and found himself soaring through it with the ease of a bird. He was the last to leave the planet, and could see the others ahead of him, the evening sun lending them its fire, so that they became red smoke sliding across the sky.

A small figure stood at the edge of his world and in his heart flew with them. He would, even now, have liked to follow them. But he didn't. He turned towards the great castle, towards his father and his people. As he neared them his light pulsed softly and the heaviness of his body fell away. He lifted into the air and floated across the golden snow and knew the feeling to be right.

EPILOGUE

GOING HOME

The song of summer coming

Silver on white. Turrets and towers. Wires thrummed softly, dishes turned, antennae sensed echoes in the stratosphere. The small glass and aluminium hut, beneath the technological odds and sods, was the temporary weather station. Here wind speeds were recorded, frequencies were measured, the density of clouds and percentage of moisture in them interpreted by the Weatherman. He was doing it now, with his eye to the sky, watching the clouds tear apart. A little world of pinnacles and cones, and a great towering castle, rose up. For a moment the orb was suspended above the highest mountain, then it pulled free.

*

Five streaks of light, five jet streams, were borne on the air. Five children landed on Earth's snow. It wasn't black anymore, but a faint grey, touched here and there by a dark rim. Cool air whistled past their ears. Their movements were graceful, like those of eagles flying. They skimmed across the surface of the snow and slowly altered their course to ski great, winding curves down Earth's mountains. They descended into the valley and stopped at last. For here the winter snow was vanishing. Spring had arrived.

The sound of streams greeted them, of water skipping stones. A choir of evening birdsong came from the forests on the slope. And other sounds. The rustle of a fox, the burrowing of a beetle, the humming of bees. Swallows darted above them. A deer stepped out of the fir trees and regarded them with tranquil eyes. Flowers and herbs crowded onto their path and nodded in the breeze, the faint blue colour of forget-me-nots lay on the fields as though a piece of sky had fallen. The emerald sheen of grass pushed its way through brown earth; there was a scent of growth, rich in the air, and a whisper of voices, the song of summer coming. Lights glowed from every hilltop, lit in welcome; starlight strung in trees. Fireflies danced.

They removed their skis in slow, stiff movements and shouldered them. They walked home, tired soldiers returning from a long, cold war. But they were not too tired to grin at one another. In single file they came into town, passing houses in the streets. Row upon neat, tidy row, hedges planed, gardens ordered. They passed the town square, and the statue of the man on the well. He was pointing at them now, as they came home. He had stopped running at last, and the expression of cold horror had softened.

They passed the railway station and Georg's father's bakery. The Grand Hotel with its many windows and flags streaming out. Cattle, flowers garlanding their horns, were being herded through the streets towards the mountain where they would graze the alpine meadows over summer. People dressed in colourful clothes were standing in doorways, leaning out of windows, calling out to one another, rejoicing in the newborn warmth.

'So, what do we do next?' asked Ziggi, not wanting to say goodbye. She turned to Manfred. 'Do we have any other worlds to save?'

'Let's start with ours,' Manfred said. 'It could do with our help'.

'I'm going home.' Anne's voice was decisive. 'I want to tell my parents I missed them. But I'll come back soon.' She was looking directly at Dieter now.

'We'll be here,' Dieter said, quietly.

'Same time next year?' Georg sounded eager. He didn't want to waste his newly found talents.

'Sounds good to me.'

'Then it's a promise.' They all shook hands on it. 'In the meantime, keep practising.'

'You too, Ziggi.' Anne shook Ziggi's hand last, and the girls grinned at one another.

'Georg… Georg… Dinner!' A voice called out. Georg's steps faltered. The rhythm of their march home had ended. Another voice joined Georg's mother's call.

'Manfred. Manfred come here at once!' They had reached 13 Nussbaum Strasse, where Manfred's grandma was waiting at the gate, a broom in hand, and a 'where-have-you-been?' forming on her lips. 'MANFRED!! Late as usual!' Manfred sighed. He was in trouble again.

They all stopped and turned towards a clear, ringing sound in the distance. It could be sheep bells in the mountain meadows, or cow bells that clanged like pots and pans. It could be church bells ringing the evening hour. But they knew it came from higher than the church steeple or the mountain meadows and mountain peaks. It was the sound of motors, humming. A cloud drifted across the face of the setting sun, more a shadow than a cloud. It passed and was gone, and the ringing faded with it. The children's eyes searched and searched, but the tranquil sky was empty.

*

On the slopes of the highest mountain, outside his temporary weather station, the Weatherman looked from the sky into the valley towards Wintersheim. His smile was hidden in his beard.

Author Note

Many years ago, I wanted to learn to ski. My mother had often told me about her childhood and the laughter she'd shared with friends on skis. So twenty or more years ago I set off to find – well – an adventure. For two years I lived and worked in a town called Garmisch-Partenkirchen, which is in Bavaria, on the border of Austria, in the south of Germany. I had a glorious second childhood.

Now, every time I read *Snow Wings* – and certainly when I wrote it – I relive that time and feel happy. There's something about mountains. The way they lift your heart when you look up at them.

There are many people I would like to thank for helping me with this book. The Wettermann family, who gave me work and treated me like a second daughter. Having a place to live gave me the time to write, and to experience the snow. I felt cared for.

I learned to ski at the Flori Woerndle ski school where I met Martin Ulkan. Martin spent many hours talking to me about technique and snow. His love for the mountains was deeply ingrained in his soul, and he inspired this book. He wanted kids to know how joyous skiing is, and how much you need to know about yourself, your body, and the environment around you. Both Martin and another teacher, Toni Sieß, helped 'the kangaroo' (as they called me) to improve her skiing technique...up to a point!

I haven't skied for a long time. Now I ride horses because I still think its very important to have a physical activity that requires discipline, and allows a person to be in touch with the natural world. I learned that from the people who made skiing their livelihood, and who can't live without having mountains in their back yard. Thank you, all of you.

And thank you Cass Carter, who gave me writing confidence at the beginning, and a special thanks to Erica Wagner and Jodie Webster, who edited this book with kindness (and a firm hand!) and whose expertise is words. Without the right words, a story could never be told.

Whether it's in skiing, riding, living, writing – I know I'll always be learning, and will always need others to help me find my way.

Jutta Goetze